TO: K...

THANK YOU...

EVERYTHING.

PEN CUSHION
PUBLISHERS

MIZ

Bishop   MIZ

2

"OH!"

PRESENTS

BISHOP

WRITTEN BY MIZ

PEN CUSHION PUBLISHERS
PO Box 85 New York, NY 10116
(718) 844-0686

ISBN# 0-9764446-0-7
SAN# 256-3533
Story by: MIZ
Presented by: "OH!"
Edited by: Mark Adams
Cover Created by: "OH!" and Dean Wiltshire
Graphic Design by: Kevin Cosme
Cover Photography by: Fatima Bloom
Transcontinental June 2006
Printed in the Canada

In memory of the realest
Brother to ever walk
the Brooklyn streets,

Tyrone "Tee Rock" Baum

Dedication

To my beautiful grandmother, Ruth "MAMA" Adams, I will always love you and keep you in my heart, may GOD bless your soul.

My ambition and sane behavior is dedicated to my young prince Willie "OH!" Jr. my precious princess Jada Mo'ne Vaughan and her big brother Danori, my god kids Jabri Moore, Javion and Tatiana Brewster, Aricelyis Turay, and Nevada Ingram. "OH! Love the kids".

R.I.P to Sharod "HOTROD" Joyner, LIL JAYO, NUTSY, Christopher "CHALIS" Williams, four year old Amayla Avian Mitchell, my aunts PRIMROSE and DELLA MAE, cousins MYRA and DAVID and every other loved one that's no longer here. GOD bless you and you will always be cherished in memories.

To the big homies on lockdown……..

My cousins Shaborn, Miz, Devine, Rakeem, Daquan, Anthony, my brother Kev Web, my good dudes Kai, Larry, Rah, Askari, Drama, Joel, Kenyatta, Mandel, Ice and Dawg. May GOD bless you and every stand up dude and female with another chance at life beyond a wall. One love………….

MIZ Acknowledgments

I would like to thank the Most High God for blessing me with many talents. I have forgiven others as you have forgiven me. Special thanks to my mother, Dot and my father, Alfred. You two created an author and there are many more books to come. I love and honor you.

Much love and respect to my twin cousin, OH, let's take it to the top champ. To my brother, Shaborn, "My Brother's Keeper." Much love and respect, how do you write so many proper books in such a short time? Dewey Hill is next.

Much love and thanks to all my brothers and sisters, nieces, nephews, uncles and aunts. Especially Aunt Shirley. You've shown me what a true aunt is about, I love you. Cousin Devon. And the rest of the Adams, Browns, etc. Love you all.

Last but not least, to all my comrades locked down. Too many to name. Oh, I can't forget my female comrade Leshawn, my boy K.B .Mel, and those I forgot to name. Rest in Peace to my Uncle Harold, his daughter Myra, and her son David. I love you and miss you.

Wow! I almost forgot my mentor, the O.G. player Randy, don't worry, Drama is part of the vision.(Smile). I can't forget Kriste, I told you I wouldn't forget- And a special thanks again, to Sister Souljah, you've inspired me to try my hand at what I do. Much love and respect to you sister. To all the haters: Let the hating begin. It's good for promotion. For anyone I forgot to name, just get in the car and ride with me. Thank you........

OH Acknowledgments

I would like to thank GOD for blessing me with the gift of being an rap artist, without you none of this would be possible. Special thanks to my mother "TOOT" and my father "FOXX" who has always supported me with my visions.

I send my love and appreciation to my twin cousin MIZ, "you're my idle champ. Thank you for putting the vision together and making this possible." To my big cousin SHABORN -my other idol, "from a youngen coming up I watched your ambition to achieve the impossible. Ain't no turning back we will make it happen together."

Much love and thanks to my aunts, uncles, nieces, nephews, siblings, cousins and the entire Adams family. "Y'all know we two hundred, fifty deep. It would take a whole book to give everybody individual shout outs." Love y'all.

Special thanks to Dean Wiltshire, Fatima Bloom, Thanks to Maine, Perry "Uncle Pee" Jones and the whole Phatfarm/Run athletics staff, A Blak and the whole Hawthorne street family, my god sister Vanessa, K DOGG and family, Sharette, Toni, Preme, Dana, Tim, Trevor, SANTA and SHIM for being a part of the movement.

And last but not ever forgotten, the whole Brooklyn U.S.A, from every block to the eighty-nine projects throughout the borough, one love ya heard!!!!!!

Chapter One

A warm summer day in 1986, was the happiest day for Pastor Richard Timothy Brown, Sr. and his beautiful wife Maria Ann Brown. They welcomed their handsome baby boy into their small house in a quiet section of Brooklyn, New York. Pastor Brown preached to his congregation in Brooklyn, while Mrs. Brown educated the youth in a public school near the Lafayette Gardens Housing Projects.

As little Richard Jr. grew, he became as intrigued with God as his father was. Richard would attend church with his father every Saturday and Sunday and relish it. At the tender age of three, he could recite the Lord's Prayer backward and forward.

Life was by no means glamorous for the Browns, their love and faith in the Lord provided them a safe, stable and humble existence. The Lord, however, in his never-ending wisdom, does have a master plan and often test his "loyal" believers. When Richard turned sixteen, Maria Brown was laid off, forcing his family to move into the notorious Fort Greene Housing Projects. Pastor Brown believed his calling was to spread the word of God. He felt that other men of the cloth were more intrigued with how they could make money rather than serving the Lord. The salary Richard's mother earned from teaching had served as the financial support for the Browns and with her lay off, Pastor Brown's meager paycheck was their only means of income. The Fort Greene Housing Projects was one of by far the worse projects in Brooklyn, but the Browns had no other choice.

The ever humble Richard did not mind being uprooted and was determined to make the best of his situation. Richard was enrolled in Sarah J. Hale High School. He had always loved school and he still did, but Sarah J. Hale was unlike any school he went to before. Sarah J. Hale had seemed more like a pick-up spot with a fashion show going on constantly. There were so many pretty girls there that as he would turn his head to look at one girl, another one prettier than the last would appear.   Even the girls that had stayed in the West-Wing part of the school, who were in Special Education, were attractive.

All of the school's playboys would hang out in front of the donut shop on Atlantic Avenue around the corner from the school, waiting to lay their game down on all of the beautiful girls on their lunch periods. Though Richard was very handsome by all standards, no one in the school paid him any attention. He was too shy to approach the girls and his church boy reputation and clothes often kept the girls far away from him. At least the girls acknowledged he was there, while the boys acted as if he didn't exist. Richard often wished that for just one day he was one of the guys that circled the school all day in their cars, talking to the pretty girls. Sadly, the only attention paid to him was by his teachers. With summer just around the corner and still with no friends, Richard knew it would be a very long and hot summer.

He continued to be in church every Saturday and Sunday with his father. He was able to recite the whole Bible back and forth with amazement by then. He loved to go to church but he did not like the Fort Greene Projects where he lived because the other children in the projects would tease him every chance they'd get. They would call him the dumb quiet church boy and laugh at his hard-bottom shoes. They also made fun of the no-name brand clothes he wore. Richard spoke softly with a serious tone and it wasn't often you would see him smile. Everyone always said he was the spitting image of his father. Dark-skinned, six foot in height, and muscular with thick, jet black, wavy hair, Richard was definitely blessed by the Lord.

The first day of the summer was a hot one. Maria asked Richard to go to the supermarket nearby on Myrtle Avenue to pick up a few things she needed. Richard got the money from her and hurried down the stairs.

As he emerged from his building he noticed four cute girls laughing and staring at him. They were all very different but beautiful in their own way. One of them called to Richard. She was five foot, if within an inch, with light complected skin that appeared kissed by the sun, and long thick black hair.

"Hey, excuse me dark-skin. Come here for a minute, please."

As Richard made his way over to the group of girls, they began to giggle except the one who called him. She gave the other girls a look that silenced their giggles very quickly. As Richard nervously approached, the one that called him began to speak.

"Hi, my name is Lisa. I think you got it going on. What's your name?"

"Richard" he replied, "I live in this building on the 9th floor."

"I know," she responded coolly. "I've been watching you. I can't front, you look good. If I was your girl I'd keep you real dipped; keep you outta those bullshit clothes you be wearing."

When she said that, the group of girls began to laugh hysterically, falling over each other, and wiping their eyes as if tears were rolling down their faces.

"Don't pay these dumb bitches no mind," remarked Lisa. "I'm just being real with you."

"I understand, but I have to go to the store for my mother and then I have to study my bible. But who knows, maybe I'll see you another time," Richard replied quietly.

"No doubt, I'll definitely see you baby with your fine ass," said Lisa as Richard walked away. "I'll see you."

As he walked away he overheard one of Lisa's friends say, "Bitch, you crazy! You fucking with that broke ass church nigga? He can't do shit for you."

"Bitch, everything gotta be about money with you. I got my own fucking money, and the nigga is fine," Lisa replied.

"And he look way better than pizza face Shameek," said another voice. The girls began to laugh again. As Richard kept walking their laughter faded.

He daydreamed about what it would be like if he were popular. As he walked on he saw a lot of good-looking girls talking to guys in the projects. Of course there were some that weren't attractive at all, but overall most of the girls were looking good. It was a hot day so all of the shorts, mini-skirts and short sleeves were out and the girls were looking good wearing them. Even a few heavy-set women were wearing the latest fashions and styling. But they did not even look at Richard twice. He was in disbelief that Lisa, the best-looking girl in the projects, had pushed up on him. It had to be a joke. Wasn't that why her friends was laughing at him? As he thought about their quick conversation, he had to laugh. He never had the pleasure of talking to such a beautiful girl that he knew what he said to her was lame. How could he ever get a girl if he keeps mentioning his Bible studies?, he thought to himself. It had slipped out because Lisa was just so beautiful he was caught off guard when she called him over. He wondered if they would still be there in front of his building when he returned from the store. If so, he planned to at least look in her direction with a smile to let her know that he was interested in getting to know her. But what could he offer her? He had no money to buy her things, take her out or even look good enough in his no-name brand clothes to be seen around her. He knew a beautiful girl like her probably had only the money-making guys with expensive cars and clothes chasing her.

As he walked to the supermarket, he kept replaying the conversation he and Lisa had shared in his mind. But this time in his mind he said all of the smooth things that he thought she wanted to hear.

He finally reached Myrtle Avenue and there were so many people out. Young pretty girls were pushing baby strollers, and all of the expensive cars and trucks driving by were playing the latest hip-hop songs. Richard wished he was one of those guys pushing one of those expensive cars. He laughed out-loud to himself because he knew that it was only a dream and he would never even get close enough to look inside one of those cars.

As he was about to enter the supermarket, he heard a deep voice behind him.

"Yo, pardon me black. You know a chick name Keisha that live in building 79?" a tall, slim, light-skinned, curly haired teenager asked. "Shorty was suppose to be upstairs."

Richard turned around and faced the boy, answering him, "No I don't know Keisha. Actually I don't really know anyone around here. My family just moved here not long ago and the only one I met so far that's cool is a girl name Lisa."

"Son, you talking about light-skin bowlegged Lisa?" the boy asked as he began to chuckle.

"Yeah that's her. Do you know her?" asked Richard.

"Yeah son, I know her. I use to fuck with her friend Pam. Lisa's cool people, but if you ain't heard already, her man Shameek is doing big things down here on the drug side. Anyway, my name is Kendu. I'm from L.G. What's your name?" asked Kendu as he gave Richard a five.

"My name is Richard. I live in building 68, up on the 9th floor in the second apartment from the elevator."

"Aiight that's cool," said Kendu. "When I come through tomorrow to check Keisha, I'll see you."

They gave each other a five again and Richard walked slowly into the supermarket with a smile on his face from the joy of meeting his first friend, as Kendu headed up Myrtle Avenue.

Chapter Two

Two weeks had passed and Richard and Kendu were inseparable like twins. Richard continued to attend church every weekend, which Kendu would joke about, but in a friendly manner of course.

"Damn son, you go to church more than your pops, and he's the Pastor in the motherfucker," Kendu said as he began laughing.

"Why do you curse so much? You need to go to church and pray to get rid of that filthy language. Plus, my mother's in the other room so keep your voice down."

"No doubt Bishop," Kendu replied quietly. "That's what I'm going to start calling you from now on. Bishop, that name fits you. Anyway, I wanna introduce you to my man Ant-live. He's a good dude son. He's from Nostrand and Gates. Bounce with me over there son. I ain't see him in a few days now."

"When now?" asked Richard feeling a bit uncomfortable with going to Nostrand Avenue. He knew a lot of thugs hung out there.

"Yeah, we can bounce over there now," answered Kendu. "That is my nigga forreal. He's a stand up dude. I met the nigga a year ago. I had beef with some kats down on his end so I rolled down there to handle my business and son liked the way I moved. And the beef was over some bullshit; one of them niggas on his end was tight that I was fucking his bitch. Ant-live deaded the beef, but you know it's always a clown-ass nigga outta the bunch that wanna front. So I'm down there one day and this nigga tried me like I was some bird-ass nigga or something. Shit, I'm the one that went down there to handle business in the first place. To make a long story short, it didn't jump off but when Ant-live heard about it he just went crazy. He shot homie's ass up. He gave duke a seat for life! One in the back, straight paralyzed him. Word, that's my dog. It's mad dime pieces that live on his block too. I fucked damn near all them bitches. What's up with Lisa? Nigga, you ain't hit that yet?"

"No, I'm not even thinking about her like that," said Richard. "But I did notice her man Shameek looking at me the other day."

"Word? Fuck that nigga. He wanna fuck everybody else girl but his bitch suppose to be off limits to every other nigga out here? Fuck that bird-ass nigga. Come on son, let's get up outta here. We'll catch a cab over there."

They left Richard's apartment and as they left the building they felt the blazing heat. It seemed as though every girl and woman down Myrtle Avenue knew Kendu. They all spoke to him with something in their eyes that made it apparent they lusted for him. He was truly a pretty thug, and his reputation with women spoke for itself.

"I wish girls liked me like they do you," said Richard. "You're the man!"

"Son, chicks like a fly nigga that can dress," said Kendu with a smile. "If he ain't holding major chips then he better have game. See I have both, I can talk and I can dress. Plus I got a crazy dick game son."

They both laughed.

"I was up in the broad Keisha's crib the other day," continued Kendu. "I was hitting that ass so good son, I had the bitch climbing the fucking walls."

"You're crazy," said Richard through his laughter. "Hey, you wanna go to church with me and my family Sunday morning?"

Kendu stopped walking suddenly and looked at Richard like he was crazy and said, "Nigga are you nuts?! I ain't seen the inside of a church since I was five years old. But then again I might go if there's some bad bitches up in there."

They resumed walking and Richard said, "Kendu, church is not a place to go and meet women. It's a place of worship, even though some people do go for the wrong reasons."

Laughing Kendu replied, "Nigga, most of the bitches I fuck go to church every Sunday and they smoke, drink, party and fuck like

15

everybody else. So I don't see why you can't meet chicks up in there. I mean I believe in God and everything but that church thing ain't about too much. A church ain't never helped me with any of my problems. So that church thing ain't for the kid. But let me ask you a question. Most of the people in your church have been going there for about how long?"

"We just got some new members, but there are a lot that's been there for over twenty years."

"And the ones that have been going there for all that time, are they perfect?"

"Kendu, no one is perfect."

"You should be after twenty years of practicing that shit."

Richard shook his head looking at Kendu with a smile on his face. Kendu never ceased to amaze him; he had an answer for everything.

"Yo, you see that chick over there?" asked Kendu changing the subject as he pointed at an attractive woman. She was in her late thirties, but could easily have passed for late twenties. She had long thick legs and a small taut waist that was enhanced by her outfit.

"That was my first piece of pussy kid," continued Kendu. "She used to be cool with my mother. One day moms wasn't home and she came to the crib and pushed up on me. I was tearing that ass up on a regular basis until moms found out what was going down and fucked her up. We got caught 'cause the bitch started getting open and possessive with the dick."

Richard looked at the woman and had to admit that she was pretty and had an exceptional body for her age. She saw Kendu and smiled and waved as if she won the lottery.

"She's still open off a nigga," bragged Kendu. "I can fuck her anytime I want. Shit, I can even get her to fuck your virgin ass nigga."

Kendu started laughing as Richard looked at him seriously and replied, "No thank you, she's too old for me. Plus I might as well wait until I'm married to have sex."

"Boy are you crazy?!" asked Kendu with his face screwed up, "All the pussy be gone by then. You don't know what you're missing baby boy. Pussy makes you strong. That's why they call me Lee Haney, nigga."

As Kendu laughed Richard said, "Don't get me wrong Kendu, I would love to have sex with a beautiful girl but they're just not feeling me. I have nothing to give them."

"Nigga, you got everything to give them, and they got every thing to give you. But you have to have confidence in yourself no matter how you dress. Material shit doesn't really make a nigga, and believe it or not, it don't really bag bitches either. It only grabs their attention. And to make girls feel good being around you all you have to do is be yourself. Trust me, I know a lot of fly dressing niggas that can't bag a bitch for shit!"

As they waited to catch a cab to go check Ant-live, Richard thought about everything Kendu said and realized it made a lot of sense. After nearly an hour, they finally caught a cab. It was early afternoon when Richard and Kendu stepped out of the cab onto the corner of Nostrand and Gates.

As they made their way down Gates Avenue, they noticed two boys fighting with a crowd of people around them. Without a word, Kendu took off running towards the fight. At first Richard thought Kendu was just running to see the fight but then he saw Kendu punch one of the guys fighting in the face and knew otherwise. Richard ran into the crowd and saw Kendu and a short, stocky guy beating up on a tall lanky boy. The boy, who was clearly outnumbered and out-muscled, appeared to be around 18 or 19. The crowd of people were laughing, as the lanky boy managed to get up and throw two wild punches before running away, right past Richard.

Richard shook his head sadly, as Kendu ran up to him yelling, "Yo son, why you didn't snuff that nigga, or trip him up when he ran past you? Damn! That punk nigga got away!"

After a few moments Kendu calmed down and softly said, "Yo, forget it son. Come on, I want you to meet my boy!"

They walked towards the stocky brown-skin guy who fought along-side Kendu moments ago.

"Son, I want you to meet my boy; he's a good dude. This is Bishop. Bishop this is Ant-live," laughed Kendu, "and the nigga stay in shit!"

"That's right nigga," said a raspy voiced Ant-live. "Punk ass nigga lucky I ain't put a shell in his ass, straight thug life. But check it homie, you down with the team. Why you ain't snuff that bitch when he ran past you?"

"No, I couldn't do that," said Richard firmly. "It's not right. You have to turn the other cheek brother."

Kendu started laughing as Ant-live looked at Kendu with a smile.

"Son, who the fuck is this nigga? Did I tell you to bring Jesus to my house?"

"Nah" Kendu said through his laughter. "Son is cool. He's a church nigga, but that's my boy."

"Aiight," said Ant-live talking to Kendu but looking at Richard. "That's cool. If he's your boy, then he's my boy too. We live and die together, but church boy next time snuff a motherfucker!"

They all began to laugh as Richard thought to himself how cool Ant-live and Kendu were. If only he could change their ways by spreading the word of God.

"Check it out y'all," said Kendu interrupting Richard's thoughts. "I was at this bitch Shantel's crib, the one from Farragut P.J.'s in building 190. She said nobody was home so I'm smashing her out right? While I'm fucking the shit out of her, I look out of the corner of my eye and I see my fucking pants slide through a crack in the closet door. I get up and walk over to the closet and the bitch is behind me yelling 'Where the fuck is you going?' I pay the bitch no mind. So I open the closet door. Son, her little 10 year old brother got my whole money stack in his hand. I'm standing there butt-ass naked looking at this little nigga."

"You off the hook," Ant-live managed to say through his laughter.

"Nah, check it son," Kendu continued with a smile. "So I reach down to snatch my money out his hands, and my dick was still hard. Shit poked shorty in the eye, he start crying and the bitch Shantel behind me yelling, talking about get out of her house and asking why I hit her brother, I'm trying to explain to her that he got hit by accident with the same thing she got hit with on purpose, but she's yelling like somebody is killing her. So, I got dressed, got my money, and got the fuck up outta there."

Ant-live and Richard laughed so hard their stomachs began to hurt.

"Kendu, you're bugged out. You need help," Richard said through his laughter. "Scratch that, you need prayer."

Chapter Three

Richard sat on the benches outside of his Fort Greene projects taking Lisa's verbal abuse in stride. He wore a pair of brown hard-bottom shoes, brown pants, and a beige short sleeve shirt. He almost seemed to be smiling. Being near Lisa had put a smile on Richard's face; he felt as though he were falling in love with her.

"What the hell is wrong with you, running around with that ho-ass nigga Kendu. He fuck any and everything that moves. He probably got AIDS. And I don't know where you pick up that grimey ass nigga Ant-live with his foul ass. You ain't like them niggas. You got things going for you, don't mess yourself up by following them niggas."

Every time Richard looked at Lisa, it was like he was realizing how pretty she was for the first time. Not only was Lisa the most beautiful girl he had over seen, but she was always dressed in the most stylish clothes. She wore white tennis shoes, little yellow socks, and a short white tennis skirt with a matching top. Richard loved the way she held her hair up with a thin yellow ribbon. As Lisa spoke heatedly, her hair swung, grazing her delicate shoulders.

"I guess you ain't feeling what I'm saying, but at least I am giving it to you real. Before you know it you'll be running around with AIDS or doing some other dumb shit."

"I appreciate your concern," Richard said sincerely. "But I have no desire to be like Kendu or Ant-live. And everything you said they are, from what I heard, your man Shameek is the exact same way."

"Don't try to flip it and beat me in the head with that bullshit! I'm just saying you're better than them niggas, Shameek included."

"Well I don't feel I'm better than anyone," said Richard leaning back on the bench. "The Bible tells me never to think I'm better than anyone else. All my life people teased me about the way I dressed. I been laughed at so much I feel like a walking joke. I'm the church boy no girl wants to talk to. You didn't have to go through what I went through so you wouldn't understand what I'm saying, but Kendu and

Ant-live showed me nothing but love from the first day I met them, and they accept me for who I am."

"Look, I'm not trying to judge your friends," said Lisa now calming down. "It's just that, you deserve better. As for Shameek you are right, but the nigga gives me anything I want."

"Oh, so..." Richard paused. "Are you for sale?"

"No, I'm not for sale," Lisa began with an agitated expression on her face, "Shameek got shit locked down on this side. The nigga is thirty-three years old. I'm only twenty-two. But the nigga is strong, whatever he wants he gets. If he don't get it he'll destroy you, straight up."

Lisa knew she was making up excuses for being with Shameek.

Richard looked into her eyes and asked, "Why are you telling me all of this?"

"Because I like you. Look, I'm not stupid. Shameek's time is limited, that's how the game goes. I want to be your girl. Matter-of-fact, let's go up to my house and talk. I don't need these nosy ass bitches out here all in my business."

Lisa and Richard got off the bench, and walked to the other side of the projects. It took them ten minutes to get to the other side. It seemed as if everybody in the projects stared at Richard and Lisa as they made their way to Lisa's. Several of the guys outside gave respectful acknowledgement to Lisa, completely ignoring Richard. Even though some of them wanted to push up on her, none of them dared to even try. They were too afraid of what Shameek would do. Trying to get with her was suicide and these brothers wanted to live. They all wondered what Lisa was doing walking with Richard, but thoughts were dismissed because they knew Richard was not Lisa's type.

The guys hanging outside were not the only ones paying attention to Richard and Lisa as they passed. The girls in the projects looked at Lisa with hatred and jealousy. As she walked by with Richard, most of them whispered to each other and giggled but they all made sure not to let Lisa hear anything they had to say. Lisa was not only beautiful but she was one of the baddest girls in the projects. They knew Lisa and her three homegirls wouldn't hesitate to pull out box-cutters and get busy. Plus they knew Lisa had enough props in the projects to get anyone of them duffed out.

When they entered building 107 they walked up the stairs to the second floor. Lisa reached into her bra, pulled out her key, and entered the apartment. Richard was surprised at how well furnished the living room was. He looked around as Lisa locked the door. She then led the way to her bedroom; the room was not too big. A queen-sized bed took up most of the room. There was just enough room left for a TV that sat at the foot of her bed, and a nightstand with a beautiful white lamp rested atop. On top of the dresser resting near the closet, were an assortment of pictures and other mementos.

Lisa sat on the bed and began taking off her shoes. "You can sit on the bed. Do you want something to drink?"

"No, I'm okay," Richard answered as he sat down on the bed. "You have a nice apartment. You live here by yourself?"

"Hell no, but I wish I did. Me, my moms, and my brother stay here. But my mother's at work and I don't know where my brother is. He hangs out in Marcy Projects mostly. He gets money. You probably heard of him. His name is Omar, but they call him Omega. Anyway, like I was telling you outside, I like you, and I think I wanna be with you."

"But what about Shameek?" Richard asked.

"Shameek? I don't know. I got thirty thousand dollars in my bank account from that nigga. So I know he wouldn't take losing me lightly. Plus, he got two of the craziest niggas in the projects running with him, T-bone and stupid ass Rashien. But I don't want to talk about them niggas."

With no warning, Lisa leaned in and passionately kissed Richard. After a moment she drew back and began to laugh.

"You never kissed a girl before?" she asked.

"No, I've never had sex before either. I was always taught to wait until marriage."

"Damn, I hope you ain't looking for a virgin. Because you definitely won't find her in the Fort, or New York for that matter."

She started laughing, and began kissing Richard again. She leaned away from him, stood up and walked to the open window. Silently, she gazed out the window deep in thought. Richard thought about a story Kendu told him, and smiled. Richard arose from the bed and walked behind Lisa. When he neared her, he got down on his knees like Kendu instructed and lifted Lisa' short tennis skirt. She wore a pale pair of yellow lace panties. Richard leaned forward and planted a soft kiss on her round, and shapely ass. Lisa giggled as she swayed her hips.

"Let me find out my little church boy is a freak."

She then turned around, told him to stand up, and began to undress him. After she had all of his clothes off, she only removed her panties. She then grabbed his hard on, turned back towards the window and guided him into her. She closed her eyes, and moaned softly as he gave it to her from the back.

The whole morning was spent having sex. She took him into her mouth and taught him how to please her orally as well, until she came again, and again. After they took a shower together and got dressed, Lisa looked at Richard with a smile and said, "I know how to treat my man. Come on, I'm taking you shopping."

Chapter Four

Richard sat at his kitchen table eating his breakfast. He wore a grey Polo robe, with matching slippers. His mother and father sat at the table in their modest garb. Like every other morning, Maria sat reading the newspaper. Richard, Sr. looked particularly tense this morning, as he ate silently. He finished his meal, placed his fork on the table and looked at his son.

"I see you got all these expensive clothes. I hope you're not selling drugs out there in them streets, like the rest of them devils. "

"No dad, I'm not selling drugs. My girlfriend took me shopping. That's where I got the clothes."

"And where is this girl getting all of this money from? Maybe she's out there selling drugs."

"Honey," said Maria interrupting, putting down her newspaper. "Lighten up on the boy. He said his girlfriend took him shopping. Let that be the end of it. He's passed all his grades in school, and Lord knows how long he's been with you in church, every Saturday and Sunday."

Mrs. Brown knew it was a blessing for Richard, Jr. to finally be able to have the expensive clothes she and her husband couldn't afford. As a schoolteacher, she knew all too well how kids harassed and teased other kids who were less fortunate. She knew what her son was going through and so she felt happy that Lisa bought her son the clothes.

Whenever Lisa took Richard shopping, she would get whatever she thought would look good on him. When Richard saw the prices of things she picked out, he told her not to get it but she would anyway and always with a smile. She enjoyed shopping for her man and did not care about the price. It was the money Shameek gave to her anyway. She knew she was Shameek's trophy that every guy in the projects wanted to touch, but was afraid to. It wasn't just her beauty and her being Shameek's girl that made her stand above the other girls. It was the fact of her being the sister of the big time drug dealer, Omar. Shameek had made it his business to covet her. It took over a year for Lisa to realize that Shameek was not loyal to her and was having sex with numerous girls in the projects. Every time she saw a pregnant girl in the Fort Greene Projects, she wondered was Shameek the father of the unborn baby. Lisa had recently found out that Shameek had sex with her best friend, Tonya. When the time was right, she would step to Tonya and see what she had to say. She found out when she overheard T-bone laughing and telling one of his workers that after Shameek fucked Tonya, they all ran a train on her. As far as Lisa was concerned, Shameek was history and Richard was in her life now. She smiled, as they entered Michele Olivieri's on Orchard Street. When Lisa picked out the dark green alligator shoes, Richard couldn't believe the amount of money she was spending for them.

There was a knock at the door and Richard, Jr. excused himself to answer the door. Before he could get out of his seat, Maria stopped him. "Sit down and finish your breakfast, I'll get the door." She then excused herself, as Richard, Sr. and his son finished their breakfast in silence.

Maria entered the kitchen and took the dishes from the table.

"That was your friends at the door, Anthony and Kenny. I told them you will be outside in a little while, you're excused."

"Thank you ma," said Richard as he got up from the table and kissed his mother on the cheek. "Have a good day dad," Richard said to his father.

"Yeah," his father mumbled as Richard, Jr. went to his room to get dressed. It was hot outside so Richard decided to put on a white short sleeve Sean John shirt, peach colored Sean John shorts, white socks, and a fresh pair of white Nikes.

As he came out of his building, he saw Kendu and Ant-live sitting on the benches in front of his building.

"Damn son!" yelled a shocked Ant-live. "Look at the Bishop. That punk muh'fucker's taking up big offerings these days!"

They all began to laugh.

"Bishop, I been hearing about you," said a smiling Kendu. "Word around town is you got every bitch down here in the Fort dressing you and giving you a weekly allowance nigga. You know I gotta step my game up now."

"Kendu, I don't know where you got your information. Only my baby, Lisa, buys my clothes. I don't have another woman. It's about me and my baby. In fact, we're going to the movies tonight. But I don't know what we're going to see."

"You hear this nigga?" asked Ant-live jokingly. "Bitch buy him a tee-shirt and now that's his baby. Matterfact, she ain't buy you shit. Them bitches she hang wit' is boosters, so technically your ass is wearing stolen goods. Now tell that to the congregation in your church, boy!"

The three boys laughed as they made their way through the projects. When they finally reached Myrtle and Carlton Avenue, they saw Shameek's 1998 Lexus Land Cruiser, sitting on 22-inch rims. The system in the truck was banging a song from the new rapper, O-Fella. Only the money getters and big time drug dealers were banging his songs. With all the money Shameek was pulling in from his organization, he had a car in what seemed every color, and his outfits always matched his ride. Shameek's tall slender body emerged from his car in a pair of maroon gators and a tailor made maroon suit. He had his sleeves rolled up, exposing the iced out Rolex on his left wrist. He also sported a pinky ring flooded with diamonds, and a long platinum chain holding a platinum medallion full of ice.

Though he was an impressive figure, he had not been blessed with good looks. There was another man who exited the car. He was of slighter height than Shameek. He stood 5'7", with a stocky build, and skin as dark as the night. He wore no jewelry except the Rolex on his left wrist, minus the diamonds. He and Shameek were both thirty-three years old and heavy in the game. Rashien was Shameek's right hand and if anything needed to be done-legal or otherwise-it was

Rashien who pulled it off.

Though Shameek's reputation preceded him, Rashien was known as the most dangerous thug in the Fort. Whenever you saw Rashien out at night, you were guaranteed to see the coroner with the body bags by morning. Rashien had a large body count. It was even rumored that he once killed a guy because everyone said the guy looked just like him. He was a ruthless killer that would not only attack the person he had beef with, but he would also attack their family and friends. No one was safe.

As a child, Rashien stayed to himself. He was a bad kid that always found trouble to get into and no one knew why he was this way. He was often found hitting stray dogs with bottles and setting stray cats on fire. He enjoyed looking into the animal's eyes as they suffered. One day, Rashien was playing a game with a young boy his age, but it was not a typical child's game. Had a man not been walking in the park that day, the boy would have died. Rashien tied one end of a rope around the boy's neck and the other end around his own and told the boy they were Siamese twins. Wherever one went, the other had to follow, but Rashien was always the leader. Rashien decided to climb a fence, and the young boy began to follow. Rashien reached the top of the fence first and hoisted himself over. Before he leapt from the fence, he removed the rope from his neck and yanked it as he kicked the boy's hands off the fence. The young boy hung and gasped for air, as Rashien held tightly to the rope with a look of devilish enjoyment on his face. A man taking a walk near the playground saw the young boy hanging from the fence and quickly ran over to help the boy. He climbed the fence and removed the rope from the boy's neck. Though the boy fell from the fence and broke his ankle, he was thankful to just be alive and out of Rashien's hands. The man climbed down and looked at the boy's injury. He then made his way over to Rashien and gave him the much-deserved beating he needed. The man was so enraged by what Rashien had done to the young boy, that he took no mercy, and beat Rashien like a grown-man.

If it was known before, then it was confirmed then, there was something seriously wrong with Rashien. Rashien stood there and received his beating without a sound or even so much as a small tear in his eye. He simply stared at the man beating him, as if he were trying to memorize every detail of this man.

When Rashien got older and was deep in Shameek's crew, he sought out the man who beat him in the park that day and served his revenge. He shot the man four times in the head.

His parents took him to counseling but it never did anything for him, and he was a loner until he went to high school. It was there he met T-bone and Shameek. T-bone was like his twin, causing just as much havoc as he was. Shameek was dangerous also, but most of all he was a thinker that always kept money in all of their pockets.

As Rashien was talking, Shameek's eyes were focused on the three young boys coming his way. He looked at Richard and as they neared, Shameek called out to Richard with malice in his voice.

"A yo, your name Bishop?"

Richard turned around and answered.

"No, but that's what my friends call me. Why?"

"Why? You better stay the fuck away from my girl Lisa, before I kill all y'all little niggas. You hear me?"

"Yeah I hear you, but I think Lisa is old enough to make the choice as to who she wants to be with."

Shameek looked at Rashien with a look of feigned shock.

"Yo son, who the fuck is this little punk?"

"Yo, I don't know," answered Rashien. "But if you want the little nigga dead I'll kill him and his homeboys."

"Nah, he heard my warning. Let 'em keep being stupid. All y'all little niggas, get the fuck outta here!"

As they walked away Kendu looked at Richard and said, "Son, fuck that old ass nigga. I fucked four of his bitches, he just don't know it yet. Hating on us young niggas coming up. Fuck that nigga kid, he ain't nobody."

"A yo Bishop," said Ant-live, "Just give me the word. You know how I get down. Thug life nigga! Just give me the word and homie is dead. Straight like that!"

Chapter Five

"Hello, may I speak to Richard?"

"Yeah, this is Richard."

"What the fuck is wrong with you?" asked Lisa, "Why you ain't come get me? You fucking stood me up for the movies two days ago. And then I call and you keep telling me you busy, and you'll call me back. But do you call back? Hell no. What's wrong with you?"

Richard laid back on his bed with the phone in his left hand, looking up at the ceiling.

"I don't know what's going on," he answered. "One day I have no enemies, the next day brothers wanna kill me."

"Did Shameek say anything to you?" she asked, as she sat on the end of her bed with nothing on except the TV. It was 10:00 on a Thursday night with nothing going on.

Before she called Richard, she thought about going to her best friend Gina's house, but she knew Gina was probably shacked up with some guy and if she wasn't all she would talk about all night was dick. Lisa didn't want to hear that tonight, because that would just put her mind on Richard. She didn't want to think about him because he was acting like a jackass, but she couldn't help it. She wished her friend Pam wasn't with her boyfriend, because Pam would definitely have cheered her up.

Pam was the funny one, who would always make Lisa, Gina and Tonya laugh. She was like the female Chris Tucker, and she stayed wearing the latest wears because she was so good at boosting. Pam could steal stitches out of clothes! Her complexion was yellow like American cheese. She was five feet five, long sandy reddish hair, slim, but with an ass and breasts that made guys drool. And Lisa wanted to smoke a blunt and chill out with her homegirl, but Pam wasn't in the projects. Lately no one had heard from her. Pam was constantly on the move with her boyfriend. Some big balla she met from Crown Heights named Big G. Lisa wasn't even thinking about calling money hungry, grimey ass Tonya. Boredom has a way of making you go back on your word. Even though, she was mad at him for standing her up, she decided to call Richard anyway.

"Yeah, he approached me and said if I keep on spending time with you he's going to kill me or have me killed. Something to that effect."

"What the fuck is wrong with him?" questioned Lisa with her pretty face screwed up. "That nigga don't own me. I would tell my brother, but a crazy war might break out. That shit will be like Marcy and Tompkins projects, against Fort Greene. Damn, why did I even fuck with this knuckle head?"

"Oh, I'm a knucklehead now?"

Lisa laughed. "No boy. Not you stupid. I'm talking about ugly ass Shameek. I hate his ass."

"Anyway, I do miss you and I love you."

Lisa was feeling the same way lately. Two days without him was torture. She never felt this way about Shameek.

"Forreal? Fuck that nigga Shameek, he don't scare me. I love you too baby. You wanna go out?"

"When?" Richard asked now sitting up on his bed.

"Now!"

"Well, my parents are sleep. I can get up, get dressed and be at your house in twenty minutes. Where do you wanna go?"

"I don't know yet, but it's my treat. So, you'll know when we get there."

"Okay big spender," Richard said with a smile. "Oh yeah, and Lisa?"

"What is it baby?" Lisa asked softly.

"Um...can we do it tonight?"

Lisa giggled as she hung up the phone.

He got up, looked in his closet and laid a black pair of Sean John jeans out, black Timberland chukkas, and a multicolor Coogi vest out to wear. He quickly got dressed and contently looked into the mirror.

He smiled; he knew he looked good.

Richard noticed that more and more girls were taking notice of him. These were the same girls who use to diss and laugh at him, but now they wanted to get with him. However, his love and loyalty was to Lisa and he couldn't see himself with anyone else.

He checked himself in the mirror once more, then grabbed his keys off the dresser and shut his bedroom door. He quietly walked out of the apartment, careful not to wake his parents. After locking the front door, he hit the staircase and took off running like someone was chasing him.

Richard flung open the door to his building and jumped down the stairs. He hit Park Avenue and was on the other side in like ten minutes. He was about to cut through the projects, but was surprised when he saw Lisa approaching him. Absence does make the heart grow fonder, Richard thought, as he laid his eyes on Lisa. She was looking good in her powder blue Dolce and Gabbana short-set, a powder blue purse, and a black pair of Donna Karen slip-on shoes. She had on diamond studded earrings, a small gold chain around her neck, and when she walked she switched her ass so sexily, even other females got wet looking at her. She walked towards Richard, kissed him on the cheek, grabbed his hand and led him down Park Avenue.

"You're looking beautiful as always," said Richard. "I'm proud to say I'm your man."

"Thank you baby," replied Lisa with a smile. "I'm proud to have you as my man."

Lisa let go of Richard's hand, looked in her purse and pulled out car keys, as he wondered what she was doing. She walked to the driver's side of a brand new Range Rover sitting on 23 inch rims, better known as M.J.'s and opened the door.

"Who's truck is this?"

"Just get in," said Lisa as she slid in the driver's seat. When the truck was started the system came on banging the song, "Guess who's back" by Scarface, Jay-Z and Beanie.

"Whose truck is this?" Richard asked again.

"It's my brother's truck. Omar got mad cars, like he's trying to compete with Baby from Cash Money or something. He let me hold this one for the first time."

"If he got so much money, why is he still in the projects?"

"Because he thinks he's a fucking genius. He said if he spends his money on a big ass house, the Feds will be all over him. He wanted to move mommy but she's comfortable. She said she's not going anywhere. But knowing my brother, he probably got a house somewhere because he's never home. He only really comes through when me or mommy call him on his cell."

Lisa eased the truck off the Major Deegan at Fordham Road in the Bronx. Richard was so wrapped up in their conversation, that he didn't even remember getting on the FDR Drive from the Brooklyn Bridge. Lisa pulled onto a busy avenue and parked the car. They got out of the truck and Lisa walked over to join Richard. They held hands and walked into Jimmy's Bronx Cafe.

They entered the cafe and a man wearing a tuxedo escorted them to their table. Richard was in awe by the elegance of the dining room. The waiters were dressed in black slacks with crisp white shirts and black bow ties. Richard walked over to Lisa and pulled out her chair, before sitting at the table covered in white linens and china. Richard ordered rice and beans with fish on the side, and Lisa ordered the lobster and potatoes with a bottle of Cristal.

"I like this place," said Richard looking around. It's nice."

"Yeah it's alright. They have a podium over there and there goes the bar," Lisa motioned with her hands. "They also have a dance floor downstairs. Maybe one day we'll come back and I'll teach you how to dance."

"You wanna teach me everything, huh?"

Lisa smiled and the waiter finally brought their food and the bottle of Cristal to the table.

After their meal, Lisa paid the bill, leaving the waiter a generous tip. As they left Jimmy's Cafe, all eyes were on them. They made a perfect couple and those in the restaurant nodded their approval.

When they got back in the truck, Lisa pulled off with Hot 97 blasting a song by Angie Martinez.

They finally reached Brooklyn well after midnight. Lisa parked the car under a street light and she and Richard exited the car. He walked her to her building and Lisa invited him upstairs.

"I know it's kind of late, but you can come upstairs. The only one there is my mother, but most likely she's sleeping. Did you enjoy the restaurant?"

"I loved it," answered Richard with a smile. "And don't forget you still have to teach me how to dance."

"I know, right?" said Lisa, grabbing his hand and leading him into the building.

As they entered, two girls came out of the building and one of them looked at Richard and winked at him. Her friend glared at Lisa with a look of pure jealousy and hatred. The girls were almost out of the building, when Lisa heard one of the girls say, "I hate that bitch. She think she's all that. She had to buy that nigga to be with her ass."

"Shit if I had the money I'd buy that nigga too. He's too fine," said the other girl with a laugh.

"Bitch you stupid," said her friend. "Fuck both of them motherfuckers. They ain't nobody."

Lisa stopped in her tracks and let go of Richard's hand. She was ready to go back outside and beat the girls up. She was not worried about them trying to jump her because she knew they knew better, and plus Richard was with her. She turned to walk out of the building, when Richard suddenly grabbed her arm, stopping her from moving.

"It's not worth it baby," said Richard. "They're just mad because they're not you."

"Fuck that!" said Lisa angrily trying to pull away from Richard. "I will beat that bitch's ass. Fucking bum bitches!"

Richard pulled her towards him and kissed her passionately. "Boo come on, you gonna let them spoil our night?"

"You're right baby," said Lisa. "Come on let's go."

She grabbed his hand again and led him up the stairs. But Lisa still thought about the two girls. She couldn't wait to see Gina tomorrow. They would definitely handle their business when they run into the girls. Lisa had a brand new box-cutter that she was dying to test on the face of one of the many girls in the projects that made it their business to hate on her. Lisa was very pretty but at times she had the temper of an out of control gangster. She knew she would see the girls another time so she pushed them out of her mind and grabbed Richard's hand tighter. She felt so good being with him, and she hoped that their relationship would last forever. When they got to Lisa's apartment, she opened the door and kissed him deeply.

"Be quiet mommy's sleeping," she whispered as she pulled him inside, locked the door and led him quietly to her bedroom.

After making love for two hours, Richard got dressed and went home as Lisa laid in her bed drifting off to sleep with a smile on her face. Richard rushed home exhausted, hoping to be in bed before his parents awakened.

Chapter Six

"Turn your bibles to 1Timothy, chapter 2 verse 9," Pastor Brown preached. "The good book said 'I also want women to dress modestly, with decency and propriety. Not with braided hair or gold or pearls or expensive clothes, but with good deeds appropriate for women who profess to worship God.'"

As soon as those words left his mouth, a young Spanish woman with long braids, a white miniskirt, gold rings on her hands, and high heeled shoes raised from the pew and stormed out of the church. The church got quiet as everyone looked around checking out the other parishioner's attire. Women in the congregation that were less than appropriately dressed began to shift nervously in their seats. They were hoping they would pass under Pastor Brown's radar.

As usual, Richard sat in the front row of seats next to his mother. Sensing the tension in the church, he too wished that his father would change the subject before even more women became uncomfortable or worse, angry. Ever the devout follower, he quickly relaxed and smiled; he knew his father spoke the truth. Richard remembered the time his father told a man to come up to the pulpit. When the man stood in front of the whole church his father openly asked the man if he was a homosexual. Some of the parishioners giggled, while others were shocked by embarrassment. They couldn't believe Pastor Brown had put someone on the spot like that. The man hesitated for a moment and then admitted that he was indeed a homosexual and had been struggling with his identity. Pastor Brown thanked the man for being honest and confessing his struggles. He then told everybody in the church that homosexuality is not right with God and you couldn't find it being acceptable anywhere in the Bible. He then went on and told the man and the congregation that everyone in the church was family and that a good family does not hide problems from one another, they pray for and help one another. Pastor Brown preached that covered wounds don't heal, and if he's praying for someone then he should know what he's praying for. Before the service was over, Pastor Brown had the whole church in tears, comforting that man with love and prayers. He knew many people came to church because they had issues in their lives, but he also knew that most of them would never have the courage to confess their daily sins and struggles to their fellow Christians. He felt there was too much pretending in church, and he prayed for the day when the church could be truthful.

Pastor Brown, Sr. continued his sermon. "I know some of the women here do not want to hear that. And I do not blame them but what I preach is what the good book says. So when I preach what is written, am I right or wrong? I know some of you are saying, 'but times have changed', but I ask you, has it changed for better or has it changed for worse? Look around you and stop pretending. The reality is, fourteen and fifteen year old kids are having babies they cannot raise; they are selling drugs; and you don't want to see what is going on until a trigger happy police shoots them down like a dog in the streets. I'm suppose to accept it because times have changed? I tell you all today, let us not become like those of this world and when we sin let's pray to come out of it and not become it. Somebody talk to me. Can I get an Amen?"

The church erupted into a chorus of "Amens", "Praise the Lords" and "Hallelujahs". Richard clapped his hands as he stood out of his seat. He made a point to only sit near his mother during service. He noticed lately how some of the women in the church would openly flirt with him. Some asked for his phone number and then there were those that actually hugged him and rubbed their private parts against him as they said their greetings. He told his mother about it and she laughed saying it was because he was growing up and becoming more handsome every day. She suggested that he stay close to her to avoid any unwanted attention.

Pastor Brown continued preaching. "I'm not here to beat you down. I'm here to lift you up with the word of God. Lord knows we all need to be lifted up out of this madness that we're living in. Can I get an Amen?"

The church replied to his request with an "Amen".

"You didn't come to church to be brought down. You came to be lifted up!" yelled Pastor Brown.

Everyone in the church shouted Amen again. He looked at his congregation and calmly said, "I want you to be lifted up because righteousness exalts a nation, but sin is a reproach to any people. And the best way to get rid of sin is to be distracted by righteousness. Touch the person next to you and say righteousness exalts a nation."

Everyone in the church touched the person next to them and said with a smile, "Righteousness exalts a nation."

"But sin is a reproach to what?!"

"Are reproach to any people," answered the congregation emphatically.

The people jumped to their feet and waved their hands in the air, as they were being filled with the Holy Spirit. The tall black man playing the piano hit the keys every time Pastor Brown finished saying something.

"You have to get rid of those batteries and plug yourself in to the real power that is God. I don't know whether or not you serve Him, but you are going to need Him. Don't look and wait for someone to come and fix things for you. God is much too wise to let your destiny be tied into the hands of someone else. Your blessings are in yourself. And when things don't go as you would like them to and when you feel weak, God will strengthen you. He increases and re-news your strength, when you praise God. That's why we come to church. We don't come to church to pick up women. We come to replenish ourselves and fight the good fight with faith!"

Everyone clapped their hands shouting "Amen" and "preach on now, preach on" to the Pastor. Richard clapped too and smiled. What his father had just said was what he was trying to tell Kendu. He felt there was nothing wrong with meeting your soul mate in church, but that should not be your purpose for going. He was really feeling his father's sermon today; he rose from the pew and clapped louder than anyone else.

"I'm going to close this sermon by asking everyone to stand up."

When they all stood up out of their chairs Pastor Brown said, "Lord, please watch over everyone in this church. Do not let the devil tempt us, but take us into your glory and show us the way. Show us your way Lord. Everybody say..."

"Amen," the congregation said in unison. The members made their way around the church greeting each other and hugging their fellow parishioners, as they all prepared to leave and go back to whatever life they had outside of the church.

$

Richard sat in the back seat of his father's car. It was a solemn ride home, as the Brown family reflected on this Sunday's sermon. Pastor Brown slowly pulled away from the curb in his grey 1983 Buick and headed home to the Fort Greene Projects.

Upon reaching home, Richard entered his room and took off his black silk tie and white Polo shirt. Before he could take off his white wife beater tee-shirt, his mother called him into the kitchen. They called the tee-shirt a wife beater because every time a man beat his wife and the police came they always brought the man out in handcuffs wearing that kind of tee-shirt.

"Yes ma?"

"I need you to go to the supermarket for me and pick up a loaf of bread and a pound of sugar."

Richard scooped the money off the table, gave his mother a kiss on the cheek and headed out of the apartment.

He was leaving the supermarket on Myrtle Avenue with his purchases and was surprised to see Shameek, Rashien and their other partner, T-bone waiting for him.

"Yo, what's up duke?" asked Shameek.

Richard silently looked at the three thugs blocking his path. This was the first time he had seen T-bone, but he quickly understood why he was feared by so many. T-bone was an impressive figure, standing six foot four inches tall, and built like a football player.

"Didn't I tell you to stay away from my bitch?" asked Shameek. "Y'all little punks just don't listen."

"No, you need to listen," Richard replied. "You just don't get the point that Lisa doesn't want to be with you anymore."

The words had just passed through Richard's lips, when T-bone punched him squarely in the mouth. Richard fell to the ground with such force and the purchases were flung about. Once he was down, the three thugs encircled him and began stomping and punching him. Richard tried to get up but the blows to his head and face were too much. He saw colors, a flash of light and then he passed out.

Chapter Seven

Dear Kenny,

I hope this letter finds you in good health, physically as well as mentally. As for me I'm definitely in tune with myself and my surroundings. I just got out the box for stabbing this kid up that was playing games with me. The nigga owed me some money and I don't play when it comes to that paper. What's up with your mother? Tell her I said hello. I don't know what the hell is wrong with her. The last time I saw you, you were a lil' fella and I hear you look just like me. Oh yeah, my girl from the next building from you told me they call you Kendu now. I know your mother don't allow that and I hope you ain't with that five percent thing. Tell your moms that I love her...

Kendu balled up the letter with Sing-Sing Correctional Facility stamped on the front of the envelope and threw it out of his window. Every time his father wrote him, it was always the same thing. He just got out of the box and wants Kendu's mother to come up north to see him. Never did he make suggestions of wanting to see his son; Kendu was tired of reading his letters. He had never met his father in person and now that he was older he definitely did not want to meet him. Every time his father got upset at Kendu's mother he would try to take it out on his son. Not writing him for months or years depending on his mood. But Kendu wasn't even thinking about him. The only time that he seemed to write Kendu was when he found himself back in a box called South Port, and over the years, Kendu's mother had made no attempts to take him to see his father since the day he had suggested they come to see him and for her to bring him some drugs. Going to see him was out of the question. She was never going to put her son's life in jeopardy over that man or anyone else. That was not going to happen.

Kendu got off of his bed, and when he walked into the kitchen, immediately the telephone began to ring. He picked it up on the third ring and said, "Hello?"

"Hey baby, what you doing?" asked his mother.

"Ain't nothing," answered Kendu with a smile. "I just now got another letter from my father."

"Oh yeah? What is he talking about now?"

"The same old thing. He just got out of the box over some money that some guy owed him."

"Boy, I tell you. Some men never grow up. He's running out of time for smarts."

"Yeah, and this girl from 433 told me, that her brother is up north with him and all they do is sniff dope and stay in all kinds of trouble. I know that's my pops and everything but I don't even wanna know him."

"I hear you and that is up to you. I have always gave you the opportunity to get to know your father, and you make your own decisions when it comes to him. But as for myself, like the guys in the projects say 'I ain't fucking wit' the dude.'"

Kendu bust out laughing at what his mother had just said. He loved her so much. She was much cooler than most moms and she understood everything he went through from not having a father figure in his life to having problems with the many girls that sweated him. She was so proud when Kendu graduated from Eastern District High School. He had plans to go to college but he really wanted to go away to college. His mother was not having any of that. She knew that he only wanted to go for the girls and that if she had allowed him to go, she would miss him too much, and she was not ready for her baby to leave her alone yet.

"Ma, you're crazy," said Kendu with a smile. "And he said to tell you that he love's you."

"Yeah, like the police love young black males."

After Kendu was done laughing at his moms he said, "So what's going on? Where are you?"

"I'm still at work. And I have to work overtime tonight. I left a few dollars on my dresser so you can buy some Chinese food for dinner because I won't get home 'til late and I don't want you to burn down my kitchen trying to cook."

"Ma stop playing, you know I can burn."

"Yeah that's the problem," she replied.

Kendu smiled and said, "Okay ma, I'll see you tonight."

"Kendu."

"Yeah ma?"

"Don't have a bunch of girls in that house and if they even so much as think about entering my bed room I'll skin you alive."

Kendu laughed and said, "Ma I told you I'm going to be a virgin until I'M at least twenty four."

"Yeah right. My so-called friend Sharon had made sure that did not happen. Anyway cutie, I love you and I'll see you when I get home."

"I love you too ma."

As soon as Kendu hung up the phone, it rang again. He snatched it up and said, "Hello?.. Oh. What's up Tina?... Nah, I can't come over right now baby...Nah, you can't either...Yeah I'm about to go out...Yeah, I can come to your crib tonight...Yeah, I love you too...okay bye, I'll see you tonight."

Kendu hung up the phone with a smile. He then walked into the living room, sat on the couch and clicked on the TV. He relaxed on the couch, wearing shorts and no shirt. He knew he was a handsome young man and was very proud of his physique. He was sporting his Tommy Hilfiger slippers and green Fubu sweatpants with the pockets. He looked down at his perfectly sculpted chest and stomach, and smiled. He knew the girls loved his body and the guys were envious. He was more chiseled than L.L.Cool J without even doing sit-ups.

Kendu understood the importance of a nice apartment so he made sure to keep his mother's apartment neat at all times. They had a comfortable living room with plush wall-to-wall green carpeting, which was accented by the clean, crisp, white walls. The rest of the apartment was nice as well. Kendu would go to some of his friend's apartments in the same building and he could not see how they allowed themselves to live the way they did. It had nothing to do with poverty. They just lived in filthy apartments because they were too lazy to clean up. Kendu made it a habit to always meet them outside instead of looking at their dirty living quarters. He told himself that he would never let his apartment become a hangout spot like so many of them had.

Kendu sat on his green soft leather sofa waiting for a girl name Christine to come downstairs from her apartment. She probably had to get rid of her boyfriend before she could sneak down here, Kendu thought to himself with a smile.

Three hours before he read his father's letter, Donna from Spencer and Dekalb was trying to wear him out. She was truly a freak. After having sex for the second time, she licked every part of his body. But when her tongue had touched the crack of his ass he leapt out of the bed like he was on fire. He told himself many times the only thing that's going to get that close to his ass was tissue. Tired of her getting too freaky, he told Donna he had to get up and take care of a few things and that he would see her tomorrow afternoon. Once she had left, he took a long hot shower planning the rest of his day. As he emerged from the hot shower, he received a phone call from Christine saying she was coming downstairs in a couple of hours. He decided to wait until she came to fully plan the rest of his day, but one thing was for sure, it was definitely going to be a long day.

Kendu flicked off the TV and began to make his way to the kitchen, when there was a knock on the door. He peered through the peephole and then ushered in the beautiful Christine. She had a petite frame and had her hair cut in a short style like Halle Berry. She favored a young Stacy Dash, and she wore tight dark-blue jeans and a low cut white sweater. Though he would never deny she was an attractive girl, he didn't go crazy over her like the other guys in the projects. Kendu held himself to high standards; all the girls he associated himself with were beautiful. He made a point not to become involved with any of the girls who lived in his building because he didn't want them in his business all the time, but he made an exception for the young lady Christine. He figured that since she already had a man and their relationship was strictly sexual, he wouldn't have to deal with any jealousy.

"What's up baby?" asked Kendu. "Come on in."

Christine walked inside of the apartment with a smile on her face and touched his stomach as she walked past him. She made her way to the sofa and seductively sat down.

"What took you so long?" asked Kendu sitting close to her.

"You know this nigga is a headache," she answered referring to her boyfriend. "I'm ready to get rid of his ass. He never take me anywhere, he can't fuck for shit, and he spends most of the money he makes selling drugs in the back of the building on these little nasty ass bitches. So you ready to be my man or what?"

Kendu laughed and smoothly said, "I like the way things are. Let's be real, right now homie gives you anything you want, which means you ain't got no problem breaking me off when I need something and duke don't know what's popping between me and you. But if you became my girl, then I'll have to let that be known. And the only reason that I wouldn't want to have your beautiful ass being my girl is because I don't want no beefs with a jealous ex-boyfriend. Any man in his right mind that's in a relationship with you would flip if you leave them. Yeah even I would," Kendu said with a straight face.

It was all part of the game. But the truth of the matter was that Kendu was not ready to be in any kind of a committed relationship. He always told himself that New York had too many beautiful women to go out like that. Unlike his father though, he knew if he got any girl pregnant, his player days were over. That is why he always wore condoms when having sex, because he did not want to face that responsibility just yet.

"I know," said Christine with a smile. "But I love everything about you Kendu."

"Like what?" asked Kendu looking into her eyes.

"The way you carry yourself, the way you talk and treat me, like I'm special. The way you take everything so calmly. It's just...everything. The way you make love to me," she said with a smile on her pretty face.

"Speaking of making love," said Kendu slyly. "Let's go to my room and be about it."

He grabbed her hand and led the way to his bedroom. When they entered, she sat on his bed and began taking off her clothes as Kendu cut on the CD player in his room. The sounds of Faith Evan's "I love you" came through the CD player loud and clear. Kendu's room was not big but it was comfortable and neat. A color TV sat on a stand next to his dresser against the wall. His closet was near the window and the door was open exposing all kinds of name brand clothes and expensive footwear. Christine laid on the bed with nothing on and moved her body to the song. Kendu pulled off his sweatpants and glanced at the clock on his dresser. He then realized he had to go check Bishop today. He grabbed a condom off of the dresser and made his way up Christine's very beautiful body.

Chapter Eight

Richard woke up Monday morning; his entire body was in pain. He then remembered the events of the day before. Shameek was walking towards him and then darkness. He vaguely remembered his mother crying over his bed, his father asking who had done this to him, and Kendu trying to comfort him by telling him that he would get the guys who did this to him. Everything was so hazy, he couldn't really differentiate what was reality and what he had dreamed. Based on the pain he was feeling, he figured the beating he received had been real for sure. As he became more aware of his surroundings he suddenly remembered that Lisa had been there too. She was crying and cursing like a drunken sailor. Richard thought about how his parents must have looked at Lisa when she started cursing. Thinking about it made him smile but the pain was unbearable.

His mother appeared in the doorway. "My baby," she said with tears still in her eyes. "Are you okay?"

"Yes ma, I'm okay. Just a little sore."

Maria sat down on her son's bed and gently wiped his face with a cool washcloth. She thought she was going to have a heart attack when the little boy banged on her door saying her son was all bloodied up and dying in front of the supermarket. She called to her husband and they rushed out of the apartment to see what happened to Richard. When they got to the scene, there was a crowd of people standing around. Richard was lying on the ground drifting in and out of consciousness bleeding from his nose and his head. As Maria stood there in shock at the scene, Pastor Brown lifted his son from the ground and helped him to their apartment.

Passersby looked at the Browns as they made their way home in shock and wonderment at the sight of Richard. Those who had saw the fight shook their heads in pity. Pastor Brown overheard two women talking about the incident.

"That's fucked up what they did to that boy. He don't bother nobody. One day somebody gonna kill them niggas. Watch! You saw how they was stomping his head into the ground?"

"Yeah I seen it," answered the other woman. "That's fucked up. But I bet you it's over that girl. A lot of niggas in these projects got killed over these little fast ass girls."

"Bitch you got some kind of nerves," said her friend rolling her eyes. "Like you forgot. Little Rob is still in jail for killing Disco back in the days over your stink ass!"

The other woman laughed, stuck her middle finger up and walked away. Pastor Brown shook his head from side to side and continued to make his way back to the building. He heard everything the two women had said and thought to himself, when will these women grow up and stop acting like teenagers? They were almost forty years old still wearing miniskirts, halter tops and doing nothing but standing around gossiping.

Maria ran to her son and husband as tears fell from her face. She held Richard's hand tightly, fearful that if she let go, she might lose him. As they neared the building, Kendu and Lisa came running towards them.

"Who the fuck did this to my baby?!" yelled Lisa angrily. "I'm telling my brother to fuck them niggas up! Watch! It's on now!"

"Young lady stop all that cursing," said Pastor Brown. "He will be alright. He just needs some rest."

"I'm sorry Mr. Brown," said Lisa. Then quietly under her breath she said, "I hate these motherfuckers."

Kendu remained still. He walked over to Richard and helped him upstairs to his apartment. He was down for whatever Richard wanted to do after he was better. If he would've gotten down to the Fort ten minutes earlier things would have been different, he told himself. He and Ant-live were on their way to see him, when a girl he knew told him what had happened. He ran to the scene, as Ant-live went back to Nostrand Avenue to get his gun.

Lisa and Maria both shed tears and when they got upstairs, Maria invited Lisa and Kendu inside. When Richard laid down on his bed, he quickly fell asleep.

"We've all been worried about you," said Maria. "Kenny and Lisa are in the living room with your father. They both had just arrived. That Lisa is a sweet girl and I can tell that she loves you. She keeps saying she needs to see you. I'll let her come in first and then Kenny can come in. Okay?"

"Yes ma. Thank you."

"Son, do you want anything to drink?"

"Yes, a cup of water please. You can let Lisa bring it."

"Okay," his mother replied. She then kissed him on the cheek, got up and walked out of the room.

Richard had just closed his tired eyes, when he heard Lisa open the door to his bedroom. She was beautiful. She wore her long hair in two braids, Indian style. Richard wanted to stand up and give her a long kiss, but his sore body wouldn't allow him. Lisa walked over to the bed, gently kissed him on the lips, and gave him the cup of water. She sat on the bed and played with his wavy hair as he took sips from the cup. He placed the glass on the nightstand and attempted to shift his body but the pain in his side was unbearable.

"Relax baby," said Lisa. "Everything will be fine. Your face is swollen on the right side but it's much better than yesterday."

Tears welled in her eyes as she continued to play with his hair. "I feel like everything is my fault. I never should've gotten with you. I mean, I wanna be with you but I don't want you to get hurt."

"It's too late for that," he said with a smile. "I love you Lisa, and no one, Shameek or otherwise, can stop the love that I have for you."

"I told my brother what happened, he said for you to keep your head up and don't tell anybody who did this to you. He said he'll talk to you soon."

"Okay," said Richard.

Just then his father and Kendu entered the room. Kendu had a smile on his face, while his eyes told a different story.

"Who did this to you?" were the first words that passed through Pastor Brown's lips. "I'm going to have the police pick them up for what they did to you. Now, who did this?"

Richard looked at the blank look on Kendu's face and then turned to look at Lisa's beautiful face. He then remembered what her brother Omar had said.

"Dad, I have no idea. I didn't see anyone's face."

His father looked him in the eyes for a full minute and then walked out of the bedroom. That was the first time that he had ever lied to his father and he felt terrible about it. But he felt it was the right thing to do.

"Yo son, you aiight?" asked Kendu. "That's my word son, that punk nigga gonna get his."

"Kendu, leave it alone. It's my problem and I'll handle it," said Richard. "I'm going to pray about it and then I'll talk to Shameek."

"Son, you buggin'. I understand you a church kat, but you can't talk to niggas like Shameek. He don't understand your language. You just got to put one in him."

"Don't tell him he gotta put one in him!" Lisa barked back. "Richard is not like y'all niggas."

"Bitch shut the fuck up," said Kendu angrily. "You the reason my son is caught up in all this bullshit!"

"Fuck you Kendu!"

Richard held up his hand and said, "Can both of you be quiet? It's nobody's fault. I said I'll talk to Shameek."

"Aiight son I'm out," said Kendu looking at Lisa. "I'll slide through later and see you, when your girl is gone. I'm going to check Ant-live right now. He's type heated and ready to bring drama."

"Just relax I got this," said Richard as he gave Kendu a five.

Kendu left, as Lisa began kissing Richard and playing in his hair again.

Kendu walked through the Fort Greene Projects, thinking about what Shameek and his homeboys had done to Richard. Kendu knew he wasn't in Shameek's league, but one thing was for sure, he definitely wasn't scared of him either.

As he turned onto Myrtle Avenue, he saw Shameek and Rashien making their way towards him. Kendu thought to cross the street because he didn't have a gun on him, but he thought he'd be damned if he let two punks intimidate him. He continued down the street until they were face to face. Shameek and Rashien both wore devilish smirks on their faces.

"What's up playboy?" asked Shameek stepping in front of him. "What's up with your homie? You see I had to discipline his punk-ass. Somebody needed to teach him how to talk to a thug nigga. "

"Duke I hate to bust your bubble but you ain't no thug nigga," said Kendu. "Actually, you're a real clown-ass nigga. Beating up young niggas because you can't control your bitch."

"What?!" Shameek asked with his face screwed up.

Kendu knew Shameek was ready to go into action, so he beat him to the punch, hitting him squarely on the chin, knocking him out cold. He quickly turned to attack Rashien, but instead found a black .9 millimeter barrel staring him down. He paused for a moment and then took off running up Carlton Avenue, but Rashien was not too far behind him. Kendu made it to the corner and turned down Willoughby Avenue. He shortly reached the corner of Vanderbilt and Willoughby Avenue when he heard three gunshots. The first shot hit him in the leg, and the other two missed. He fell hard to the ground and when he rolled over on his back, Rashien held the nine millimeter pointed at his head and fired four shots at point blank range.

Chapter Nine

Fear not the terror of the night, nor the arrow that flies by day, nor the pestilence that stalks in the darkness, nor the plague that destroys at midday. A thousand may fall at your side, ten thousand at your right hand, but it will not come near you. You will only observe with your eyes and see the punishment of the wicked. If you make the Most High your dwelling-even the Lord who is my refuge-then no harm will befall you, no disaster will come near your tent. For he will command his angels concerning you to guard you in all your ways; they will lift you up in their hands, so that you will not strike your foot against a stone. You will tread upon the lion and the cobra; you will trample the great lion and the serpent. Because he loves me, says the Lord, I will rescue him; I will protect him, for he acknowledges my name. He will call upon me, and I will answer him, I will be with him in trouble, I will deliver him...

The church was near Dekalb Avenue and Adelphi Street. People from all over Brooklyn, especially young girls who had sexual relations with him, attended Kendu's funeral. They were crying and yelling more than anyone, even Kendu's family. Richard sat in the back of the church wearing a pair of alligator shoes, a dark blue suit, white dress shirt, dark blue tie and a pair of dark sunglasses; but they could not hide the tears that streamed down his face. Lisa sat next to him wearing black Prada shoes, black stockings, a black Gigi Hunter dress that came to her knees and a black pair of Versace shades. As the tears rolled down her face, all she could remember was the argument she had with Kendu just before he was killed. Remembering the day he pushed up on her before she met Richard, but after turning him down how quickly he started talking to her friend Pam. Kendu was like that, he didn't wait for girls to change their minds. He simply moved on and got with someone else.

"He was a good boy," the preacher continued. "All he wanted to do in life was have fun and make people happy. He was very well liked and easy to get along with. It's a shame that so many of our children are being gunned down in the streets. Kenny Tyrone Patterson was a good boy. He never been in trouble, he graduated high school and was about to attend college. We lost one of our brightest children to violence. But God called him home on July 25th. I believe God wanted that strength in Heaven. And He called him home."

Richard listened to the preacher and he believed that he could have given a better sermon, but he knew he was not strong enough to take on that task. He would break down just thinking about the times that he and Kendu shared. He loved no one outside of his father and mother as much as he did Kendu.

"Kenny is in a much better place now," continued the preacher with his Bible in front of him. "I'm going to open to Psalm 91 and read from there."

Richard knew the chapter by heart and recited it silently as the preacher opened his Bible to the page and began reading.

"He who dwells in the shelter of the Most High will rest in the shadow of the Almighty. I will say of the Lord, He is my refuge and my fortress, my God, in whom I trust. Surely he will save you from the fowler's snare and from the deadly pestilence. He will cover you with his feathers, and under his wings you will find refuge; his faithfulness will be your shield and rampart and..."

Richard recalled how he first met Kendu and how they had clicked as soon as they met each other. Kendu was more like a brother to him than a friend. He never felt so angry as he did now and he knew in his heart that no matter how much of a Christian he was, he would never be able to forgive Shameek for what he'd done. Richard felt that it was because of him that Kendu was murdered. Maybe he should've told Ant-live to handle the situation, but he didn't want anyone else to die on account of him.

When Richard first heard what happened to Kendu, he went looking for Shameek. He was still in pain from the beating he took, but it could not compare to the pain he felt in his heart. Lisa was finally successful in talking him out of searching for Shameek. She argued that he didn't have a gun and that Shameek wasn't the kind of person to just sit and talk things out; they would try to jump him again or even kill him this time around. Lisa told Richard that she'd talk to her brother Omar and see what he could do. She said it was a street beef, and street niggas would handle it.

Richard hadn't seen Ant-live since Kendu's death. He knew Ant-live would be out for blood. All Ant-live ever talked about was robbing or killing someone. Richard couldn't understand why he was not at Kendu's funeral; didn't he love Kendu? Wasn't Kendu his homie? Richard had no answers, but he knew it had to be a good reason why Ant-live was not here today.

The preacher completed his sermon in tribute of Kendu and invited his friends to memorialize him. After some of his friends finished speaking, Kendu's mother made her way to the pulpit.

"Hello everyone," she said. "My name is Gloria Patterson for those who don't know me, and that is my son in that casket. I would like to thank everyone for being here today. Even those who I do not know."

Gloria Patterson was a beautiful woman. She had a beautiful clear complexion and long black hair. People often mistook her for Kendu's sister, rather than his mother. Everyone always said that she looked like a young Phylicia Rashad from the Cosby Show.

"My son is very special to me and it's hard to deal with the fact that he is no longer here," she continued. "But he will always be in my heart, and I hope in yours as well. He had a wonderful sense of humor and he meant many different things to many different people. He would always tell me, that if he could not be real to himself and those he loved, then he didn't want to live. He was very loyal to his family and friends. He also had a lot of girlfriends, as most of us can see that many of them are here today. And I want to thank all of you for coming. It wasn't about disrespect with my son; he just loved women. And not to try to justify being with different people, but sometimes when we love something, we have a problem of wanting more of what we love. My sons' favorite rapper was Tupac Shakur and like Tupac, my son lived his life for those around him. That's how deep his love was for those he cared about. So it would only be right to recite a poem written by Tupac because this is the best way I can pay tribute to my son."

She unfolded a white piece of paper, looked at the people in the church and smiled. She then turned her eyes to the paper and began reading the words of Tupac that she dedicated to her one and only son Kendu. After reciting the poem, "In the Event of My Demise" from Tupac's poetry book, Gloria folded the paper, put both of her hands over her face and cried.

An older man, in his sixties, walked to Gloria and helped her from the pulpit. He hugged her and kissed her on the forehead as he led her back to her seat. She dried her tears and within minutes she looked as if she was never crying; she was definitely a very strong woman.

When the funeral was over, Richard wanted to go speak with Gloria, but was petrified. What if she blamed him for her son's death? Richard felt it was his fault, but he didn't want Kendu's mother to yell and scream at him. Before he could decide what to do, Lisa grabbed his hand and led the way towards Gloria. She had just finished speaking with a tall slender woman, when she turned to face Richard and Lisa with a smile.

Richard took off his glasses and revealed that his eyes were red and puffy from shedding so many tears.

"Hello Ms. Patterson. My name is Richard Brown and this is my girlfriend Lisa. I was a very good friend of your son, Kendu. I mean Kenny."

"It's okay you can call him Kendu," said Gloria with a kind smile. "He preferred that name. I use to call him that as well. Are you the Richard that he used to call Bishop?"

"Yes ma'am," answered a surprised Richard.

"He always spoke of you. My son and I were very close and we would talk about everything. That was my son and my best friend. Sometimes he would tell me a few things about you and we would laugh together. He always said he loved you like a brother, and you were the only friend that he said he truly trusted. He would call you his church brother."

"Ms. Patterson," Richard interrupted with a frown on his face. "I may be the blame for your son dying. I have problems with the guys that killed your son. And I believe they killed your son because he was my friend. I feel so terrible, I can't even sleep."

"Kendu told me about some guys you had trouble with," said Gloria again surprising Richard. "Don't blame yourself Bishop. Kendu always knew he had choices to make in life. I always taught him to make choices that he felt right with. And he wouldn't have felt right not being your friend because you have enemies. He made his choices, he lived with his choices and died with them. There are not many young men like that anymore with morals and principles and I'm proud of him. Now I'm telling you, be careful out there in the streets and make the right choices in your life. If I can do anything for you, you know where I live. Feel free to stop by, and be careful. You hear me baby?"

"Yes ma'am," answered Richard.

Gloria kissed Richard on the cheek and walked out of the church with sorrow on her face, accompanied by two women.

Richard and Lisa walked out of the church shortly after and were surprised to see Ant-live leaning on a car outside.

"What's up Bishop?" asked Ant-live.

"What's up Ant?" replied Richard. "Why you didn't come inside?"

"I don't wanna see my dog like that. Plus I don't like funerals, only sending people to them. I heard Rashien is the one who killed

Kendu and the word on the street is me and you is next. But I ain't going out like that baby."

Ant-live lifted his shirt to expose a black three fifty-seven. He then looked at Richard and said, "A-yo, give me two days. I'll be down your end to handle this little situation kid."

Ant-live then walked away up Dekalb Avenue, as Richard and Lisa looked at him silently, both knowing that somebody else would soon die.

Chapter Ten

"Hello, may I speak to Richard?"

"This is Richard, who's calling?"

"My name is Omar, Lisa's brother, but you can call me Omega. I don't like talking on phones, so if you can come to my house in like twenty minutes that would be cool. Okay?"

"Alright, I'll be there in twenty minutes," Richard said and hung up the phone. He'd been waiting to speak to Omar for a week now.

When Lisa told Richard that Omar wanted to see him, he was overjoyed. Maybe Omar would talk to Shameek and stop the unnecessary killings.

Richard went to his room to get dressed. He put on a white tee-shirt, grey Iceberg sweatpants, grey track Adidas and grabbed his keys off of the dresser and headed out the door.

He made it to Lisa's building in ten minutes and made his way to the second floor apartment. He knocked on the door and a tall, muscular man appeared at the door. He was wearing a money green Tommy Hilfiger robe, and money green slippers also made by Tommy Hilfiger.

"Come in and have a seat," said Omar.

Richard entered the living room and sat on the sky blue couch. Omar sat opposite from him in the sky blue leather recliner in the corner of the room.

"My sister is in love with you," said Omar. "That's why I called you over here. You got beef with Shameek and them niggas. I'm telling you like I told them, nothing better not happen to my little sister. But I ain't call you to diss you, I don't get down like that. And I hear you been going through a lot already with these kats."

"Yeah, Shameek just doesn't know when to give up," said Richard leaning back on the couch. "Lisa loves me, and he can't stand the fact he lost his girl to a church boy."

"Well listen here church boy, these niggas wanna kill you. And I'm not telling you to go out and kill, but you do have to protect yourself. Why would you let Lisa, and your family feel the sadness of attending your funeral? They already gave you a beat down, they killed your right hand man, and given the chance you're dead also. Fuck that turn the other cheek bullshit. You tried that already and they killed your man afterwards. Keep turning the other cheek and your whole family may die. Yeah, even your Pastor pops. That's how them niggas get down."

"What do you think I should do?"

"Do the only thing you can do," answered Omar. "Protect your motherfucking self. Don't worry about my sister. My rep protects her. The reason I told Lisa to tell you not to let anyone know who jumped you is because you don't need the cops involved. The worse thing a person can be is a snitch. And once you tell not only are you dead, but those who associate with you is dead as well. Dig? Maybe not physically, but you'll never be respected. A reputation means a lot. Trust me kid, it's easier to cope with a bad conscious than with a bad reputation. Like I said, protect yourself. You need a gun?"

"No, I don't want a gun," Richard answered. "But if I need it I'll give you a call."

"Okay that's cool, I'll assist you as much as I can."

"Can't you talk to Shameek and just tell him to leave all of this alone?" asked Richard, hoping that Omar would say yes.

Omar rubbed his beard thoughtfully and then said, "I don't really get into nigga's beefs. And I'm not doing that peace making shit for the simple fact you don't get busy. That puts me out there to one day do them clown ass niggas a favor and that's not happening. I don't like them kats at all. I don't even know why Lisa started dealing with that bird. So like I said I'll give you a gun and assist you as much as I can by letting you know on the low what's going on."

"Omega, I never shot anyone in my life."

Omar folded his arms and asked, "You ever been shot?"

Richard just put his head down without answering.

"I thought so," said Omar. "That's the name of the game, shoot or get shot. But don't look so down, Shameek will get over my sister. I just don't wanna see you get killed. That shit will fuck my little sister head up, but I just can't take your beef, because a lot of good niggas will get killed over some bullshit."

"I understand and I know what you mean about protecting me and my family. If I need a gun, I'll come see you. I just hope and pray I don't need it. I'm not that kind of guy. There's nothing tough about me, but I do have to protect myself if I really have to."

"Let me ask you something Rich," said Omar leaning back in his chair. "Is my sister the first girl you had sex with, and do you love her?"

Richard nodded his head with a serious look.

"I thought so," said Omar smiling. "You gonna be alright homie. Niggas in love, will do what the average nigga doesn't have the balls to do. I can read people pretty well and I can tell you ain't no clown ass nigga."

Omar stood up and Richard did the same. For some reason, Omar liked the young boy's style. He was different. He wasn't like the other dudes he saw everyday, fascinated with being around gangsters and pretending to be tough. He really wanted to help Richard out but he wasn't used to being the peacemaker, especially after someone had already been killed. In the streets that made the one that lost the loved one look soft. He did not want Richard to live off of his name because he would be stuck in that shadow forever. But Omar did want to help him, so he decided to think about it and then get back to Richard with his decision. It was all he could do, he told himself.

They shook hands, Omar gave him his cell phone number, and Richard walked back to his building.

$

It was 10:30 on a Tuesday night and the remaining glow of the sun was just beginning to dissipate. People were outside enjoying the warm weather. A gentle breeze blew; it was the most beautiful night of the summer. Little kids were playing as their parents and friends sat outside on the benches conversing. It was a near perfect scene, except for the drug dealers on the avenue, selling their wares to those who did not want to see the world through sober eyes.

Richard wanted to run and keep on running, but he knew he could not escape his problems. He would have to stand up like a man and face them. He thought Omar would take care of the situation, but all he really did was offer him a gun. Richard knew how to shoot one; he remembered being on the roof of his building with Ant-live and Kendu. As usual, Kendu was talking about the girls he had sex with as he and Ant-live passed a blunt back and forth. Richard didn't like the smell of marijuana, so he stood a few feet away from them as they smoked their weed. When Kendu took the blunt, Ant-live pulled out two guns from his waist. Richard's heart began to beat faster and faster. Ant-live walked towards Richard and handed him one of the guns. Once Richard calmed down, Ant-live showed him how to shoot the nine as well as the three fifty seven he was holding. They both went off like cannons, and Richard dropped the gun to the roof like it was burning his hand. Kendu laughed so hard, he cried. Those were the good old days when Kendu was still alive.

Richard approached the front of his building and saw Ant-live standing there smoking a blunt. He was surprised to see him; Ant-live had made himself very scarce since Kendu's death.

"What's up Ant?" asked Richard. "Why are you smoking that junk in front of my building? You know if my moms or pops see you, I'll never hear the end of it."

"My bad son," said Ant-live as he put the blunt out and put the remainder of it in his shirt pocket. "Did you see that nigga Shameek yet?"

"No, I didn't see him yet. I just came from Lisa's building but I know I'll see Shameek and his friends soon. I don't know what's going to happen, but we have to end this nonsense somehow. I'm getting scared Ant, and I don't like the feeling."

"I feel you dog, but I'm not scared. I just wanna see them kats before they see me. I keep my gun on me. I'm just ready to see these niggas. Son, walk with me to Myrtle Avenue."

"Why? Who's on Myrtle?"

"Nah, I just wanna see something. Come on son, let's ba-dounce."

They walked to Myrtle Avenue and when they got there Ant-live could not believe his luck. Rashien was standing on the corner of Myrtle and Carlton Avenue talking to a girl, Michelle Jackson. She was twenty-five years old, slim, brown-skin, chinky eyes, five foot six, and her hair was cut the way Toni Braxton used to wear hers. Rashien didn't notice Richard and Ant-live standing behind him, but when he saw the look on Michelle's face, he turned around and smiled at the two boys. Ant-live's face was screwed up, as he held the three fifty seven to Rashien's chest.

Rashien knew he had no chance of getting his gun. He figured if he bluffed them right, they would slip up and he would have a chance to murder them both.

"What y'all little punks tryin' to get heart now?" asked Rashien.

"Bitch get the fuck outta here," Ant-live told Michelle. "Before you die with this nigga."

Michelle quickly made her escape, and ran down Myrtle Ave.

"Listen," Rashien said with a smile. "If you kill me, you are dead. And if you don't kill me, you're dead. Y'all fucked up pulling that gun on me. Pull the trigger Ant-live, and my niggas will kill everybody in your family. Your moms work in the welfare building on Dekalb and Skillman. You didn't think I knew that, huh? Your man Richard there, his parents are dead already. I just didn't pull the trigger yet. But Ant-live, you can save yourself and your moms by stepping off. That's my word, I have no beef with you."

"Shoot him Ant," Richard said angrily thinking about his parents.

Ant-live still had the gun pointed at Rashien but he looked scared now and his hand began to shake.

"I said shoot him Ant," repeated Richard. "Kill 'em. He's not fit to live."

Ant-live just stood there not knowing what to do.

Rashien continued smiling, hoping Michelle had alerted his crew to what was happening.

Ant-live's hand was shaking so bad, you could hear the bullets rattle in the gun. Rashien had that kind of effect on people. They knew if they shot him, they had to make sure he was dead because if he lived through it, by some kind of miracle, it would be bodies dropping all over Brooklyn. Rashien didn't really like people; he only tolerated them. Ant-live was beginning to regret pulling the gun out on him. Rashien felt confident he would be able to bluff Ant-live into not shooting him.

Richard grabbed Ant-live's gun and moved closer to Rashien.

Rashien didn't think Richard had the heart to pull the trigger, but then he looked in his eyes and realized he would have to pay for his mistake. The smirk was wiped off Rashien's face.

Richard pulled the trigger and the first shot entered Rashien's eye socket as he fell to the ground screaming. The second shot hit him in the side of the head as blood colored the sidewalk.

Ant-live took off running down Myrtle towards Nostrand Avenue, as Richard dropped the gun in a sewer and walked back to his building in a daze.

Chapter Eleven

"Hello, can I speak to Omega?"

"Yeah, this is Omega. Who dis?"

"It's me, Richard."

"My nigga, Bishop?"

"Yeah, it's me."

"Yo, I was just about to get in touch with you. I heard what happened. Nigga, you're a hero. You just don't know it yet. I just spoke to Shameek, dig? He wanna murder you kid. Him and his clique was ready to run up in your house and kill everybody. But I told him not to do that, leave your parents out of it and respect the rules of the game and see you when he see you. I told him my sister be up in your house, so your crib is a safe haven for now kid. But all you really have to do is come out of the crib and get busy. You still have the gun you and your man used, right?"

"No, I threw it in the sewer."

"Alright, my little man from Harlem gets busy. I'll have him and a few of his niggas from the Polo Grounds come down, give you a gun and get busy with you. Nobody down here can tie them to me. They'll think that's your cousins or something. Like I said duke, I would never tell you to kill someone but you have to protect yourself. Shit is deeper now that Rashien is dead. Shameek still got that crazy nigga T-bone with him, so somebody's gonna die. It's just a matter of who-you or them. Don't let it be you."

"Omega, I'm not ready to die. I don't even wanna kill again but I know you're right. I have to protect myself. How did you know what took place?"

"That's something else you will learn about the streets," Omar answered with a laugh. "Niggas can't keep their mouths closed. Your boy Ant-live talk too much, but niggas want him too. So, he's in hiding. But check it, play the crib until I get back at you. You're gonna be alright fam. Oh yeah, my sister left from here twenty minutes ago.

She said something about coming to see you. The streets are talking about you kid, but your reputation depends on your next move. Just lay low, and I'll holla at you in a minute."

"Alright thanks Omega," replied Richard. He hung up the phone and laid back on his bed, looking at the ceiling wondering how he got himself into this situation.

It was scorching hot outside, and Richard knew everyone would be out today including Shameek and his clique. He also knew they would be gunning for him, hoping to catch him outside. Richard felt like a prisoner locked in the confines of his apartment, which made him want to go outside even more, but he knew the price to do that would be too costly. What if his mother wanted him to go to the store? What about attending church services? His father would drag him there if he had to. Involving the police was definitely out of the question. Omar had already told him that if he told, everyone would be against him. Would Lisa stay with him if he went out like that? Would anyone still respect him? All of these thoughts were going through his head, and he came to the conclusion that he would just have to stay strong and ride the situation out. He would have to let his parents know a little bit of what happened, so they wouldn't send him to the store or drag him to church. Maybe he could go and stay with his cousin in New Jersey. He decided to wait and see what his parents would say about everything. Richard got off his bed and went into the kitchen where his mother was.

He walked into the kitchen and found his mother sitting at the table reading her newspaper. As he looked at her, he made a promise to himself that he would never let any harm come to his mother, no matter what he had to do.

"Hey handsome, what are you doing in the house on such a nice day? I thought you would be outside with one of your friends by now. I know you miss Kenny. He was such a sweet boy."

"Yeah ma, I miss him," said Richard as he sat in a chair facing his mother. "I really wish I could talk to him right now."

Richard truly meant what he said. He loved Kendu like a brother and just seeing him right now would have been enough. He loved Ant-live too. He didn't blame him for being scared to shoot Rashien because he too was scared. Richard just knew what he had to do, and looking at his mother helped him realize he made the right decision.

"Where is dad?" asked Richard.

"Your father went to the church. He had to open the doors for the plumber to fix the bathroom. They were suppose to fix it last week. This is the second time he had to go and open the door for them. Hopefully everything will be done today," said Maria spreading her newspaper on the kitchen table. "This is crazy, look at this. A guy in the Bronx suffocated his baby because he was upset with his wife. This doesn't make any sense."

Richard half listened to his mother because he was into his own thoughts. He wondered was Rashien's murder also in the same newspaper. Richard didn't even feel like he was the one that had killed Rashien. It was as if he was watching someone else pull the trigger. Everything happened so quickly, but he remembered the whole incident like it was all in slow motion.

As he walked back to his building, people ran past him to the crime scene not knowing he was the one that pulled the trigger. That was the first night in his life he couldn't fall asleep. He kept tossing and turning and every time he closed his eyes he could see Rashien screaming, covered in blood. Richard got out of bed and went to the bathroom to wash his face with cold water. As he exited the bathroom, the phone rang. He quickly grabbed the phone to prevent his parents from waking up. It was Lisa on the other end screaming frantically into the receiver.

"What the fuck happened?! Baby, are you okay?! Somebody told me you shot Rashien. I just came from over there. My brother said as soon as you can, call him. What happened?!"

Her questions were bombarding him so quickly, he didn't know where or how to begin. Richard took a deep breath and said, "I don't know, I don't know... Everything just happened so fast. Me and Ant-live was walking and we..."

"I knew it!" Lisa said angrily cutting him off. "I knew that motherfucker had something to do with this. He told you to shoot Rashien?"

"No baby," Richard answered sadly. "Everything just happened so fast. Baby, I'm just so tired. I'll tell you everything tomorrow. Okay, boo?"

"I'll come over in the afternoon. I love you."

"I love you too," said Richard before hanging up.

"That baby had nothing to do with anything that they were arguing about," said Maria angrily folding her newspaper snapping Richard out of his thoughts.

"It's a shame what happened to that baby. Some people just don't deserve to have children. They don't love themselves and have some nerve to have kids."

"Ma, can I talk to you about something serious?" asked Richard deciding that now was the time to tell her some of what had taken place.

"Of course baby, you know you can talk to me about anything that's on your mind. What's going on?" she asked.

"Well, the same guys that killed Kenny are out to get me as well."

"Oh my God! Why?! What happened?! What they want you for?!" she asked becoming hysterical.

"Relax ma, everything will be okay."

There was suddenly a knock on the door. Richard began to rise from the table when his mother stopped him.

"I'll get the door son. When I come back I want to know everything. That's it, we are moving from here. I'm getting you away from these projects. I'm not losing my baby to the streets."

Maria quickly exited the kitchen. Richard thought it was Lisa at the door, but it seemed to be taking too long for his mother to come back to the kitchen. His heart began to race, as his mind conjured up the unthinkable. What if T-bone and Shameek were at the door holding a gun to his mother's head? He knew he should have answered the door.

As soon as Richard got out of his chair to see what was going on, his mother entered the kitchen with two white police officers. The first one's name was Officer Tom O'Ryan. He was six foot two, stocky, blond hair, blue eyes and clean-shaven. The other officer's name was Officer Martin Harrison. People in the streets called him Rambo, because he was known to have shoot-outs and had arrested some of Brooklyn's most notorious gangsters alone. He was also known to put drugs on guys in the projects and start drug wars by putting false information out on the streets, that someone was a snitch. He was six foot three, muscular, baldheaded and wore a thick mustache and beard. He was the first officer to speak upon entering the kitchen.

"Is your name Richard Brown, also known as Bishop?"

"Yes, I'm Richard."

"You are under arrest for the murder of Alex Stewart, also known as Rashien."

"Oh my God!" cried Maria. "I thought you only wanted to talk to my son Richard. He didn't kill anyone. My baby would not kill anyone. Lord, please don't let them take my baby. "

"Excuse me Mrs. Brown," said Officer O'Ryan. "We'll have to question your son at the precinct. If he didn't do it, he'll be home before you know it."

Officer Harrison put the handcuffs on Richard and patted him down. After reading him his rights he asked, "Where's the gun?"

"Didn't you just say I have the right to remain silent?" asked Richard. He knew he would not be coming home anytime soon.

"Excuse me ma'am," interrupted Officer O'Ryan. "Do you mind if I search the apartment?"

Maria stepped out of his way without a word as tears fell from her eyes and her hands covered her mouth.

Officer O'Ryan searched every room in the small apartment.

"It's clean Marty," he announced when he was done. "Let's go."

"What precinct are you taking my son to?" asked Maria with a look of terror on her face.

"He's going to the 88th precinct," answered Officer O'Ryan.

Maria took a good look at her son to make sure that he had no scars. She knew from reading the newspapers how police would beat black men after having them in custody. The two officers realized what she was doing and quickly brushed past her, leading Richard out of the apartment. They got onto the elevator, took it down to the lobby and escorted him to an unmarked car parked in front of the building.

Everyone was outside on this hot summer day. The officer shoved Richard in the back seat and closed the door behind him. Richard looked out of the window, and was surprised to see Shameek, T-bone and at least ten young boys with them. They all appeared to be concealing guns. The crowd of people in front of the building looked at Richard wondering why he was arrested. A few of them whispered that he was the one who killed Rashien. Most of their reactions were of surprise and disbelief. Richard saw Shameek smiling, and pointing his finger at him as if he had an imaginary gun. He then heard a loud, screaming voice, and when he turned his head he saw Lisa running towards him. She was yelling and cursing at the officers.

"Where the fuck are you taking him? He didn't do shit! Y'all cracker motherfuckers always fucking with people!!!"

Shameek and his boys started laughing, as the cops drove away with Richard in the back seat handcuffed. Lisa pulled a cell phone out of her red Gucci bag and dialed frantically.

Chapter Twelve

Richard sat in the bullpen at the 88 precinct. He had already been fingerprinted, and he paced the small cell back and forth. This was the first time that he felt truly alone. The cell reeked of piss and he couldn't wait to get out of there. He sang all the church songs he could remember to pass the time. He was about to lay back down on the hard bench, when a tall black man carrying a briefcase came to the bullpen. He was a brown-skinned man, sporting a small afro, clean-shaven, and looked as if he were rich. He was donning a white Armani dress shirt, a brown double breasted Brooks Brothers suit, and a pair of brown alligator shoes. He sported a pinky ring full of diamonds, and the Rolex on his left wrist had so many diamonds in it, you couldn't see the hands that told the time.

"Are you Richard Brown?" asked the well-dressed black man.

"Yes I am," answered Richard. "Who are you?"

"My name is Jeffrey Atkins. I'm your lawyer. Actually, I'm Omar Thompson's attorney; he keeps me on retainer. He called me and said to get down here to represent you. Omar wants you out of jail, as soon as possible. So, what I'll do is put in for a bail and push for a speedy trial. The arresting officer told me that you are about to be placed in a line-up. I'll be present to make sure that you get a fair one. Have you made a statement?"

"No. I chose to use my right to remain silent."

"Good," smiled the lawyer. "I wish my other clients would use that right more often."

When he left, Officer O'Ryan came to bring Richard to the line-up. Even though Richard's attorney were present, the line-up still did not seem fair; the other five dark-skin boys in the line-up looked dirty, and it was not hard to tell that they were from a shelter, where as Richard looked freshly clean.

After being picked out of the line-up by two witnesses, he was put back into the smelly bullpen.

70

Richard remained in the bullpens for two days before being taken to Brooklyn Criminal Court for arraignment. The sandwiches he were served were disgusting! The bread was so hard it was like eating baloney and cheese on two giant crackers. He sat in the court's crowded bullpens with other black and Puerto Rican men waiting to see the judge. Most of them were dirty and smelled. Even Richard was a little smelly from sleeping in the dirty bull pen. Some of the guys were sleeping on the dirty floor, while others sold anything they had for cigarettes.

Richard relied on thinking of his beautiful Lisa to get him through the days and nights of confinement. When he was about to think of her for the hundredth time, a black corrections officer came to the gates and began calling out names in a loud booming voice.

"Kenny Johnson, Michael Walker, Juan Gomez, Tito Garcia, John Doe, Richard Brown, and Thomas Lopez, step to the gate, it's your time to shine!"

Richard and the other prisoners called were handcuffed, and escorted to the 9th floor by elevator. There they were put into another pen. This one not smelling as bad as the others because it was near the court rooms.

"Yeah kid, that was my girl," said one of the prisoners. He was a short, dirty Hispanic guy. He wore dirty sneakers, dirty pants with oil on them and a dingy orange tee-shirt. He looked as if he smoked crack. He was talking to a well-dressed Hispanic guy who didn't look interested in what the dirty guy had to say.

"Papi, I mean she was bad!" he continued. "I'm talking Jennifer Lopez bad. No bro, Selena bad!"

"Yo, shut the fuck up," interrupted a young black guy sitting on the bench. "Nobody wanna hear that shit; your dirty ass. Who da fuck want your crack head ass?"

There was another black guy in the pen and he had his face screwed up like he smelled something foul or he really thought he was the toughest guy in the pen. He kept looking at Richard, and then he asked, "A-yo, where you from?"

"You talking to me?" asked Richard.

"Yeah," the guy answered. "You look mad familiar."

"I'm from Fort Greene."

"Word?!" the guy said excitedly. "I got mad people down there. You know my son Big Duke?"

"No, I never heard of him."

"Word? Everybody know my son. I know you know my son Bishop from down there. My boy get busy."

Richard wanted to laugh at the guy and since there was nothing to do he decided to have a little fun.

"No, I don't know Bishop, but I heard a lot about him."

"Yeah son," the guy continued. "He's dangerous. You know he killed crazy ass Rashien from down your end the other day right? A lot of niggas don't even know how my son look. Between me and you, that's my man. We go back like fat crayons and car seats."

Richard started laughing, but was interrupted by a fat black corrections officer.

"Richard Brown? Richard Brown?" she yelled out.

"Right here," Richard answered.

The heavy-set woman opened the pen and as Richard stepped out she locked the pen, handcuffed him, and escorted him to the court room. Before he entered the courtroom, he said a little prayer, "Lord, please have mercy on me and let me get out of here because I don't belong here."

Richard heard the bailiff call his name out as he entered the courtroom.

"Richard Brown," yelled the bailiff, "docket number 20K4765."

The first person Richard saw in the courtroom was his mother. She had tears of joy in her eyes, because she was happy to see that he was okay. She hadn't slept since Richard was arrested. His father sat next to her with an expression on his face that was unreadable. Then he saw Lisa; his heart filled with joy as he laid eyes on her.

Excited to see him and to know that he was okay, put a big smile on her face. She blew a kiss and mouthed 'I love you' to Richard as he walked to the defendant's table.

Richard's lawyer, Mr. Atkins, had on something similar to what he had on two days prior. The only difference was that his Brooks Brothers suit, his tie, his briefcase and alligator shoes were now dark blue. The district attorney was a fat white guy in his late forties. His name was Henry Hudson and he wore cheap shoes, a cheap suit, a white shirt and a cheap tie. The judge was a fat white man with grayish hair. He was in his early 60's and his name was Joseph Clark.

"This case, 20K4765, the charge of murder in the second degree," said the judge, "and the charge of possession of a weapon in the second degree against the defendant, Richard Brown. How does the defendant plea?"

"Not guilty your Honor," answered Mr. Atkins. "My client has never been involved with the law. He comes from a very good family. His father is a pastor, and his mother is a school teacher and they are both present. I request that he's given a reasonable bail."

"Your Honor," interrupted the DA. "The defendant is a threat to society. He has no regard for human life, and I request that bail be denied."

"Your Honor, that is not true," said Mr. Atkins. "The outcome of this case will show that my client is innocent and until then he should be given a reasonable bail until trial. There is no reason to assume that he will jump bail and we all know that he is innocent until proven otherwise."

"Your Honor," interrupted the DA again with an agitated look on his face. "A man was gunned down violently in the streets and the defendant was identified by witnesses as being the gunman and the facts will come out that he is indeed guilty and I feel that for the safety of society the defendant should not be given any bail."

"Remand," said the judge slamming his hammer down. "Bail denied. Court date set for August 15th. That's two weeks from now. Court adjourned."

Richard turned around and looked at his father, mother and Lisa before being escorted back to the pen. Lisa and his mother sat with tears welling in their eyes. His father stood up, waved to him and walked out of the courtroom holding up both of the women.

Richard felt as if his whole world was crashing down around him. When he got back to the pen, one of the guys asked him, "Yo, what's up with the judge? He on some bullshit or what?"

Richard sat down on the bench without answering. He was still in shock from not being granted bail. He couldn't get Lisa's and his parent's sad faces out of his mind. He felt as if he let them down. What if he never walked to Myrtle Avenue with Ant-live that night? What if he never snatched the gun and shot Rashien? All of these 'what ifs' were going through his mind.

"That's a dumb ass question to ask homie," said another guy in the pen. "It's evident the judge is on some bullshit. You see they remanded him. But you might be good 'cause you look like one of them loitering ass niggas."

Everyone in the pen laughed except Richard. He was not in a joking mood. He stared at the floor wondering if his life would end in prison. He thought about how easy it was for a person's life to be turned upside down from one out of control action. He thought of every alternative he could have chosen over murdering Rashien. But he kept coming up blank because he knew Rashien was crazy and it was just a matter of time before Rashien killed him or his parents. All Rashien understood was death, so the only way to deal with him was to kill him before he killed you.

Chapter Thirteen

It was 7 pm on a Thursday evening. Richard sat in the back seat of the Rikers Island bus handcuffed, looking out of the window. When the bus turned onto the Brooklyn-Queens Expressway, he knew this may be the very last time that he would ever see the Fort Greene Projects. Well, at least until his next court date. But he wouldn't be able to walk through it for a very long time. Richard heard stories about Rikers Island and he knew he had to stay strong to survive. He had never been arrested before and was nervous because he didn't know what to expect.

"Yo son," one youth said to another. "As soon as my homies hear I'm back in the building it's on! Every time I come through I'm treated like a king."

"I just need a gun," the youth he was speaking to responded "I know I got crazy beef in the four building."

Richard sat listening to the bus full of young boys talking tough. He knew that most of them were really scared just like he was; they didn't know what awaited them.

"Don't worry about it par," one youth in the front of the bus was heard telling another. "Something pop off we just stick together kid."

"Nigga what the fuck you talking about?" questioned the youth he was talking to. "I'm thick like quick. If you don't know what that mean, I'm Blood homie. My dogs hold me down."

"That shit is corny," said another youth sitting in the back of the bus. "I hold myself down. Niggas know my gun go off. I just left the four building."

Richard continued to look out of the window as they crossed the bridge to get to Rikers Island. Before he knew it, they were in front of C-74, the building that housed wild adolescence as well as adults. They entered the receiving room and after being uncuffed, they were told to step into the open gate pen.

There were three correction officers in the receiving room. CO Cook was a tall dark-skinned man in his late forties. He had a thick mustache, a nappy afro, and a deep Barry White's voice. CO Green stood next to him processing the new arrivals. She was above average height with shoulder length hair and a body that everyone in the building lusted after. The third officer in the receiving room was CO Smith. She was a short, fat, ugly light-skin woman. She couldn't get a man to save her life, but in here, there were a few inmates who would push up on her. That was the main reason she loved her job, and every now and then, she would pick a handsome inmate of her choice to have fun with on the down low.

There was also a prisoner preparing food to serve to the newly arrived inmates in the receiving room as well. He was a porter that everyone called Big Lord. He was in his mid-thirties and was a very impressive figure. He had a thick body and spoke in a very deep voice. He kept his mustache and beard well-groomed and he had a curly Steve Harvey type afro. He was rocking a brand new pair of white on white shell toe Adidas, blue Guess jeans, a white long sleeve Gap shirt, and a thick Platinum chain with a medallion flooded with diamonds. He also rocked two rings with diamonds in them.

"When I call your names," CO Cook yelled out holding a bunch of yellow cards in his hand, "step out. Get your food and go back into the pen. Kenyatta Jones, Michael Williams, Juan Gomez, Thomas Perry, Tito Rodriguez, Richard Brown." As soon as Big Lord heard Richard's name he looked to the open pen waiting for Richard to step out.

"Kenneth Harris," continued CO Cook. "John Doe, and uh, uh, Joseph Diaz."

When Richard was getting his food, Big Lord looked at him and asked, "Is your name Bishop?"

"Yeah," Richard answered. "That's what they call me."

"I'm Big Lord. I talked to Omega earlier. He told me you were coming through. After you get searched, I'll see you."

"Alright," Richard replied. He then got his rice, beans, Kool-Aid and bread and walked back into the pen. He then realized how strong Omar was and that he knew people everywhere. He had a whole new respect for Omar.

After eating and getting strip searched and being put into another open gate pen, Big Lord came to the pen when the CO's weren't looking, about twenty minutes later.

"Listen," said Big Lord. "They're sending you to the north side of Mod 5. A kid name Supreme is in there. He's your enemy. He's one of Shameek's soldiers and he got shit locked down in that house. But my little man Krazy Kay is in there also. He's expecting you and he got food and everything for you. Here take this, stash it on you."

Big Lord handed Richard a sharp knife-like shank. Richard looked around nervously and stashed it in his pants. "Listen," Big Lord continued, "after you blow him up give the gun to Krazy Kay. He'll stash it for you. Supreme don't know about you yet, but in twenty four hours he'll get on the phone. And once he find out, him and his boys will stab you up viciously down there if you don't handle your business. Omega said you ain't the violent type but he said to tell you to protect yourself and you'll be aiight. So, you got twenty-four hours to get busy."

"I just got here," said Richard. "I can't do that in one day. It's not enough time."

"A day is more than enough time. Is not a day divided into twenty-four hours, each hour into sixty minutes and every minute subdivided into sixty seconds?" asked Big Lord quoting the Count of Monte Cristo. "Now, in 86,400 seconds very many things can be done. So get busy, I'm behind you kid."

"Alright," said Richard with a frown.

Big Lord stepped out of the open pen, and walked back to his housing unit. All the other young boys in the pen looked at Richard with respect. They hadn't heard anything Big Lord told Richard, but they knew Big Lord was dangerous just by the chain he wore. Not just anyone can wear jewelry in this building without getting yapped or stabbed up for it. The medallion Big Lord wore on his thick Platinum chain was embellished with diamonds. They figured if Big Lord had love for Richard, then Richard had to be someone important too. Some of them saw Big Lord give Richard the shank and they knew he was the only one in the pen that had a knife, so they stayed out of Richard's way and gave him much respect.

Everybody in the pen was quiet until CO Cook came to the pen with his yellow cards.

"Okay," he yelled out. "When I call your name, step out, stand behind the camera and smile. Richard Brown."

Richard stepped out, took his picture for his ID card and when he was done, he was asked a few questions.

"What's your religion, Muslim or Christian?"

"Christian."

"Do you have any enemies?"

He wanted to say, 'Yeah this kid name Supreme,' but instead he said, "No."

"You eat regular meals or Kosher?"

"Regular."

"Do you have any gold you want to put in property?"

"No."

He then was given an orange ID card, and was told to grab a set-up off the table. The set-up consisted of two sheets, a pillowcase, toothpaste, toothbrush, bath towel, washcloth, and a green plastic cup all rolled up in a green army blanket.

After all the other inmates followed the same routine, they were escorted to the clinic for a full checkup, which included giving blood and urine. Richard took the shank out of his pants when no one was looking, and slipped it into his blanket. While he waited in the clinic, a light-skin baldhead guy came inside holding his face with blood dripping everywhere! Richard was filled with fear and realized he would have to get Supreme because he had no plans to have his face ripped up like the guy who was just rushed in.

It took two and a half hours for everyone to get their check-ups. Once they were complete, they were escorted by CO Smith down a long corridor to Mod 5. When they reached their destination, young boys on the north and south side were perched on the window looking at the new arrivals. Some of them even began to yell through the window with looks of malice on their faces.

"Don't come in here homeboy."

"Yo, that's my man , CO put 'em on this side."

"I'm getting that chain scrams got on."

CO Smith looked at the cards and said, "All the names I call out are going to the north side. Kenyatta Jones, Thomas Perry, Juan Gomez, Richard Brown, and Joseph Diaz. All the rest of you are going to the south side."

The doors on both sides opened and Richard stepped inside of the big dorm. He noticed a group of boys standing around a stocky boy with wavy hair. He was of average height and was no older than seventeen or eighteen. He wore a thick chain around his neck. Richard knew the guy had to be Supreme. He was wearing beige sweatpants with no shirt on. The other guys paid close attention to him when he talked. He moved his hands dramatically with every word spoken, and when he looked around the dorm at all the newly arrived inmates, he squinted his eyes making him look tougher than what he was. He and Richard made eye contact but Richard quickly glanced away. He did not want to put Supreme on point. First, he had to find out who Krazy Kay was. As he scanned the dorm, he overheard Supreme talking to his soldiers.

"Yeah I got them bitches coming this week. They gonna pull both of y'all down," said Supreme nodding his head at two of the guys that were standing around him, "and they gonna hit y'all off with some dope and weed. I don't give a fuck if y'all push up on 'em, just take care of business first." Supreme looked around the dorm again and said, "Damn, nothing but crab niggas came up in here today."

The guys circling him looked around and laughed. There were at least seven of them and Richard wondered how he was going to be able to get close enough to hit Supreme. When he left the clinic, he put the shank back into his pocket when CO Smith wasn't looking.

Richard had less than twenty-four hours to make his move. He wished he could phone Omar and ask for advice, but guys in the dorm had the telephones locked down. Images of the guy in the clinic clutching his bloody face kept flashing through Richard's mind. He looked around and put his hand in his pocket thumbing the sharp shank. Richard went to his bunk and sat down, as everyone in the housing area looked and talked to the new inmates that just came in.

Richard rested on his bunk and thought about his situation, until a short curly haired boy approached him.

"Yo par," said the youth. "What's your name?"

"They call me Bishop."

"You're the nigga I was looking for," said the youth. "My name is Krazy Kay. Big Lord told me about you. You see that kid right there wit' no shirt on?"

"Yeah, I see him."

"That's Supreme, he's dangerous. You have to get him tonight, before we go to sleep. "

"Okay," Richard replied. "But what about his soldiers?"

"I don't know kid," Krazy Kay answered. "Big Lord only told me to hit you off with the food and cosmetics he gave me for you, and he told me to hide the gun if you need me to."

Krazy Kay then walked away, and sat on his own bunk. Richard knew that he was definitely on his own now. Omar, Big Lord or Krazy Kay could not help him. He would have to pull this off on his own. He was upset that Shameek had put him into this situation in the first place.

It was getting late and he knew he would have to make his move as soon as the opportunity presented itself. He was ready to do what he had to do to survive, and he wasn't going to sleep until he or Supreme left the dorm; they both could not stay in the same dorm together. He was scared to make his move but he feared getting stabbed or cut in the face more than anything. Lisa and his father would go crazy, and his mother would probably have a nervous breakdown. Richard was determined not to let that happen.

An hour had passed and everyone was getting ready to go to bed. Richard jumped off his bunk and entered the bathroom while Supreme was at the urinal taking a piss. He looked at Richard with his face screwed up and continued pissing. After he washed his hands, he turned around and was surprised to see Richard standing there with a sharp shank in his hand.

"Do not suppose that I have come to bring peace to the earth," said Richard. "I did not come to bring peace but a sword. Matthew 10:34."

Richard then stabbed Supreme in the face, and when Supreme tried to run, it cost him dearly. Because Richard then hit him five times in the back. Supreme fell to the floor and Richard stepped over him and walked quickly to Krazy Kay's bed, handing him the shank with blood all over it.

Chapter Fourteen

Every inmate in the building was talking about Bishop. Four days had past and with all the snitches in the building, it was miraculous Richard had not been caught. After blowing Supreme up that night, he speedily passed the shank to Krazy Kay and prayed to God for forgiveness all night. Shameek still had soldiers in the building, but they knew Richard was dangerous so they moved around him cautiously. Word was all over the building that Big Lord was holding Richard down, keeping him even safer. Big Lord had previously stabbed two of Shameek's soldiers to make a statement that he was not playing. All of Supreme's homies in Mod 5 began sweating Richard. They gave him food and offered phone time. But Richard spent most of his time talking to Krazy Kay or laying on his bed reading his Bible. He did not trust any of Supreme's so-called friends. None of them did anything after their boy had been attacked; Richard even saw two of them stealing some of Supreme's stuff before the COs came and packed up his belongings. Richard knew he would see Supreme again and when he did, he would be ready to do what he had to do to protect him self. He was determined to get out of prison unharmed. He had seen so many young black men walking around with stitches in their faces. Some of the young men had been very handsome and that often caused them to be targets of the slashings. Jealousy and egos were the main reasons inmates would hurt each other and Richard learned that it was safer to stay close to his bunk and keep to himself. Despite being in jail his thoughts were still on positive things, so listening to the guys in the yard telling war stories did not interest him at all. Whenever he went outside for recreation, he would walk around the yard by himself getting his thoughts together. The other inmates in the yard would call out to him but he would never stop to talk. He would simply put his fist up in greeting and keep on walking. Once he was tired of walking, he would stand by himself, waiting to go back inside and study his Bible.

This particular day, Richard sat on his bunk reading his Bible, hoping his mother or someone would bring him some clothes and underwear. He was still wearing the same clothes he wore when he was arrested and was tired of washing his underwear without having a second pair to put on. Big Lord offered him some clothes but he declined the offer; he didn't feel comfortable taking anything from anyone he didn't really know. Richard continued reading his Bible when CO McCartney called his name out. CO McCartney was twenty-three years old, five foot six, light-skinned, slim, with very long hair.

Richard laid his Bible down and walked over to the bubble to see what she wanted.

"You have a visit," she said as he approached the bubble.

"Thank you," said Richard as he went back to his bunk to get ready for his visit. He could hardly contain his happiness. He had hoped and prayed that someone would come to visit him, and the good Lord answered his prayers.

CO McCartney smiled and thought to herself how different Richard seemed in comparison to the other inmates. He was quiet, handsome, and well-mannered. She was even further intrigued that he didn't lust after her like the other inmates did. Maybe he's gay, she thought to herself. That couldn't be it; he was too much respected by the other inmates. She wondered what a friendship or better yet, a relationship would be like with him. She had never had sex with an inmate but there was something about Richard that stirred something deep within her. She checked what he was in jail for, and she was shocked to find out he was being accused of murder. She was not concerned about that; she was only concerned with people finding out about the sexual relationship she so badly wanted with Richard. What if her co-workers, or even worse, her superiors, found out. She would have to be very careful because she did not want to lose her job. Richard didn't seem like the type to kiss and tell and she took comfort in that. She figured that Richard would jump at the chance to be with her. After all, she was the most sought after CO in the building.

She was truly a beautiful woman; her only flaw was that she didn't believe it herself. Her walk radiated sex and every inmate in the building lusted for her. The inmates were not the only men who yearned for her; she had sex with several of the COs. And secretly they would talk behind her back about the different sexual positions they had her in and laugh. CO McCartney felt the only thing she had to offer was her body and she gave it up so easily. Though she knew her fellow COs were talking about her, she didn't stop having sex with them. Though she had never done it, she did fantasize on occasion about having sex with an inmate she found attractive, and she never looked down on her female co-workers who actually did it on the down low. She felt it was just human nature to have sex with someone you were attracted to no matter where they were or what they were being accused of.

As a young girl, Robin McCartney was considered one of the baddest girls at her high school. At sixteen, her life, however, changed and she was never the same person again. Robin sat in her living room after school watching television when her uncle came into her house. Pete was her mother's brother and he was a common fixture in the house. Robin's parents wanted to be able to provide her with the luxuries they had not been afforded growing up and were always working. Pete was her favorite uncle. He would often bring her little gifts and she loved him so much because he showered her with the attention she so desperately craved. Her uncle walked into the living room and sat down on the couch next to her. He moved closer to her and laid his large hand on her young breast. She froze for a moment, uncertain of what to do. Once she regained her bearings, she tried to get up to escape her uncle's grip. He grabbed her, pulled her back to the couch and laid his body on top of hers. Pete finished raping her and as he dressed himself he warned her not to tell anyone what had happened. 'If you tell them, no one will believe you' were the words that echoed in her head for years after the incident. If you tell them, no one will believe you...It was then that she viewed herself as having no worth to anyone other than being a sexual object. And as she grew into adulthood she continued to believe that she could only attract a partner by giving sexual favors. In addition, the only pleasure or satisfaction she came to appreciate was what she was traumatically exposed to in her formidable years, which was sex. Whenever she was stressed out about anything, she would have sex with one of the various men that sweated her. Before she knew it she was addicted to the point of not even being able to sleep without having sex or masturbating. Sex became a powerful and addicted drug that acted as her get high self-medication.

$

Richard finally approached the CO's bubble. CO McCartney gently caressed Richard's hand as she handed him a visiting room pass. Richard did not notice her invitation as he scooped up the pass and headed down the long corridor. Richard walked cautiously down the corridor, aware that his enemies may take any opportunity to attack him. As he walked to the visiting room, guys he didn't even know greeted him with much respect as if they'd known him for years. He wondered was this what celebrities lives were like. He didn't mind the attention, but he had to be on point so every one that tried to give him a handshake or five, Richard would ball up his fist and touch their hands with his fist. He once saw a guy stab another guy while holding his hand from a handshake. Richard made sure not to shake any hands and to keep his distance.

After reaching the visiting room, he put on the jump suit and beige slippers he was given. There were so many people in the visiting room he was overwhelmed. Lisa stood in the corner looking as beautiful as ever. She had her hair down to her shoulders, and she was wearing a pair of red leather Gucci shoes, red leather miniskirt, red leather vest, and a soft red leather jacket. Her hair was pushed between her diamond-studded ears. A diamond necklace rested on her collarbone and a tennis bracelet encircled her delicate wrist. Lisa walked towards Richard and they met at a table in the center of the room. All heads turned to glance at the beautiful Lisa as he swayed past the tables. The girls yelled at their boyfriends, who blatantly stared at Lisa. But even they had to admit that Lisa was quite the sight.

Richard pulled Lisa close to him and held her body in his strong arms. He leaned down and gave her a long, deep kiss. He released her from his grasp and they sat across the table holding hands and staring longingly into each other's eyes.

"Look at my baby. Are you okay?"

"Yeah I'm okay," Richard answered. "I just need to get out of here. You're looking as beautiful as ever. I really miss you...and my parents."

"I miss you too boo-boo," said Lisa touching his face. "And you know I love you. Your mother said she will come see you next week. I just came from your house. I brought some clothes and shoes and put it in the package for you. My brother also told me to tell you that he'll be in contact."

"Okay that's cool," said Richard taking Lisa's hand back into his.

"Do they have church in here?"

"Yeah, they have services. I'm going tomorrow. If I blow trial, are you going to leave me?"

"Never! We will just have to get married. I'll just have to teach you a few things on them trailer visits."

Lisa smiled and they sat hugging, kissing, and talking until the visit was over.

"I love you boo," said Lisa as she stood up to leave. "Call me later. My brother said tell you he's behind you. You know, you are the only boyfriend I ever had that he likes."

"Oh yeah?" Richard asked with a smile. "Tell your brother I said what's up, and I'll call you tonight after I speak to my parents. Thanks for the package baby. I love you."

Richard passionately kissed Lisa and then turned to walk to get strip-searched. He turned around and saw Lisa standing there still staring at him with tears welling in her eyes.

"Don't cry baby," Richard yelled out to her. "Smile for me baby."

Lisa wiped her eyes and smiled as she walked out of the door. Richard smiled; walking to the back to get strip-searched.

After the humiliating search, he got dressed, retrieved his package, and it was then that he spotted Big Lord doing the same.

"What's up Big Lord?" asked Richard. "I didn't even see you on the visit floor."

"I guess not. You didn't look away from baby girl the whole visit," smiled Big Lord. "Lisa's pretty kid. She spoke to me when she first came in. Yo, I hear you twisted that bird Supreme up something proper. I'm feeling you kid. Big Lord and the Bishop, I like the sound of that. Let's make these niggas in this building believers."

Richard laughed and said, "I'll see you later." He gave Big Lord a five and made his way down the same long corridor back to his dorm.

As he carried his two big bags of clothes, he thought about Lisa. The visit with her was a quick one. The time flew by so fast. It definitely didn't seem like an hour. Richard wished he had at least another hour on the visit floor. He finally got back to Mod 5, and he just wanted to lay down and think about Lisa for the rest of the day.

When he entered Mod 5, he noticed CO McCartney was still working and she was looking at him with a smile. After putting away his clothes, shoes and underwear, he laid on the bunk just staring at the ceiling thinking of Lisa. Most of the inmates were in the dayroom watching rap video's and when the door opened, you could hear Nas dropping jewels on a song called "One Mic. "

"Did you enjoy your visit?" Richard looked up and saw CO McCartney standing there with a smile on her face.

"Yes," Richard answered. "It was definitely pleasurable. I wish it never ended."

"I hope you don't mind me asking but was that your girl?"

"Yeah, that was my baby Lisa."

"Oh," said CO McCartney, not really caring who came to see him. It was her time now. "I think you're handsome. I don't deal with inmates, but um, I was hoping you and I could get together on the quiet tip. How would you like that?" she asked with a devilish smile.

"I don't think you were listening. I told you my girl came up. No disrespect to you, but I'm loyal to her and she's loyal to me. I truly love her."

"How the fuck you know she's loyal to you? You're in jail and you don't know what she's doing out there," said CO McCartney becoming annoyed. "Plus, you ain't all that. Like your shit don't stink."

"Sister, it's not about that," said Richard. "I know my girl is loyal to me. I have to trust her. Plus, it's unfair to women out there for you to assume they all cheat on their men in jail. Even if they did, they're our biggest supporters, so they do what they have to do to stay strong. Furthermore, I don't think I'm better than anyone. But what I'm saying is, you're a very beautiful sister and if I was your man I'd be loyal to you. I wouldn't put any woman before you and I would treat you like the queen that you are. Wouldn't you want a man to treat you that way?"

"To be honest, I would," answered CO McCartney. "But I don't think loyalty exist. All men are dogs."

"Well, I'm living proof what you just said is not true. I've never cheated on my girl and I never will. If I cheated on her with you or anyone else it wouldn't be fair to her. Besides, you shouldn't belittle yourself and be used as just a sex object. You're way too pretty for that."

CO McCartney had an angry look on her face as tears formed in her eyes. She never experienced anything like this before. No one ever refused to have sex with her, and to add insult to injury it had come from an inmate who was locked up twenty-four hours a day. She didn't even know how to come back at what Richard had said, so she turned around and walked straight to the COs' bathroom. She locked the door to the bathroom and cried. She turned on the faucet and splashed cold water on her face. She could not stop thinking about what Richard had said. She then looked up and smiled at her reflection in the mirror.

Chapter Fifteen

Pastor Brown delivered yet another heartfelt sermon to the church crowded with his devoted parishioners. Maria sat in the front row with her Bible occupying the empty spot where Richard once sat. Was he okay? Was he eating enough? Had someone attacked him? Did he still have a place in his heart for the Lord and trust in Him that He would lead him through these troubled times? So many questions ran through her head. She constantly worried about her son, especially if she had just gotten off of the phone with him or seen him during one of their visits. It was also unsettling to her that everyone in the church knew her business and they talked about she and her family in hushed tones.

"I want us to be a church that follows the word of God," preached Pastor Brown. "You have these so-called activist reverends, phony bishops, and these Pentecostal pimps preaching Jesus as a business. That's not the word of God. I said that's not the word of God!"

"Go 'head and preach Pastor," shouted a woman sitting in the front row.

"Turn your bibles to Matthew 23," continued Pastor Brown looking at the open page in his Bible. "Then Jesus said to the crowds and his disciples: 'The teachers of the law and the Pharisees sit in Moses' seat. So you must obey them and do everything they tell you. But do not do what they do, for they do not practice what they preach. They tie up heavy loads and put them on men's shoulders, but they themselves are not willing to lift a finger to move them. Everything they do is for men to see: They make their Phylacteries wide and the tassels of their prayer shawls long; they love the place of honor at banquets and the most important seats in the synagogues; they love to be greeted in the market places and to have men call them 'Rabbi'. But you are not to be called 'Rabbi' for you have only one master and you are all brothers.

And do not call anyone on earth 'father', for you have one Father, and he is in heaven. Nor are you to be called 'teacher', for you have one Teacher, the Christ. The greatest among you will be your servant. For whoever exalts himself will be humbled, and whoever humbles himself will be exalted.'"

Pastor Brown enjoyed preaching the Word to his congregation and he despised preachers that preached the Word of God as a business to buy houses and cars for themselves and their women. The Word of God was his life and he took it very seriously. But things weren't always this way for him. He could remember the days when the Bible did not exist in his world. As a young man living in Charleston, South Carolina, he was one of the biggest gangsters to come out of the South. They used to call him Blacker because of his dark complexion. He was so notorious that whenever he came around men feared him and the women flocked to him. He was sharp, wearing the latest suits, alligator shoes, and drove   a dark blue four door Cadillac.

He had two older brothers, Frank and James, but he was the wildest of the Brown boys. His father was a very dark-skinned man and his mother was Indian. He had his father's very dark complexion and his mother's thick wavy hair and eyes. Every teenager his age and even men older than him showed their envy and jealousy whenever he was around. He made his money selling dope, doing robberies and doing hits for those who paid well. One hot summer's day in 1971, Blacker entered a pool hall near his house. The pool hall owner sat behind a counter cradling a shotgun in his lap. His name was Fat Hank and he was known to shoot first and ask questions later. He was brown-skinned, five foot eight, 280 ponds, baldheaded with a thick mustache and thick glasses. He always wore blue jeans and a long sleeved blue shirt no matter how hot it was outside. Everyone knew not to bring any trouble around Hank's establishment. Blacker greeted him with a nod of the head.

"Hey Blacker. A few girls came by here earlier looking for you. The last one to come by was the Sergeant's daughter. That policeman is a real pig. Blacker, I think you should leave that girl alone. You know how they feel about us being with white girls and that being the sergeant's daughter doesn't make things any easier."

"Hank, I don't tell you how to run your business," smiled Blacker. "Don't tell me how to run mines. But if it'll make you feel better, let me say I'm not thinking about that cracker anymore. Daddy ain't giving her enough money for me to keep giving her this big black snake. You know what I mean?"

Hank laughed as Blacker headed to the nearest pool table and began racking the balls. He shot a few balls around when suddenly, the pool hall door opened causing a hush to fall over the room. It was as if time had stopped; no one even dared shot another ball. Blacker placed his stick on the table and turned towards the door. Standing in the doorway, as if ready for a showdown in an old western, stood Sergeant Billy Joe Turner. Sergeant Turner swaggered towards Blacker's table.

"To what I owe this honor, Sergeant?" asked Blacker cheerily.

"Listen boy," Sergeant Turner said in a thick southern drawl. "I know you been creeping around my daughter and I don't like my daughter around coloreds. Now you stay away from my daughter or it's going to be trouble, boy."

"Sarge, I don't want your daughter. She wants me like the rest of the women 'round here."

Sergeant Turner's face turned red as a tomato and everyone in the pool hall including Fat Hank stared silently hoping things would not get out of hand. He shook his big head and called Blacker all kinds of fools, in his head.

Sergeant Turner eased closer to Blacker. Spit covered his lips as he yelled, "I will kill you nigger so help me God if you ever lay your nigger eyes on my Susan again! You hear me boy?!"

Blacker lifted the pool stick off the table and cradled it in his

92

hands.

"Sarge, with all due respect, don't ever call me nigger again."

Everyone in the pool hall looked around nervously. They knew Blacker was sure enough a gangster, but they also knew Sergeant Turner would never back down from a black man. They stared at each other and not one word was exchanged.

"You're going to jail nigger," Sergeant Turner said as he reached for his gun; but he was too slow. Blacker pulled his gun and shot the Sergeant in both legs before running out of the pool hall. He jumped into his Cadillac and headed for New York never to see the south again.

Blacker stopped long enough to call his brother Frank to say good-bye and find out what was happening. Frank told him the police were looking for him everywhere and had beaten up Fat Hank pretty badly and closed down the pool hall. Blacker's feelings of remorse for Fat Hank were short-lived, he never liked him anyway.

Once he arrived in New York, he hooked up with other tough gangsters and it wasn't long before he started using the drugs he now sold. In a matter of months, he went from a gangster with money to a junkie with nothing. He slept wherever his high left him.

But his whole life changed when he saw her. Blacker had always had the best looking women, but he never saw a woman so beautiful in his life. He just knew he had to possess her love, no matter what it took. She walked with the gracefulness of a dancer. She held her head high and had a look on her face as if she was not to be tempted by the evil that surrounded her. Blacker came out of his inebriated stupor and boldly approached the beautiful petite woman.

"Hello beautiful," said Blacker walking beside her. "I was wondering if I can uh... if I can uh..."

It was then that he had realized that he had nothing to offer her.

She stopped walking and looked into his eyes and asked innocently, "Are you on drugs?"

He nodded his head affirmatively. There was something about her that demanded the truth.

"I thought so," she said. "So many of our black men are on that stuff. You know, you would be a handsome man if you stop using those drugs. I can look in your eyes and tell you weren't always like this. What's your name?"

"Bla...Blacker," he stammered.

"No, I mean your real name."

"My name is Richard...Richard Brown."

"Richard, I can never be around you," she said matter-of-factly. "Because I'm not into what you're into. I'm in college to become a teacher, and the only way that we can become friends is if Blacker dies, because I don't like him or what he stands for."

She then left Blacker standing there with his mouth hanging open.

"Wait!" he yelled before she could turn the corner. "What's your name?"

"Maria," she yelled back before disappearing around the corner.

He found out from the people in the neighborhood where she lived, but he made no attempts to see her. He knew there was only one way to have her, so he didn't bother her yet. Instead he worked on kicking his habits and before long he was clean and working in a material factory. The job did not pay much but it was better than going back to the streets. He had an uncle in New York that had a big church in Brooklyn, so he began attending the services and learned everything he could about the Bible. His uncle was so proud of him and encouraged him to become a preacher for God. It wasn't long before he started preaching in his uncle's church. When his uncle died from illness, the church was left to him. It was then that he pursued Maria and captured her heart.

Pastor Richard Timothy Brown, Sr. knew all about the street life and sympathized with what his son was going through. He told himself that some day he would tell his son about his past.

$

"'Woe to you, teachers of the law and Pharisees, you hypocrites,'" continued Pastor Brown reading from his Bible. "'You shut the kingdom of heaven in men's faces. You, yourselves do not enter, nor will you let those enter who are trying to. Woe to you, teachers of the law and Pharisees, you hypocrites! You devour widows' houses and for a show make lengthy prayers. Therefore you will be punished severely.'"

Everyone in the church shouted their "Amens", "Hallelujahs" and "Praise the Lord". Pastor Brown closed his Bible. "I would never ask you to do anything that I'm not willing to do. I feel your happiness, and most of all I feel your suffering. I live where you live. Right now my son is in prison like so many of your sons and daughters. I struggle to pay my bills just as you do. I'm not one of those reverends that will only help you if it's something in it for me. We see them on TV all the time. They march only to gain a following, and then they're off to Hollywood. In this church, when you put in your offerings you know what's being done with your money. Unlike some of these preachers taking your hard earned money buying new cars and spending it in strip bars."

Most of the people in the church laughed, nodded their heads saying, "That's right" and "Amen".

"I know a lot of you are looking forward to our bus trip next week to Bear Mountain," continued Pastor Brown. "The kids need to get out of the ghetto when the opportunity presents itself. So, everyone should try to make an effort to go. And don't wait too long to start cooking, you all know how much I love them sweet potato pies."

Everyone in the church laughed and when the laughter died down Pastor Brown said, "Let us close this service. Everyone bow their heads."

Everyone did as Pastor Brown directed.

"Lord, thank you for blessing us and taking us into your hands. Continue to watch over us and our families, and if we suffer Lord let it be for you. Keep us in your good graces, Lord. You are the Kingdom, the Power and the Glory, forever. Everybody say Amen."

The church erupted into a chorus of Amens, lifted their heads, and walked around the church greeting one another before going home.

Chapter Sixteen

"I missed you baby," said Lisa. "Please boo make love to me."

Lisa laid back on the big queen sized bed with no clothes on. She spread her legs and held her arms wide open for Richard to come to her. He didn't feel this good in so long. He kissed her lips, and gently played with her left nipple with his thumb. When she turned her head to the side with a look of passion on her face, Richard kissed her behind the ear and whispered sweet words to her. He then dropped his face to her breast and began licking, sucking, and gently biting. He then lowered his head to her vagina and made her cum so many times she thought she was going to faint, but Richard was only getting started. He turned her onto her stomach and kissed the back of her neck and went down with kisses until he reached the back of her knees. She cried out, "Give it to me Richard, please baby," and raised her ass in the doggy style position.

"Bishop. Bishop. Bishop. Bishop."

He looked down at Lisa but it was not she who was calling him; the voice belonged to a man. "Bishop. Bishop." Why was this guy shaking his shoulder and calling him while he made love to Lisa, he thought to himself. Richard turned around to face the guy and when his eyes opened he saw Krazy Kay standing there with a big smile on his face.

"Damn Bishop," laughed Krazy Kay. "Your mattress might be pregnant now. You was calling Lisa's name and humping your bed. I woke you up before anyone else saw you. That was some funny shit though. Yo, they about to call chow. You going?"

"No, I'm not going," answered Richard with a smile. "I wasn't sleep that long. We went to chow before I took that nap."

"So, what's up?" asked Krazy Kay. "You getting up or what? Your homegirl Ms. McCartney is on." "Alright, I'm getting up," said Richard. "I have to call my girl's brother Omega anyway. Watch out."

Krazy Kay got off of Richard's bed and Richard grabbed his toothbrush and toothpaste and headed to the bathroom.

Richard emerged from the bathroom just as an inmate was getting off the phone. He placed his toothbrush and toothpaste in his pocket and began dialing Omar's number. He looked to the COs' bubble and saw CO McCartney on the telephone, laughing and talking loud. "Yeah, we had a good time...Girl, you should've came...No girl I didn't see any of them, and I'm not trying to be around any of them."

She probably went to a party or something, Richard thought to himself. Everyone in the dorm was in the dayroom watching TV except for four guys standing around Krazy Kay listening to his war stories. "I got hit a few times," said Krazy Kay lifting his shirt to show a few scars on his back. "They sent me to a fucking Bronx house when I first came through, but I represent Queens to the fullest, baby. As soon as I came in the dorm, niggas tried to rush 'cause they knew where I was from. So I pulled out my fiber glass glock I made and it was on! I was airing them kats out and then a big nigga snuffed me and that's when a Puerto-Rican kid poked me a few times. I ain't gonna front son, he fucked me up. But when I first came through I did a few favors for the nigga Big Lord getting weed to his man and 'em. So when he heard how shit went down he caught the Puerto Rican kid coming off the visit and aired him out crazy. I love that nigga Big Lord son."

Krazy Kay was from the south side of Jamaica, Queens. He lived on South Road and Liverpool Street and everyone around his way knew who he was because he stayed in trouble. He was not always a troubled kid. He lived with his mother and aunt and life was modest but good until his mother became addicted to crack. She became so addicted Krazy Kay lost all respect for his mother; when he lost respect for her, he lost respect for everyone. He started hanging in the streets robbing people and selling drugs. He did time in a youth corrections facility and he came out of there worse than when he entered. At times his mother would steal money and crack out of his pocket when he was asleep. One day, he screamed on her and she saw the murder in his eyes. She knew it would be safer to beg or have sex with someone outside to get high. Krazy Kay was now serving time for gun possession. He figured it had to have been his mother who turned him into the police. Shortly after his arrest, he called his house and his aunt said the money and drugs he had stashed in the house were now gone.

Before Krazy Kay started his second war story, he and Richard made eye contact. Richard smiled and put his fist in the air in greeting, before dialing Omar's number.

"Hello, may I speak to Omega?"

"This is Omega, who dis?"

"Yo, what's up Omega? This is Richard."

"Rich kid, what's the deal homie?"

"I'm okay. I figured I'd call and give you an update on what's going on with me. I talked to the lawyer, Mr. Atkins yesterday. He said the speedy trial motion went through, so I'll be in court next month. My trial date is December 9th. I can't believe I been in here going on six months."

"It seems like you been gone longer than that," said Omar. "But what else did the lawyer say?" "He said that one of the witnesses against me is a girl named Michelle Jackson."

"Michelle?" interrupted Omar.

"Yeah, and I still can't believe the other witness is Anthony Parker."

"Who the fuck is Anthony Parker?"

"That's my man Ant-live," Richard answered. "I can't even believe it. I got his number, so when I hang up from you I'll call him and see what's going on."

"Damn kid," said Omar. "Anyway, I know who Michelle is. I'll talk to her. She used to be my little girlfriend. Yo, get back to me about Ant-live. Give his info to my sister and I'll see what I can do. Oh yeah, Shameek and T-bone put a high price on your head. I heard that stupid nigga T-bone was about to catch a bullshit case just to come in there and try to run into you, but Shameek told him he needed him on the outside. Them niggas is retarded. But fuck them niggas. I'm all the way with you fam. We gotta get you outta there. Hit me back later, I'll be here for a while. One!"

"Alright," said Richard. He hung up the phone, immediately dialed Ant-live's number and hoped he would be able to catch up to him. It was the middle of the winter and Richard figured Ant-live would be inside; cold weather was the only thing that kept people indoors. The last time Richard talked to Ant-live was four months ago long before he discovered that Ant-live was telling on him. Ant-live had made up a story saying he didn't shoot Rashien because he thought he saw a cop car riding by. Richard knew Ant-live was lying but he didn't let it bother him because he still had mad love for his friend. He wanted to tell Ant-live that being scared was a natural thing and it was nothing to be ashamed of, but Richard knew that some men's egos forced them to say things their hearts didn't agree with- So Richard had said nothing at all. He let Ant-live ramble on.

The phone rang three times before someone picked it up and said, "Hello, who dis?"

"Can I speak to Anthony?"

"Dis Ant-live, who dis?"

"It's me Bishop. What's up Ant?"

"Oh shit, what's up my nigga?" asked Ant-live.

"Let me get to the point," said Richard. "You was always my boy Ant. Remember it was me, you and Kendu? Well, I still love you like I love Kendu. But why me, Ant?"

"Why what, nigga? What's going on. Talk to me."

"Ant, I already know you're telling on me. Why me? Don't do me like this Ant."

There was a moment of silence before Ant-live said, "Yo listen man, I'm doing me kid. They was trying to have me as your co-defendant. Fuck that kid, I ain't doing time for nobody! Plus how I know you wouldn't had flipped on me?"

"Because I don't get down like that Ant."

"Well, I get down like that and I had to get down first," said Ant-live. "Yeah, I'm on the team now, and if you're smart you'll cop out."

"You're on the wrong team Ant. You betrayed me but I'm not surprised, Judas did it to Jesus."

"I don't wanna hear that Bible shit!" Ant-live fired back.

"I understand," Richard said angrily as tears streamed down his face. "But understand this Ant. 'The son will go just as it is written about him. But woe to that man who betray the son of man! It would be better for him if he had not been born', Mark; 14:21."

"What nigga?!" asked Ant-live angrily. "You threatening me? You bitch ass nigga!"

"Ant-live, I can never be what you are."

"Oh yeah? Fuck you and Kendu nigga! Write me from Attica you bitch ass nigga!!!"

Richard hung up the phone and walked back to his bunk. He laid down and couldn't get Ant-live out of his head. How could Ant-live do this to him? He shot Rashien for the safety of both of them and their families. It was something that had to be done, Richard thought to himself. He was so wrapped in his thoughts, he didn't notice CO McCartney walk up to his bed carrying a small brown paper bag.

"Hey baby," she said smiling. "What's up?"

Richard looked up and saw the beautiful woman smiling.

"Oh, how are you Ms. McCartney?"

"I'm okay, but you don't look so hot. Is everything okay?" she asked. She and Richard had become very close friends during the last six months.

She even once told Richard that he made her feel so good about herself that she no longer had sex with men upon first meeting them. She told him everything she went through in her youth and it made her feel so good to get it all off her chest. She didn't even want a sexual relationship with Richard anymore. She now truly cherished their friendship and she didn't want anything to come between that.

She stopped having sex with the male COs and she looked even more beautiful to them than she ever did. She owed her newfound self-confidence to Richard. He acted as her psychiatrist. She knew she was a sexaholic, but she was well on her way to recovery with the help of Richard and her new fiancé. She was now engaged to a doctor and Richard was truly happy for her, and that made her feel good. She cherished the friendship Richard offered her; she had never met a man like him. He seemed so much older than his age, she thought to herself. Now it was her turn to be there for him.

"I'm okay Ms. McCartney," said Richard. "I just need to get out of here."

"I understand. Here I brought you a sandwich. It's your favorite," she smiled. "Turkey and cheese with lettuce and tomatoes."

"Thank you, I appreciate it," said Richard as he took the bag from her outstretched hand. "Did anybody you loved ever betrayed you?"

"Of course," she answered. "That's the story of my life. But you have to stay strong and keep doing what you're doing. You know, God has a special plan for us and sometimes He makes us go through some tough times, but He always makes sure that we come out of it even stronger."

The phone in the bubble began ringing.

"Hold on. I'll be right back," said CO McCartney walking towards the phone. "Ms. Higgins must be in the bathroom."

She entered the bubble and answered the phone. After saying a few words, Richard could see her walking back to his bunk with a smile on her face, as the other inmates looked at her with lustful stares.

"You have a visit," she told Richard. "I'll still be here when you come back."

"Alright," said Richard as he got up to go and get ready.

Who could it be, he thought. Lisa couldn't make it today. His parents always let him know ahead of time before they came up. There was only one way to find out.

He made his way down the long corridor to the visiting room. Upon reaching his destination he put on the jumpsuit and beige slippers. When he stepped out onto the visiting floor, he looked around and saw his mother Maria. As he made his way to the table where she sat, he noticed the bags under her eyes and knew she'd been crying probably all morning. Something was definitely wrong. He got to the table, gave her a big hug and sat down opposite of her.

"I thought you were coming next week. I hear you went back to work. You took the day off?" Richard was bombarding Maria with questions, when he suddenly stopped. "Ma, what's wrong? Is it me being in here? What's wrong mommy?" Richard slid his chair over closer to his mother. He laid an arm on her shoulder.

"Your, your..." Maria stammered. "Your, your father. He had a stroke and he died yesterday."

"Oh my God!" cried Richard. He pulled his mother tighter and they cried together. Richard never imagined that something like this could happen to him.

"Son, things are hard for me right now. I need you home baby. The funeral is next week. Will they let you come?"

"I hope so," Richard answered sadly. "I'll look into it when I go back to the dorm."

They sat in silence, holding and comforting each other. When the visit was nearing end, Maria gave her son a big hug and kissed him gently on the forehead. He stood from the table and wiped the tears from his mother's eyes.

"Ma, please try to stay strong. You know daddy would want you to remain strong. Stay strong for me as well as daddy, ma."

"I know son. Please call me tonight. I love you baby. Take care of yourself in here."

"I love you too ma," said Richard as he hugged her, kissed her and then walked away to be strip-searched. He held his head down as he walked away. He didn't want his mother to see him shed anymore tears. He wondered how he could tell her to remain strong when he may not be able to.

Chapter Seventeen

Ant-live sat in his apartment watching an old episode of Sopranos on TV and smoking weed in a Dutch Master cigar. He was waiting for a girl named Lashonda to come to his house. They had gotten off the phone ten minutes prior, and she said she would be right over. Ant-live thought about the conversation he had with Richard, as he waited for Lashonda. As far as he was concerned, he was 100% right for turning on Richard. If Richard was smart he would cop out to whatever time they offered him, Ant-live thought to himself. He had no plans of doing not even one day in jail for something that Richard had done. Ant-live was not going back to jail.

Two years ago he served eight months in C-76 on Rikers Island and he had no plans of repeating that performance. He was so stressed out during his stay, that he began to lose his hair. He knew he did not have it in him to do any more time in prison and made up his mind long ago to do anything it took not to go back. He wasn't concerned about being called a snitch, because guys would still deal with him being that he did not tell on them. Plus so many guys were telling nowadays to save themselves from doing jail time, that it was becoming acceptable to 'do you' so to speak.

Ant-live was never taught to care for anyone but himself and death before dishonor had nothing to do with his life. When he was born, his mother was attending college but things were rough for her. She was a single mother with no job and was on welfare. She didn't drop out of school because she was determined to improve her life not only for her, but also for her son. While her intentions were noble, they had an adverse effect on Anthony. He was left to fend for himself and was often hungry.

Left to fend for himself, that is exactly what he learned to do. Anthony began his life of stealing at the age of seven and never looked back. He would go to the grocery store and look into the freezer as if he was looking for a specific tem and then walk out of the store with a look of disappointment on his little face. Meanwhile, his coat sleeves were filled with ice-cream sandwiches. By age thirteen, he had graduated to selling crack for whatever drug dealer offered to pay him twenty dollars off every hundred he sold.

He had always done well in school, but he dropped out after making it to high school. By then, his mother had gotten her Bachelor's and Master's degrees and was working in the welfare building on Dekalb Avenue. The hard work she put in had finally paid off, but her son was so out of control he was lost to her forever. She had gone to school to learn how to help others and the person she wanted to help the most was unreachable and that troubled her. Ant-live loved his mother to death, but he also loved the streets and was not giving that life up for anyone, not even his mother. It didn't concern him that his mother could provide for him now; the streets had supported him for all those hard years. He had never known his father and the streets became that to him. But like a disobedient son, he didn't follow the rules of the streets either. All was fair to Ant-live and he was out for himself.

He heard a knock on the door and got up to answer it with his blunt still in his hand. He opened the door and Lashonda came inside. Lashonda was a chubby, young girl with chocolate brown-skin and eyes the color of a copper coin.

"What's up baby?" asked Ant-live. "What took you so long to get over here?"

"I had to wait for my cousin to come home," answered Lashonda as she followed Ant-live to his bedroom, "so she could watch my little brother."

They entered Ant-live's small bedroom. There was a single bed against the wall and a small television atop a brown dresser. There was a wooden folding chair situated in the corner with a nine millimeter and two full clips rested on top of it. Lashonda sat on the bed as Ant-live cut off the TV. He sat next to her and began kissing her neck.

She pushed him off of her and said, "I need to talk to you."

"I want some pussy. Fuck talking. Fuck you wanna talk about any-motherfucking-way?"

Lashonda looked at him for a few seconds and then said, "My cousin said her man is on the Island and he told her that you got mad beef and that you told on somebody that's in there."

"Fuck your cousin's boyfriend and the nigga I was suppose to had told on," said Ant-live with agitation in his voice. "I'm not thinking about them niggas."

"But did you tell on the guy?"

"Let me ask you something," said Ant-live ignoring her question. "Would you do twenty-five years for something that you didn't do?"

"Hell no!" answered Lashonda with her face twisted up. "Are you crazy?!"

"You're smart. That's what I'm talking about baby. That's what I'm talking about," said a smiling Ant-live as he took his shirt off.

He took a blunt and a lighter out of his sweatpants pocket and after lighting his blunt he laid back on his bed. Lashonda knelled down and began to pleasure him, as he puffed his blunt with a smile on his face.

Ant-live's body began to tense up and Lashonda could tell he was about to peak. Lashonda tried to pull her head away but Ant-live grabbed the back of her head and pumped upwards into her mouth. She began to gag and struggled to pull away. After he was done cumming, he let her head go and Lashonda looked at him very angrily as she wiped her mouth.

"Why the fuck you held my head like that for?!" asked Lashonda angrily. "That's the second time you did that shit to me!"

"Bitch knock it off," smiled Ant-live. "You do the same shit when I'm eating your pussy."

Lashonda laughed because she knew what he said was true. She began removing her clothes when someone knocked on Ant-live's front door. Ant-live threw on some clothes and went to see who was at his door. He looked through the peephole and saw Magic and Slim, two guys he knew from the block. He opened the door partway but did not invite the two men in; he didn't trust any guys to be in his apartment.

"What's up y'all?" asked Ant-live.

One of the guys was five foot eleven, light-skin, stocky, wavy hair and they called him Magic. The other guy was five foot nine, brown-skin, baldhead and they called him Slim.

"Yo kid I need a burner," said Magic. "We got a vic around the corner."

"Word?" asked Ant-live. "What he got?"

"He got a platinum chain and a coupla rings wit' ice in 'em," smiled Slim. "But we gotta hurry up before he bounce. He's around the corner talking to some bitch."

"Hold up, I'm coming, give me a minute," said Ant-live as he closed the door and walked quickly to his room.

Lashonda laid naked under the covers with a smile on her face as Ant-live entered the bedroom. Without even glancing at Lashonda, he opened his closet door and took out his jacket and a pair of sneakers.

"Where you going?" asked Lashonda.

"I gotta take care of something," answered Ant-live as he finished getting dressed. "Get up and get dressed and come see me tomorrow or something."

"Come see you tomorrow?" asked Lashonda with an attitude. "I can wait here 'til you come back."

"Picture that. I don't leave bitches in my crib baby."

"Oh, I'm a bitch now? I come over here and suck your dick and now you kicking me out?"

"Yep," answered Ant-live as he picked her clothes up off the floor and tossed them to her. "Hurry up and get dressed. I ain't got that much time for you girl."

"You foul motherfucker," said Lashonda as she put on her clothes. "I hope somebody kill your ass. You ain't shit nigga. My cousin told me don't fuck with your punk telling ass!"

Ant-live grabbed his nine and clips off the chair with a smirk on his face and stuck it in his jacket pocket. If he had time he would've beat Lashonda's ass for talking to him like that, he thought to himself. But it was time to get paid.

After Lashonda was dressed they walked out of the apartment and Lashonda stormed past Magic and Slim angrily as Ant-live locked his door. He didn't care about Lashonda or any other woman that wanted to be with him. His money came first. They headed out of the building and he smiled. He then looked at Slim and said, "Money over bitches." Slim laughed as Magic led the way to the guy they planned to rob.

They rounded the corner onto Monroe and Nostrand Avenue where they spotted their victim. The tall, clean-cut guy stood in front of a brown house talking to a very pretty girl, not expecting what was about to happen. Sticking out of his sweat-hooded shirt was a long chain with an iced out cross hanging heavily from it. The slim, pretty girl was the spitting image of the late great singer Aaliyah. The couple was deep into their conversation as the three men crept up on them. When they finally noticed the three thugs, it was already too late.

"If you move, I'll kill you," said Ant-live pointing a gun at the pair. The girl had a frightened look on her face as her boyfriend held up his hands to show them that he had no gun on him. "Yo, y'all search the bitch down," Ant-live told Slim and Magic. "I got homeboy over here."

While they searched the girl, Ant-live took the guy's chain and two rings and then began searching his pockets. Ant-live pulled out a large bankroll of money; there had to be at least two thousand dollars in the roll. He looked over to see what Slim and Magic were doing and quickly stuffed the money into his back pocket. He placed the jewelry he stole into his front pocket and then called out to his partners.

"Yo, come on. Fuck her, let's get outta here."

The three men started running down the street and did not stop until they reached Ant-live's apartment. They stood outside of his apartment door. Ant-live pulled the chain, cross and two rings out of his pocket.

He handed the chain and cross to Slim and said, "Yo the nigga didn't have any money on him, so y'all take the chain and cross and I'll keep the two rings."

"Aiight, that's cool," said Magic. "The rings are kind of small anyway."

"No doubt, baby," said Ant-live. "I'll see y'all niggas later."

He gave both of them a five and entered his apartment as Slim and Magic went off to sell the chain and cross. They never realized they too had been robbed.

Chapter Eighteen

"I don't understand that, that's crazy. How can they deny you from attending you father's funeral?"

"Ms. McCartney, I don't know. They claim my life is in danger due to my case, but I don't care about that. I just wanted to see my dad for one last time and be there to comfort my mother."

Richard continued attending church services, reading his bible, and praying to God but he had already made up his mind to make T-bone and Shameek pay if he ever got out of jail.

"I know baby," said CO McCartney. "But you have to try and stay strong. I know it's easy for me to say, but what can you do?"

"I know it's nothing I can do. That's what hurts me the most, not being able to do anything," said Richard sadly. "And to be real with you, even if I beat this case and go home, I don't know if I'll be able to do anything. But one thing is for sure. When I do get out of here I wont let anyone harm me or the people I love."

"I hear you," said CO McCartney. "But we have to think positively and like you always say, put God first."

The day Richard's mother came to tell him of his father's death was the saddest day of his life. When he got back to the dorm everyone knew something bad had happened just by the look on his face. Even CO McCartney noticed something was wrong and she was hoping that everything was okay. Deep down she knew that it was not. She cared about him so much that she wanted to go to him and hug him and kiss him and assure him that everything would be okay, but she knew she couldn't because it would not look right. Just from little hug of comfort and care, someone would open their mouth and if it got to the wrong person it would put her in a position to be fired for fraternizing with an inmate. She knew the male COs she no longer gave play to would definitely spread the false rumor.

Before she became a CO, Robin McCartney wondered how could she work day in and day out with young black men that could be her family, for months and not have some kind of relationship with them. It had nothing to do with having sex, because she never thought seriously about having sex with an inmate until she met Richard and that was only because he had proved to be like no other man she ever met. Her heart broke that day as she watched someone she cared so deeply for, be in so much pain. She sat there for hours watching him suffer silently on his bunk.

Krazy Kay and the rest of the guys in the dorm gave him his space to let him have time to himself. A few guys in the dorm who had experienced the same tragedy gave him their condolences, and stayed out of his way. Richard cried himself to sleep and woke the next morning hoping that the previous day had simply been a nightmare, but he knew it hadn't. He had to face reality and stay strong, as he had told his mother to do. As the days went by, he found the strength to talk to Krazy Kay and CO McCartney about his father's death.

"It's time for me to leave. My shift is over," said CO McCartney. "But keep your faith in God. All things work together for good for those who love God. Remember that. I'll see you tomorrow. If you need anything let me know."

CO McCartney was beginning to sound like Richard more and more as the months passed by.

"Okay, I'll see you in the morning," said Richard. "You have a good evening."

"Thank you baby," said CO McCartney as she headed to the bubble to get her belongings.

Since his incarceration Richard had changed and was beginning to see a few things a little differently. He made it his business now to speak to the other inmates. They were full of so much information and he wanted to learn as much as he could from them.

Krazy Kay and several other inmates were in the back of the dorm telling war stories. Richard decided to take a walk back there and as he approached, the young men stopped talking to respectfully acknowledge him.

"Bishop, what's up?"

"What's the deal Bish?"

"Bishop, what's popping baby?"

"Alight Bish."

"Son, what's up?"

"Okay, okay Bish."

"What's cracking baby?"

"My man Bishop," said Krazy Kay last. "What's popping?"

"Ain't nothing," answered Richard. "Don't let me stop y'all flow."

"Yeah son, so like I was saying right?" said one of the youths. "I couldn't get the nigga out of his crib. So I ain't have no other choice but to wait 'til I caught the nigga outside. Mad bitches on the benches and everything son. When I saw that nigga, I pulled out the desert and homie saw me and tried to run. I hit 'em in the back four times. Bong,bong,bong,bong. Yo, I straight laid 'em out. I know them dirty bitches on that bench told on me son."

No wonder this dude got caught, he did it in front of the whole projects, Richard thought to himself.

"That's why I don't leave no witnesses," another youth replied. "They got me on some bogus shit. Nobody saw me do anything. They just heard shots. I got this beat son. They just making me lay up 'cause they know I had beef wit the nigga that got murked."

Richard listened to all the young boys tell their stories and he thought about how everyone of them had got caught. Their biggest problem was they talked too much. The Bible said that a man needs to control his tongue, and because of that, Richard learned early on not to talk too much. Of course, he knew some of the young boys were lying, but he had to admit the stories were entertaining. He'd been thinking of many ways to kill Shameek and T-bone without getting caught, if he was fortunate to beat his case. He knew he had a good chance of beating the case but listening to most of the inmates, it seemed as if they all got railroaded by the courts in one way or another. Most of them had court appointed attorneys that did not fight hard enough for the prisoner they were representing. You couldn't even call the prisoner a client because the lawyer took the case from the court and didn't get any money from the prisoner; in return they'd receive half-assed representation which explained why most of the court appointed lawyers didn't give a damn if the prisoner beat the case or not. Most of them made deals with the prosecutor to get a conviction even when they knew the prisoner was innocent but Richard felt good about his case because he had what inmates called a 'paid lawyer', and he knew whether he beat the case or not, Mr. Atkins, would fight the case with all the experience he had. That was the advantage of having money, or knowing someone who had it.

"Excuse me a minute y'all," said Krazy Kay. "Bishop, let me holla at you for a second."

Richard and Krazy Kay walked away from the group of young boys.

"What's up Kay, what's going on?"

"Yo Bishop, you see that dark-skin, baldhead kid that came in today?" asked Krazy Kay. "Niggas gonna blow him up tonight."

"Why?" asked Richard.

"Niggas just ain't feeling his style," answered Krazy Kay. "Homie is too quiet."

"That's stupid!" said Richard. "Homie seems cool."

"Yeah well, if he ain't, niggas gonna air his ass out tonight," said Krazy Kay as he walked back to the group of young boys.

Richard shook his head sadly, and went back to his bunk. He laid down and began reading his Bible.

The young guy the other boys planned to stab, laid back on his bed looking around with a smirk on his face as if he knew what they were planning. He would occasionally get up to do some push-ups and then sit back on his bunk and just look around.

Richard looked at him and noticed the guy did not look scared. He did however look as if he was getting bored. Richard hated troublemakers, and wanted to warn the guy of the trouble that was soon to come. He then decided to wait it out and see what happened.

Later that night, five young boys in the dorm approached the guy. "Yo my man," said one of the youths. "Where you from?"

"What?!" the guy asked with his face screwed up. "Y'all faggots better get the fuck away from me,"

Before they could respond, the guy pulled out an ice pick with white cloth around the handle and began chasing the five youths around the dorm. They ran to the CO's bubble and the guy went back to his bunk and sat down with a smirk on his face staring at the five boys.

Richard was the only one in the dorm that was laughing at the five youths standing near the bubble. All the other inmates had a look of shock on their faces.

Richard got off his bunk and walked up to the five boys standing near the bubble and said, "Tell the CO y'all can't stay here."

"Yo, Bishop," said one of the youths. "What's up? Why you flipping?"

"I'm not gonna tell you cowards again," replied Richard as he walked away. He went back to sit on his bunk and began reading his Bible again.

The five youths packed up their belongings and the CO had escorted them out of the dorm to move to another house. Richard got off of his bunk and walked over to the guy who had earlier wielded an ice pick.

"I apologize for the idiots who came at you," said Richard. "Usually these guys listen to me when I tell them to chill, but there's always some clowns who don't listen. Anyway, they call me Bishop. If you need anything let me know."

"So you're the church-boy Bishop, huh?" the guy asked with a smile. "I've been hearing a lot about you and from what I've heard I definitely dig your style. They call me Moe-dog. I'm just waiting to get bailed out right now. I should be out of here in another hour or so."

Moe-dog was a five foot six, stocky, dark-skinned baldhead guy that wore a mustache and a thick beard.

"Yeah kid," continued Moe-dog. "I heard about the Shameek and T-bone beef you got. They get down, but between us, they're overrated. I'm all about paper and for the right price...Hey man, shit can happen."

"I hear you," responded Richard. "They'll pay for what they did to my man Kendu, rest in peace."

"I knew Kendu. Son was from LG. He use to fuck wit' my cousin Shawnette. He was definitely cool people."

Richard and Moe-dog sat on Moe-dog's bed talking for hours, until the CO in the bubble called Moe-dog's name out.

"John Simmons, let's go. You're outta here."

"Okay Bishop," said Moe-dog. "I'm out. Take this number and call me."

Richard took the number and gave Moe-dog a five. Moe-dog then pulled the ice pick out of his pocket and handed it to Richard before walking out of the dorm with an evil smirk on his face.

Richard walked back to his bed, grabbed a pen and copied Moe-dog's name and phone number into the back of his Bible. He then laid back on his bunk and stared at the ceiling with a smile on his face, as plans began to form in his mind. Richard was definitely changing into a different person. Prison and death have a way of doing that to people.

Chapter Nineteen

"Hello, may I speak to Ms. Patterson?"

"This is she. Who's calling?"

"I don't know if you remember me. My name is Richard. I was a friend of your..."

"Bishop?" interrupted Gloria Patterson.

"Yes, this is Bishop," answered a surprise Richard. He thought she probably would've forgotten him by now. But that was not the case at all.

"Are you okay baby? Where are you?" asked Gloria.

"I'm on Rikers Island. I'm about to start trial. They said I killed the guy that killed your son, Kendu."

"What was that guy's name? Ra something, Rameek?"

"They called him Rashien."

"Yeah, I heard his awful ass got killed. That's good for him. When you do bad it always comes back. Anyway, are you okay? Do you need anything? Do you think you can beat this case or what?"

"No, I don't need anything, and I think I have a very good chance of beating this case. But I just called to see how you were doing, Ms. Patterson."

"Boy if you call me Ms. Patterson again," she said threateningly, "I'll come see you personally and straighten you out. Call me Gloria. And I better not hear that Ms. Patterson stuff again. You hear me boy?"

Richard smiled and said, "Yes, Gloria."

"So, when you get out are you going back to Fort Greene? 'Cause I think you're gonna beat this case."

"I hope I do beat it, but to answer your question, I have to go back to Fort Greene. I still have enemies over there but I don't have anywhere else to go."

"You are always welcome to come and stay with me. You hear me?"

"Yes, I hear you. I do appreciate the offer and I may take you up on it."

"Do that baby. And keep me informed about your trial. I'm praying for you."

They said their goodbyes and Richard hung up the phone. He smiled to himself and felt good, despite being in prison for a murder case. He felt as if he had just got finished talking to Kendu himself. He enjoyed his conversation with Gloria. Everything was going according to plan. All he had to do was talk to Omar, if he beat the case. Everything would depend on what Omar had to say.

Richard stood near the phone thinking of all the things he wanted to do if he ever saw the outside again. He then thought about Ant-live and realized that he never knew him. He only knew the guy Ant-live pretended to be and when he finally saw who the real Ant-live was, he wanted to laugh and cry at the same time. He never felt so betrayed in his life. If only Kendu were here to see who the real Ant-live was, Richard thought to himself. How could Ant-live say fuck him and Kendu? That cut at Richard's heart like a knife because all three of them were like brothers. Richard decided to put his plans together and told himself that he would represent Kendu to the fullest. Things were going just as Richard predicted. He was finally able to get in touch with Kendu's mother. He had hoped she would invite him to stay in Lafayette Gardens with her and she had. If he was freed, going back to Fort Greene was like putting his head on the table to be chopped off. It would be too easy for Shameek and T-bone to get to him. Not that they couldn't come to Lafayette Gardens to get him, but he had a better chance of survival because he knew people in LG knew who killed Kendu and they had too much love for him to let the same guys who killed him come into their projects and kill someone staying with Kendu's mother. Richard knew T-bone and Shameek were stupid enough not to care, but that was his best chance if he beat the case. He first thought about asking Omar to find him a place to stay but he decided against it. He had other important favors to ask of Omar.

Never far from his mind, Richard then began thinking about Lisa. He loved her so much and there was nothing he wouldn't do for her. She came to see him twice a week. Sometimes she would come with his mother, and when she didn't come alone, she would drag her friend Gina with her. Whenever they both came to see him it would be the talk of the jail. Inmates and COs' alike would look at them lustfully because they were always the best looking women on the visiting floor. Lisa once told Richard that two COs tried to push up on them, saying that they were too beautiful to be wasting their time visiting an inmate. Lisa and Gina had embarrassed the COs so badly, everyone that was waiting to see their loved ones started laughing and snapping on the two CO's.

Just thinking about Lisa made Richard smile. A very loud commotion in the front of the dorm snapped Richard out of his thoughts. Krazy Kay and six other inmates were laughing and talking excitedly about something.

"Yo Kay," said Richard. "Come here a minute. What's going on?"

"Yo kid, niggas about to come through," Krazy Kay answered as he walked up to Richard. "I just got the wire that my man, Divine, is coming down here."

"Is that the Divine from Brownsville with the big body-count everyone talks about?"

"Yeah that's him, but fuck what niggas say. He's a good dude and a funny motherfucker too, kid."

"Yeah alright," said Richard as he walked away and sat on his bunk. Krazy Kay rejoined the group of young boys and they all were looking through the glass waiting for the newly arrived inmates. Ten minutes went by when CO Smith finally arrived with twelve new inmates.

"There go my son!" said Krazy Kay excitedly. "Yo Divine, what's up baby boy?"

Richard looked to the front of the dorm and shook his head. He hoped that Krazy Kay would not change just because Divine had arrived. Richard saw a lot of guys that were cool become real rowdy because their homeboys came around. He continued to look at the front of the dorm to get a good look at the infamous Divine.

Other inmates on the glass began calling out to Divine, as he looked at them with a big smile on his face. Most of the new arrivals looked kind of scared. Except Divine, it was maybe two others that looked as if they weren't having it. One of the two even looked back through the window like he was scheming to rob someone in the dorm. He was light-skin, tall with a frown on his face. However, the inmates in the dorm paid him no attention as they continued yelling to Divine through the glass.

"Divine, what's up boy?"

"Yo Divine, that's your man next to you with the chain on?"

"Oh shit, wait 'til niggas see Divine is back up in the building."

CO Smith began calling out names. Divine and five other inmates stepped to the north side of Mod 5, as the other six inmates were sent to the south side. As soon as Divine entered the dorm, he dropped his set-up to the floor and began to speak.

"Fuck y'all niggas on the window like y'all about to buy a puppy or something."

All of the inmates standing around began laughing.

"No nigga," said one inmate smiling. "I was window shopping and maybe I saw something I want."

"Yo Krazy Kay," said Divine. "This little bitch is still here, huh? You was doing the same thing in New York. You no-getting-money motherfucker, with your petty, chain-snatching ass. Grab my set-up and put it on my bunk, you lame duck."

The inmates laughed as the guy smiling took the set-up to Divine's bunk.

Richard laid on his bed looking at Divine. He had to admit, Divine was definitely a funny dude, but if he had plans to change things in the dorm he had something else coming. Richard heard a lot about Divine. But none of the stories matched the way he carried himself.

Everybody spoke of Divine as being a ruthless killer, but looking at him he seemed as if he was more of a comedian. Divine was a tall stocky man, with thick wavy hair. He wore a thick platinum chain and a large diamond stud in his ear. He was wearing a pair of brown and black Clarks , black Roc-A-Wear jeans, a brown long sleeve shirt, and a snorkel type coat.

"Yo Kay get me a walk-dog," said Divine with his DMX type voice. "I gotta listen to Hot 97 and catch my girl Sunny, with her fine ass."

"No doubt kid, I got you homie," said Krazy Kay. "Matter of fact, I got two walkmans. Yo, you need to check out that new Power 105 station. They be banging that proper shit. They got Ed Lover and Dr. Drew on there."

"Man, fuck all that shit! I ain't wit" that Hip-Hop and R&B bullshit. I just wanna hear my wife on Hot 97 nigga. What bitches they got on that Power 105 shit?"

"They got Step Lava, and Monie Love."

"Monie Love? Shit, that's my baby right there. I wanted to fuck her since that 'Monie in the middle' shit came out. Kay, you too young to know about that shit boy. Your little nuts was still in the sand nigga."

Krazy Kay laughed and said, "You're bugged out. Get the walkman out my locker with anything else you want. But check it, walk wit' me over here real quick. I want you to meet my man."

"Son, don't introduce me to no derelict ass nigga."

"Nah, Bishop is the real deal."

"Bishop from the Fort?"

"Yeah, you know him?"

"Nah, but I heard a lot about son."

Krazy Kay and Divine walked over to Richard's bunk and as they approached, Richard sat up.

Krazy Kay said, "Yo Bishop, this is my man Divine. Divine, that's Bishop."

"Aiight, what's popping?" asked Divine as he gave Richard a five.

"So, you're the infamous Divine, huh? I heard a lot about you. You can sit down," said Richard as he moved over and patted his bed. Divine sat on Richard's bed and Krazy Kay sat on the bed across from them.

"Likewise my nigga," said Divine. "I heard a lot about you too kid. You fighting that Rashien case right?"

Richard thought to himself how quick Divine was to get personal. He might be cool with Shameek.

But reading Richard's thoughts, Divine quickly said, "Yo son, I don't know them niggas like that. I just keep my ears to the streets that's all."

"Nah, I'm not thinking like that," lied Richard. "Yeah I got that Rashien case. I hope and pray I get around it."

"Yeah I hope you do too. But check it, I heard you're real deep into the Bible. Can I get like two pages?"

"What? What are you talking about?"

"I saw my man Big Lord in the receiving room. He hit me off wit' some trees. I need something to smoke it in homie."

Krazy Kay started laughing holding his stomach as Richard said, "Man, you ain't ripping no pages out my Bible to smoke drugs. You bugging kid. The book is to lift you up, not bring you down."

"I'm saying Bishop, forget reading the word. Let a nigga inhale the scriptures and trust me it won't bring me down. I'll be high as a fucking kite!"

Krazy Kay and Richard were laughing so hard, tears rolled down their faces.

"See y'all laughing," continued Divine. "I'm dead ass serious. Fuck it, yo Kay go get me some short-eye-books. I'm horny as a motherfucker,"

"Nigga, you just came through!" Krazy Kay said through his laughter. "Damn nigga, you want naked girl books already. You still a freak!"

"You damn right I'm a freak. Right before I got locked up I saw a dog licking his own nuts and son, I was extremely jealous."

"Krazy Kay, get this dude away from my bed," said Richard through his laughter. "This dude is crazy."

A loud sound in the back of the dorm stopped Richard and Krazy Kay's laughter. Half of the inmates in the dorm were stomping out the newly arrived tall light-skin inmate who was scheming earlier.

"I tried to tell that idiot in the pens, niggas ain't playing," said Divine. "He got a few muscles and the nigga think he's incredible stupid! Fuck that nigga. Yo Kay, go get them books!"

Chapter Twenty

"The last time I got pinched, I was fucking that CO bitch," said Divine. "I remember I was fucking her and she farted. She said, 'excuse me I farted'. I said that's alright baby, usually I make 'em shit."

"You're stupid," said Richard through his laughter. "You remind me of my man Kendu, rest in peace. But check it Divine, how did you get locked up?"

"It's a long story kid."

Richard and Divine sat on Richard's bed talking while the other inmates watched TV or stood around talking. Despite their different personalities, Richard and Divine had become very close friends. Richard didn't have a friend like Divine since Kendu was alive. And just like Kendu, Divine was a real individual. He was also very humorous and if you could not deal with him cracking jokes on you, then you couldn't be anywhere around him because he didn't care who you were; if he saw something funny he would speak on it. To make things worse, he would know certain things about you but would wait until a crowd was around before he'd expose you. Like the day when most were in the dayroom watching television, Divine singled out a light-skin tough looking guy who had a few guys in the dorm shook.

"Yo, this nigga is a fucking fraud," Divine had said. "Yo, y'all letting this bird front on y'all like he's tough. He ain't built like that. When I first came through a year and a half ago, the nigga was fucking wit' a homo name Shorty Jamaica."

The whole dayroom was in tears laughing. Even Richard was doubled over laughing and holding his stomach. The guy Divine was dissing had a frown on his face and was pissed off. He never felt so embarrassed in his life. If it had been someone else, he would've pulled out his shank and it would've been on. But he knew Divine was not the one to front on.

Everyone knew Divine was strong, and got busy in jail and out. The guy didn't even say anything back. He looked straight ahead at the TV and took the verbal abuse.

"Shorty Jamaica was an ugly motherfucker too," continued Divine as everyone continued to laugh. "The nigga looked like a gay Shabba Ranks. That's why bitches in the streets think niggas in jail get down like that; because of faggot ass niggas like him. My man Jason can't even get his hustle on braiding hair, 'cause some dumb ass bitch might think a homo did it. If y'all niggas don't believe what I said about duke, ask Big Lord or the nigga Thor in 5 Main."

Everyone laughed but knew Divine spoke the truth. He never put anyone out there if he couldn't prove it.

$

"Yeah Bishop, it's a long story how I got locked up," said Divine shaking his head.

"It ain't like we're going anywhere?" smiled Richard.

"You right, you right," said Divine. "What happened was, my sister was fucking wit' this kat named Smooth from B-more."

"What's B-more?" asked Richard.

"Damn nigga, you ain't up on no slang," answered Divine. "But I bet you know where Nazareth is motherfucker."

"You stupid. Just tell me how you got locked up."

"Anyway, like I was saying, she was fucking wit' this bird ass kat. The nigga didn't like me. At first, I thought it was because he knew he couldn't treat my sister any old way because he knew I'll kill his ass. But the real reason was most of them B-more niggas don't like us New York niggas. They hate the fact that we go all over the globe and set up shop. Them DC niggas can't stand us either, kid. I don't know if it's over that snitch ass nigga from uptown but I ain't got beef witnone of them kats as long as they don't step on my toes. Anyway, I asked the nigga Smooth to take me out there 'cause I heard there's crazy paper down there and I go wherever the paper is. So we get out to B-more and I got like four ounces on me. So we're riding around and he shows me the strip where I can move my drugs and shit. I had two guns on me, but the nigga didn't know I was strapped. The nigga tells me he'll get me a few workers from down there that knows everybody. So you know, I'm thinking everything is love. He took me to some empty ass house and said he'll be right back. I'm waiting for like two hours and shit just didn't seem right. I started feeling funny and shit, and the only time I feel funny is when I ain't got my babies on me or when something is about to pop off. Then I heard the door open. That's when I pulled my deserts and sure as shit, niggas up in the house wit' guns drawn. The first nigga that stuck his head in the room got it bad. It turned into the fourth of July in that motherfucking house. They busting they little heaters and shit. But son, my babies was spitting and crying like a motherfucker boy. I'm spitting; they spitting. I'm running outta shells so I jumped through the window, Glass was flying everywhere kid. I bust two more shots behind me and got away and shit. I make it back to New Yitty and the first person I see in my house sitting on the couch is this nigga, Smooth. You should have seen this nigga's face when he saw me, son. It was like he saw a ghost. I heard the shower running so I knew my sister was in the bathroom. I said to the nigga, 'You was waiting for my family to get the news that I got killed outta town, like a lot of New York niggas huh? But your family's gonna get that news instead kid'. His mouth was moving fast son, but I couldn't hear a word he said. All I hear is this 'yo shit'. I pulled and hit that nigga two times in the head and bounced. I know my sister was fucked up when she saw the nigga laying there staining my mom's new carpet and shit. The only reason I got arrested was because he died in my house and the cops said killing is my M.O."

"Wow, if you had a good lawyer, you wouldn't be here," said Richard looking at his friend.

"Yeah I know."

"Divine, if I beat this case and my plans go as expected, I'll get you a paid lawyer."

Richard then told Divine about all of the events that led up to his incarceration. They both felt comfortable discussing their cases with one another because they knew neither would say a word to anyone else.

They've become more like brothers than friends and made plans to see each other on the streets, where everything counted.

"Bishop, you know Big Lord was bailed out right?"

"Yeah, I know. He made two hundred thousand dollars bail."

"Word?" a surprised Divine asked. "He got paper like that?"

"There's a lot you don't know," said Richard ignoring his question. "But you'll know soon enough if things work out right."

"Oh shit, son that's Ms. Davidson in the bubble wit Ms. McCartney," said Divine changing the subject.

"Yeah," said Richard. "That's her."

"I told you I was fucking her the last time I got thrown in the can. And I hit it before in New Yitty. But she wasn't trying to be my main girl, because my money was funny. She's on some real high maintenance shit."

"Yo kid, she probably saw your card. She's coming in here."

As CO Davidson stepped into the dorm, the inmates stepped out of the dayroom to ogle her. Some of them hid where she could not see them with their hands in their pants jerking off. Others with photographic memories took mental pictures to remember for later on that night so they can jerk off privately in one of the many bathroom stalls.

CO Davidson was five foot eight, thick thighs, brown-skin, long shoulder length hair, chinky eyes, thick eye brows, nice round breasts and a Black Tail magazine ass.

The male COs in the building stayed sweating her, but she could not see herself with any of them. She liked big money getters, and these male COs received the same paycheck that she received so she definitely wasn't messing with any of them. She liked the new rapper out of Brooklyn named O-Fella. And of course Jay-Z and Cash Money Millionaires because she could relate to the real stuff they rapped about. Money, money, and more money. The only guy that did not have big paper that she gave play to was Divine. She loved his style, his ambition to get money, and his thugged out ways. She just saw no way that she could be in a committed relationship with a broke brother, no matter how good he made love to her. Inmates stood around missing their favorite videos, as a bold young boy stepped to CO Davidson and began laying his game down.

"Damn Ms. Davidson, you're looking good. Shit, I'll drink your bath water."

"If you do that, then how will I be able to take a bath," she asked with a smile. The young boy did not get the joke and CO Davidson felt like she was being rescued when she saw Divine walking towards her with his Mike Tyson walk.

"Okay shorty, your time is up," said Divine. "Haul ass you lame duck."

The youth felt disrespected, but he knew he had no wins against Divine so he stepped off with an angry look on his face.

"What's up Divine?" asked CO Davidson. "You're crazy, why did you do that to him?"

"Fuck shorty. You know I don't like niggas all up in my baby's face."

"Oh, I'm your baby now?" she asked as she folded her arms and stuck her ass out.

The young inmates loved the way she was standing now and some began to jerk off frantically as they looked at her with lust filling their eyes.

"So what's up baby? You miss that thug passion or what?"

"You know I miss that Divine," answered CO Davidson.

"So I'm saying, see if your girl Ms. McCartney will hold you down while we slide in the CO's bathroom. I'm horny as a muh'fucker. I ain't had sex since the last time we did it."

"Stop lying nigga! That was six months ago and your freak ass definitely did not go without pussy for that long."

"I'm saying ma," Divine said smiling. "See what's up with your friend."

CO Davidson just couldn't resist Divine's smile and he knew it. She loved his dimples.

"Okay, I'll see what's up," she said. "If the door clicks, come out and meet me in the CO's bathroom. Bring a washcloth with you."

"Okay ma, do me a favor."

"What?"

"I'ma drop my ID card. Bend down and pick it up."

"Boy, you crazy. I'm not doing that."

"Come on ma, do that for me," said Divine as he dropped his ID card on the floor with a smile on his face.

CO Davidson bent over and picked the ID card off the floor.

"Oh my God, son," chorused the inmates with their hand in their pants. "Oh shit, damn!!!"

Richard watched the whole scene with amusement. He had to admit that CO Davidson was definitely gorgeous, but she didn't compare to Lisa. Richard looked in the bubble and noticed CO McCartney waving to him with a smile. She knew she broke him out of his thoughts of Lisa and began laughing. Richard laughed and waved back. He figured he'd wait for a little while before going over to talk to her.

Richard looked to the front of the dorm and knew without a doubt that CO Davidson had truly made the inmates day by bending over like that.

She stood up, slapped the ID card on Divine's chest and walked out of the dorm with a smile on her face. She walked into the bubble and said a few words to CO McCartney. They began laughing as CO McCartney gave her a high five.

CO Davidson looked at her watch and went to the CO's bathroom. Divine went to his bed, grabbed his white washcloth, and put it in his back pocket. He walked to the door and when he heard the click, he walked out of the door and entered the CO's bathroom.

CO Davidson dropped to her knees taking Divine's penis out of his pants and began sucking him.

"Yeah, that's right baby. Do the damn thing."

"Hold up," said CO Davidson taking his penis out of her mouth after five minutes of sucking him. "We don't have that much time. I want you to fuck me."

She then pulled down her pants and panties, and Divine drove her crazy hitting her doggy style, her favorite position. She held onto the sink with both hands as Divine slapped her ass with each stroke. As he pumped, he kissed her behind the ears knowing her weak spots. After they both came, Divine gave her the washcloth and she cleaned herself. He then wiped his penis and nuts off with the same washcloth, and then returned it back to his back pocket. He gave CO Davidson a kiss on the cheek and slid out of the CO's bathroom.

He knew he was safe when he stepped back into the dorm. He walked over to his bed, and began smiling when he saw a brand new white washcloth hanging on the locker belonging to the inmate in the next bed from his. Being the funny guy that Divine was, he took the new washcloth, and put the one he and CO Davidson used on the boy's locker.

Chapter Twenty-one

Lisa emerged into the warm sun's radiance. The glare bounced off her beautiful skin. She was walking through the projects towards the new car her brother had just bought her. She had recently enrolled in the Borough of Manhattan Community College to study Business Administration. Her long ponytail swayed from side to side in the gentle winter breeze. She was rocking a pair of black Antonio Berardi high heel boots, a black Junya Watanabe skirt, a white short sleeve v-neck Christian Dior shirt and a long black mink coat. She had her books, her cell phone and her purse in her black nap sack strapped over her left shoulder.

As she walked through the projects, she sucked her teeth with an attitude when she saw Shameek sitting on a bench talking to one of his soldiers. Lisa couldn't understand what she ever saw in Shameek. He was ugly with little craters on his face. She realized she was only with him because of the power he had over so many of the people in the projects; but their respect for him was only out of fear. He had money and murderers on his team and that's all you needed to grab the attention of others. Lisa knew that as she neared, Shameek would speak to her. She hoped that he would just say hello and let her keep walking. She had no time for him. What made him think she would give him another chance, she thought to herself. He was repulsive to her now. Lisa wanted nothing to do with him. Every time he saw her he would ask the same questions. "What happened between us? Can I take you out to dinner? Who are you with now? Where are you going? When are we going to get back together?" And of course, the question that made her sick to her stomach, "Can we have sex just for old time sake?" Lisa told herself that she wouldn't have sex with him again, even if he was the last man on Earth.

Lisa walked on and suddenly realized who the young boy sitting on the bench with Shameek was. He was the nephew of a girl named Shaniqua who used to do Lisa's hair.

She struggled to remember the little boy's name. Every time Lisa went to Shaniqua's house to get her hair done, she would say how cute the little boy was and give him five dollars to spend on candy. Lisa figured he couldn't be older than thirteen or fourteen. That made Lisa hate Shameek even more. He was always snatching up little kids and replacing toy guns and candy with real guns and drugs. He would take some of them out of state with him. They all had hopes of returning to New York in brand new cars and clothes, but sadly many of them returned in body bags. Shameek did not care about them. They were expendable. He saw it as being part of the game and would simply find new spots and recruit new workers. It was all business and nothing personal to him. That's why a lot of guys in prison up north doing life had secretly hoped Shameek took a fall and came up state. They sought revenge because he had sealed many of their fates and the fates of their sons, brothers and nephews. But none of this concerned Shameek; he had no plans of going up north anyway. All he was concerned with was stacking his money. To Shameek, all was fair in love and war.

Shameek got off of the bench and stood directly in front of Lisa as she attempted to walk past.

"What's up baby?" he smiled. "You act like you don't know me anymore."

"What do you want?" she asked with an air of disgust in her voice.

"Me and you, that's what I want. Let me take you out to dinner tonight and we can work on the relationship that we had."

"Shameek, I've got a man."

"Who? That little bitch ass nigga that killed my boy Ra?" asked Shameek angrily.

He really wanted Richard dead. He could not understand why his solders on Rikers Island had not gotten him yet. He figured, if Richard was lucky enough to beat the case it would only be a matter of time before he had him killed. Maybe he would let T-bone do the honors, he thought, as a smirk appeared on his face.

"That little boyfriend of yours is dead. The boy better hope he stays in jail, but it won't be long before my people in there touch him. He's lucky I didn't shoot up his pop's funeral."

"Excuse me, I'm late for school," said Lisa not wanting to hear anymore of Shameek's nonsense.

As she walked past him, Shameek yelled out, "Lisa, you know I still love you baby. That little corpse can't do shit for you."

Lisa paid him no mind and when she got to Park Avenue she got into the dark blue Honda Civic LX her brother Omar gave her for her birthday.

Lisa found it hard to concentrate on her school work that day because her mind kept drifting back to Richard. She never thought she would fall in love with him so quickly. She thought about their future and had already made up her mind to marry him if he blew trial.

Lisa was no stranger to supporting someone doing time. The same year her father died of cancer, Omar was doing time up in Elmira, New York for selling drugs. Lisa and her mother would take the long ride twice a month to see him. Her mother always complained about the buses that took them to the correctional facility. When it snowed, it seemed as if the bus was going to slide off the road. She would also complain about the girls that rode on the bus to see their boyfriends and husbands. But Lisa, conversely, found the rides interesting and the girls that rode the bus even more exciting. It was like watching the Jerry Springer show right in front of your eyes. It was always drama on them buses. Like when some old white lady talked about the young handsome black Muslim inmate that she was about to marry and how the COs did not like to see white women coming up to see black men. The black women on the bus would laugh because they figured there was no way in the world that a young handsome black man would even glance at the old white woman if he was fortunate enough to have his freedom. So they figured the young brother was only doing what he had to do to survive. But other black women on the bus saw it differently. As far as they were concerned, the brother sold out. Some women would talk about the sex they had with someone else before visiting their boyfriends or the sex they were going to have after seeing him. There were often fights on the rides up north. The jails were always located in a poor white town and racism was rampant, making it unsafe for the mostly black visitors. You knew not to stay in a hotel alone when planning to see your visitor for a few days because it was a big possibility if you were a woman, that you would get raped, and the COs in these far away facilities would had played a part in the incident.

Lisa would speak to Omar on the phone and every time she would begin to cry because she desperately wanted her brother to come home. One of the happiest days of her life was the day Omar was released from prison. Lisa was only four years old when Omar went upstate, but they grew very close through his incarceration. When Omar came home he hooked up with a few big time drug dealers he had met in the pen. Within four months, Omar was no longer the small time, petty drug dealer he once was, he was now moving kilos of cocaine in New York, Connecticut, Virginia and DC. 1988 was the year people were making serious money selling crack. Things got crazy when one of Omar's soldiers got killed in DC. There was a big war in DC at the time, and Omar and his clique began killing DC boys. A lot of Omar's people got killed as well, and some were arrested for homicides. Omar knew it was time to pull up out of DC. It was then that he realized that murder and money just did not mix. Fourteen years later, Omar was still in the game but his mind was on pulling out and getting into the music business by starting his own record label. He had no plans of telling his story in Don Divas magazine from a jail cell or reading about what a snitch said about him in Feds magazine. Omar was a millionaire, but not even his family could estimate how much money he possessed. He never wore expensive jewelry, because he didn't want the attention. But today Lisa's mind was on Richard and not Omar.

Lisa packed her books and headed back to Brooklyn. Since his incarceration, Lisa had become very close to Richard's mother and decided she would pay Mrs. Brown a visit. She neared Mrs. Brown's building and was startled to see Tonya walking in her direction. This was the second person today Lisa saw but did not want to see. First Shameek, and now this grimey ass money hungry bitch Tonya, Lisa thought to herself. But nothing could take away from the fact that Tonya was extremely beautiful. She had a jet-black shiny complexion, long hair, chinky eyes, five foot five, slim body with beautiful African lips.

"What's up girl?" asked Tonya.

"You got some nerve asking me 'what's up" replied an agitated Lisa.

"What are you talking about?"

"You know what the fuck I'm talking about. A bitch can't even have a man around you without you wrapping your big ass lips around his dick!"

"Oh no you didn't," said Tonya as she placed her hands on her hips. "I don't know what the hell you're talking about. All I know is-"

"Bitch, you know what I'm talking about," said Lisa cutting Tonya off. "You think I don't know about you fucking Shameek and then letting them niggas run a train on you?"

"Yeah, I fucked Shameek, but it didn't go down the way you think it did."

"You know what? I don't even wanna hear it. You can have Shameek and his homeboys. Don't say shit to me ever again."

Lisa then turned and walked away, leaving Tonya and their ten year friendship behind her.

When Lisa entered Richard's building, she decided against going to see Maria. Instead she took the elevator up to the seventh floor and knocked on her friend Gina's door. Gina opened the door with a blunt in her left hand, and a smile on her face. She was a dime piece, and she stayed wearing the latest fashions. She was five foot five, brown-skinned, thick in all the right places and she had long black hair. She stood in the doorway wearing a long white tee-shirt, and white panties.

"What's up bitch? Come on in," Gina said as she widened the door to let Lisa enter.

"You sound like a fucking pimp," said Lisa as she walked into the apartment. She laid her bag and mink coat across the couch before sitting down.

"Where you coming from with that big ass bag?" asked Gina sitting next to Lisa smoking her blunt.

"Those are my books," answered Lisa patting the black leather bag. "I'm coming from school and I'm tired as hell. I just had to cut that bitch Tonya off."

"Come on, that shit ain't about nothing. We go too far back for that bullshit to come between us. I knew you would run into her; she just left. I'm not getting involved in that shit."

"Fuck that grimey ass bitch. Before you know it, she'll be trying to suck on Richard's dick too. And that stupid ass nigga Shameek stepped to me this morning talking shit."

"Say word?"

"Word."

"What did he say?"

"He was talking some dumb shit about me and him getting back together, and how he's going to kill Richard when he gets out of jail."

"Word? Yo, I don't know why you put that young boy through all this shit. You know Shameek and T-bone is not going to squash anything."

"Bitch, you act like everything is because of me. Shameek is just mad 'cause I don't want to fuck with his ugly ass anymore and for your information, Richard is not a young boy. He's more of a man than any of these niggas around here. That's for sure."

"I hear that, but what if he blows trial? I know you ain't trooping no bid for the nigga. Shit, a nigga up north be lucky if he gets a picture of me, let alone a visit."

"Bitch stop lying. That nigga Wise from Red Hook had your ass bouncing to Attica every weekend."

Gina started laughing between hits on her blunt. "I'm saying though, that was different. The nigga's dick was golden and girl, that nigga knew how to eat a pussy. Shit that nigga was worth waiting for."

"Well, if my boo blows trial, bitch I'm getting married."

"Yeah, that shit do sound good, but all those trips upstate will take a toll on your ass. I applaud a bitch that's strong enough to do it. You can't be no weak bitch. I've been through it. Anyway, I just hope Shameek don't kill Richard if he comes home. Richard is too much of a sweetie to go out like that."

Lisa took the blunt from Gina, took a pull and thought about what Gina had just said.

Chapter Twenty-Two

It was 6:00 am on a cold Tuesday morning when Mrs. Maria Ann Brown got up to go to work. She had been up all night grading school papers for the class she taught at PS 270 and after only four hours of sleep she was still tired. She wanted to just stay in bed today, but she had to get up and get ready for work. It seemed as though everyday was a struggle to get pass. Things were really hard for her now. She had lost her husband to a stroke and her son to prison and it caused her to stress so badly that she had to go and see her doctor. Her blood pressure was high and her doctor told her to stop worrying so much, but that was easier said than done. She was determined, however, to not let Richard see the effects his incarceration was having on her health. She acted and looked happy whenever she went to visit him, but when she got home, her reality sunk in and fell back into her hopeless despair.

The only thing that kept her going these past rough months was her going back to work and the belief that her son would be home soon. She still couldn't believe that the prison didn't allow Richard to come to his own father's funeral. She knew he was so hurt that he could not pay his last respects to his father and she noticed there was something different about him, every time she went to go see him. He seemed so much tougher and quieter than he'd ever been. It was as if something inside of him had died and the innocence he possessed before arriving on Rikers Island was stolen away. He always managed to smile and talk during their visits, but Maria was not fooled. She saw the look in his eyes.

The last time she saw that look in someone's eyes was when she first met her late husband. He had that same look of hopelessness. But just as her husband got rid of it, she knew that in time her baby would also get rid of it. She was still confused by the events that lead to Richard's arrest. She figured it had something to do with his friend Kendu's murder and his beating in front of the supermarket.

Since Richard's arrest, she noticed that people in the projects looked at her differently. Lately, a few guys in the projects began to say hello to her with respect in their voices. She didn't know them but they all seemed to know her and addressed her as Mrs. Brown. One of them stopped to say how sorry he was to hear about her husband's death. A few guys even asked about Richard with concern, but she gave them no information, because she didn't know who she could really trust. However, there were also a few guys in the projects that looked at Maria as if they wanted to kill her. She remembered two weeks earlier, on her way home from work, a group of boys stood in front of her building talking. As she neared the building, the boys got quiet except for one. He looked at her and boldly said, "Her son killed my boy, Ra. I should shoot this bitch in her face right now."

"Yo T-bone, give me a gun I'll do it," said a young boy.

"Nigga, get your little punk ass outta here," said T-bone as Maria walked bravely past them as if she did not hear a word they said. She was scared of what they might do to her but she did not show it. She entered the elevator, hoping no one would be waiting for her when she exited. The elevator doors opened and she took a deep breath before exiting. She took her keys out of her bag and she walked to her door. She quickly slipped it into the hole, turned it and entered safely into her apartment with a sigh of relief. She had just taken off her coat and laid her purse down when the phone began to ring.

"Hello?"

"Hey ma."

"Hey baby," said Maria. "What's going on? Did you try to call earlier?"

"No, this is my first time calling you today," answered Richard.

"Oh, I just came in from work," Maria said, taking off her shoes. "I'm coming to see you this weekend with Lisa. Do you need any money or anything else?"

"No, I'm okay. I still have the money Lisa left in my account."

"Oh okay. That was nice of her to leave you money."

"You're right about that," smiled Richard. "I don't have that much time to talk because they're about to call chow. I just wanted to see how you were doing and to let you know I'm about to start trial soon. "

"I'm fine, and we'll talk about your case when I see you this weekend. If you need anything before I come, make sure you get in touch with me."

"Okay ma, thanks. I love you."

"I love you too baby," said Maria before hanging up the phone. She began taking her clothes off when the phone began to ring again.

"Hello?"

"Hi mommy."

"Hey Lisa, what's going on? I just got off the phone with Richard."

"Oh yeah? I talked to him earlier. He calls me everyday, 'cause he knows if he doesn't, I'll break his neck," said Lisa as Maria laughed. "Are you still going to see him this weekend?"

"Yes," answered Maria. "On Saturday."

"I called you earlier but I got no answer. You just came from work?"

"Yes, about ten minutes ago," answered Maria. "I'm going to tell you something but don't say a word to Richard because I don't want him to be worrying up there in that place."

"I promise, I won't tell him. What's going on?"

"I was just coming in the building," began Maria, "and these boys were standing out there in front. One of them said, 'Her son shot my boy and I should shoot that b-i-t-c-h in her face right now."

"What?!" Lisa yelled into the phone. "Mommy, what did he look like?"

"He was a tall brown-skinned boy. His friend called him T-lone or T-bone or something like that."

"What else did he say to you?" Lisa asked hurriedly. She was so mad and worried at the same time, but she was trying not to curse on the phone because Maria did not tolerate filthy language. Lisa knew that T-bone would be stupid enough to try something.

"He didn't say anything to me," said Maria. "He was talking to his friend. One of the young boys told him that he'd do it if he gave him a gun, but he screamed at the boy instead."

"Mommy, I'll call you back later," said Lisa. "I have to call my brother, Omar. He'll take care of it."

"Lisa, I don't want any shooting going on around here. It's bad enough that Richard is in jail."

"Mommy, there won't be any shooting," said Lisa in a rush, trying to get off the phone. "I'll call you later."

"Remember, don't tell Richard about any of this."

"I won't mommy. I promise."

She wasn't sure how, but after her conversation with Lisa everything went back to normal. T-bone and his friends never said anything to Maria again. She saw them many times since that day but they would either turn their heads or walk away when they saw her coming.

Maria wished that her son was still with her at home. She hadn't felt this lonely since she attended college nineteen years ago. She missed her husband so much that she doubted at times if she would be able to go on without him. He and Richard were all that she had in her life. Maria did not have any close relatives and Richard was the only person that mattered to her now. She told herself that she would have to stay strong for him.

Maria got out of bed, took a shower and got dressed. She walked into the kitchen and made a bagel and a cup of coffee. The phone began ringing and she wondered who could be calling her this early in the morning. She reached for the phone and said, "Hello?"

"Good morning, mommy," said Lisa. "You told me yesterday that your car was in the shop. I'm on my way to school. Do you want a ride to work?"

"Oh boy," smiled Maria. "I can definitely use that ride. This way I won't have to wait for the bus in the cold. Where are you?"

"At home," answered Lisa. "I'm about to eat breakfast but I'll be on the side of your building in like five minutes."

"Okay, I'll see you then," said Maria hanging up the phone. As soon as she put the phone down it began ringing again. She figured it was Lisa calling back for some reason. She picked it up and said, "Hello?"

"Don't worry about anybody doing anything to you Mrs. Brown because you are safe," said a strange voice. "But tell Richard that he's a dead little nigga. Don't worry about me calling you anymore because I won't, but if your son goes upstate that's where he'll die and if he comes home, I'll send you a piece of his body every motherfucking month."

"Why are you doing this?" cried Maria into the phone. "I beg you, please don't kill my baby. He's all that I have-"

The phone went dead and a stunned Maria stood looking at the receiver. She hung up the phone and began to cry uncontrollably. She grabbed her purse and coat and headed out of the apartment. She wished she could take the day off because she knew that call would be on her mind all day. She exited her building and walked to Lisa's car. Before she made it to the car, she saw T-bone walking by. He looked at her and quickly turned away. She knew it was his voice that she heard earlier on the phone. She would never forget his voice. Maria wanted to call the police but she knew they would do nothing to protect Richard. They would say he's perfectly safe in jail, but Maria knew that men died in jail as well, and most of the time, it stemmed from something that happened in the streets.

As a teenager in Harlem she grew up around gangsters, drug dealers and number runners. She just never allowed herself to fall victim to what the streets had to offer her. But she knew everything that went on. Her father was a gangster and her mother used to hold card games and almost everyone in the neighborhood knew who their family was. After her father got killed by another gangster on the streets of Harlem, her mother moved to Tampa, Florida. Maria stayed in Harlem, got a job and stayed in school to pursue her dream of becoming a teacher.

Lisa knew something was on Maria's mind when she got into the car. She leaned over and gave Maria a long hug before driving away. She had also seen T-bone making his way through the projects.

Lisa turned to Maria and said, "Don't worry about anything they say. They're not going to do anything to Richard. If they were strong enough to have something done to Richard in there, it would've happened already."

Chapter Twenty-Three

Tonya sat in her apartment watching the 60-inch television her ex-boyfriend bought for her. He bought it when they were trying to get back together, but he ended up going to jail for selling drugs to an undercover cop. The idea of rekindling their relationship was over because Tonya definitely wasn't checking for him now. Once a guy went to jail, that was a wrap, as far as Tonya was concerned. She moved on to the next big baller with a big bankroll that had no problem separating himself from some of his money.

As a child, Tonya was very spoiled. Her grandmother gave her anything she wanted. Her aunts and uncles praised her for her beauty and showered her with gifts. They told her that if she ever needed anything all she had to do was ask. She had four uncles who were very successful in their own right. Between the four of them, they owned several restaurants, liquor stores and apartment buildings. Tonya always wondered why her grandmother didn't move into one of their beautiful apartment buildings far away from the projects. She later learned that her grandmother would not leave Fort Greene because she was stubborn and wanted to do things on her own. Tonya would have jumped at the chance to move out of the projects, but she couldn't even think of leaving her grandmother behind.

Tonya's grandmother was her mother. She never really knew her mother and father and her grandmother had raised her from infancy. As a small child, her father went to prison and shortly after, her mother moved to California with her new boyfriend. During the beginning of his incarceration, Tonya and her father kept in contact, but as the years went by they drifted farther and farther apart. Twenty years was a long time to spend away from someone you hardly know, and Tonya's father became nonexistent in her life.

But her mother, Valerie, was still very much a real part of her life. Tonya's mother would come to visit her mother and her sisters often, but never treated Tonya like a daughter. She had acted as if

Tonya was her niece. Tonya once heard her aunts talk about how Valerie hated kids and only had Tonya because her man Troy wanted a baby. They just could not understand how Valerie could be so distant, cold and insensitive to her own daughter.

Tonya's aunts watched her grow up and taught her everything they knew. They were all gold diggers and had married very rich and successful men. Tonya was told at a very young age never to deal with a broke man and that only ugly girls messed around with them. Tonya knew she was beautiful and felt that any guy wanting her time should be willing to spend money for it. As Tonya got older, she noticed that only the prettiest girls hung around the drug dealers and that they wore the best and most expensive shoes and clothes. It was then that she told herself that she would never deal with a man that did not have serious money.

Tonya called her grandmother 'Mommy', and called her mother by her first name. She didn't know her as anything but Valerie. But her grandmother had never talked bad about Valerie or her father Troy. She simply just took the responsibility and raised Tonya as if she was her own daughter without a complaint.

Tonya had her long hair in a ponytail and she was wearing a white short sleeve Gap tee-shirt and white Polo shorts. She was eating chocolate ice cream out of a big white bowl as she watched an old episode of the Steve Harvey Show with her dark beautiful legs folded underneath her on the couch. She had a thing for the guy on the show that they called Romeo. Tonya thought he was very handsome and she knew that he had money because he was on television since being a little boy on the Cosby show. When she heard he'd been killed in LA, she cried as if she knew him personally. But when the show went off, he was quickly forgotten because Tonya had her own problems to deal with.

Tonya started thinking about Lisa and how much she missed her. She missed Lisa more than anything and being with Gina from time to time could not even make her forget about Lisa. Tonya didn't understand why Lisa was tripping so hard. She was money hungry, there was no debating that, but she hadn't intentionally had sex with Shameek.

Shameek called her from the fifth floor window and told her to come upstairs. Thinking Lisa was up there, she went up to the apartment. She got off of the elevator and was already in the apartment, when she realized Lisa was not there. T-bone had opened the door for her and she saw Shameek sitting on the couch.

"Tonya, come here," Shameek said, nodding to the empty spot next to him on the couch. "I need to talk to you."

"Where's Lisa?" Tonya asked with an attitude as T-bone locked the door.

"This ain't about Lisa," answered Shameek. "It's about you. Now come here."

Tonya wanted to leave but she figured she'd give him a minute to see what he had to say. She walked over to the couch and sat down next to him.

Shameek put his arm around her and said, "Fuck Lisa, it's all about you. Everything in these P.J.'s are mines and if you act right you can be my main lady and floss like no other bitch in these bullshit ass projects."

"What do you think you're doing?" asked Tonya removing Shameek's arm from her shoulders.

She then said angrily, "I don't get down like that! Lisa's my girl. Now get off me!"

Shameek pulled out a gun and calmly said, "Take your shit off before I fuck around and kill you. You think I'm a joke or something? I told you everything in these projects is mine."

Shameek was playing with her in the beginning, but now he wanted to see how far he could go with his little game. He had always wanted to have sex with Tonya but knew she would never give in to his advances. He smiled as Tonya looked around the living room in a panic. When T-bone walked into the room, she quickly got undressed because she knew he wouldn't hesitate to kill her. Shameek then noticed T-bone and laughed as he threw Tonya's clothes to the floor.

"Yo homie" smiled Shameek. "Slide into the back room for a few. I can tell, she don't like crowds."

"Man, you're a hater," said T-bone as he walked to the back room laughing.

Tonya was happy that T-bone was no longer in the room, but she knew he was only a holler away.

"Shameek, why are you doing this to me?" asked Tonya as tears formed in her eyes.

"What, you don't want this nigga? You know how many bitches wouldn't hesitate to be you right now?" he asked as he slid his hand between her legs.

She closed her legs tightly and softly said, "Please don't do this to me Shameek."

He held up his gun and undid his pants with his other hand. He then took all of the bullets out of the gun and when he was sure he had her attention he pretended to put one bullet back into the gun but he palmed it instead. He pushed the barrel back into place, pointed the gun at her head and pulled the trigger. She jumped when she heard the click.

Shameek wanted to laugh but instead kept a serious look on his face and said, "You're lucky but next time you might not be. Now spread those legs for daddy."

"Why are you doing this? You can get any girl in these projects," said Tonya crying as she spread her legs open.

"Fuck them bitches baby, I want you. Shit, you should feel honored. Plus I had most of them bitches already anyway," said Shameek as he entered her with the gun still in his hand.

After twenty minutes of raping her, there was a knock on the door. T-bone entered the front room and stopped as he watched Shameek have his way with Tonya.

"Oh shit! Look at her facial expressions," T-bone laughed

excitedly. "Damn she's sexy!"

He looked through the peephole and said, "Yo Shameek, that's the workers at the door. All the work is bagged up."

"Good, I'm outta here," said Shameek as he got up off of Tonya and pulled up his pants, as T-bone let the workers in.

Tonya got up from the couch as tears streamed down her face and picked up her clothes.

"Bitch, drop those clothes and sit your ass back down," T-bone said as Shameek's two workers stared with their mouths open. "I want some of that pussy too with your Janet Jacme facial expressions."

Tonya dropped her clothes and sat back on the couch with her hands covering her tear-soaked face. T-bone didn't have to pull out a gun; his words were enough. He never threatened anyone because when he pulled out his gun, someone was always shot. Shameek laughed and walked past T-bone and his workers, slamming the door behind him as he left the apartment.

Tonya relived the whole incident as she sat on her couch thinking about Lisa. She tried to clear her mind by watching TV, but she kept drifting to that day. She wanted Shameek and T-bone dead but all the thugs she knew, also knew and respected them. What happened to all the black men that would kill you if you raped a black woman? Maybe they were all in jail and if that was the case, then the state needed to let their asses out, Tonya thought to herself. She wanted to tell Gina what happened but she wasn't ready to share the story with her yet. Before she could even tell Lisa what happened, Lisa accused her of sleeping with Shameek behind her back. Where in the hell was Pam, she thought. Pam would be able to cheer her up and understand the situation.

Tonya looked at her ladies Rolex watch and smiled as she grabbed the remote off of the couch and clicked on the cable station. She laughed to herself just thinking about the show that was about to come on. It was called "The Gangster Larry Show'. The host was a brown-skinned, five foot ten, Trinidadian gold tooth stocky guy with braids name Larry who interviewed Rap celebrities. Larry had just come home from jail for murder and he did not hold his tongue when it came to his interviews. The show was very controversial and a lot of rappers did not want to come on the show but the streets loved the show so much that a few rappers came on the show to prove that they had some kind of street credibility.

Tonya smiled and increased the volume when she saw the tattooed baldhead rapper from Queens with the raspy voice sit down next to Gangster Larry on a soft butter leather red couch.

"Murr-der," the rapper yelled as the audience at the show went crazy.

"Shut the fuck up with that murder shit," said Gangster Larry with his face screwed up. "You ain't never murder nothing nigga."

"Nah dog, you have to understand, " smiled the rapper. "I got too much money to be in the streets murdering niggas. But the 'hood is in me."

"No nigga, the 'hood is in your pockets."

The audience laughed as the rapper tried to explain.

"Nah dog, I still be in the streets and I love my street niggas."

"How the fuck you love street niggas," said Gangster Larry, "and you was on the news talking about street niggas is trying to get in the industry and extort you rap motherfuckers?"

"Damn dog, you hard on a nigga. That shit I said I didn't mean it like that. I was just saying that nobody's taking nothing from me. I'm just trying to eat and take my niggas wit' me, feel me? I got a new movie out, but what I really wanna-"

"Hold the fuck up!" Gangster Larry cut him off. "This is my show! What's this shit about you having sex with a homo fashion designer?"

"No he didn't," said a wide eyed Tonya with her hand over her mouth. "This nigga is worse than Star from Hot 97 -I can see this show won't be on too long," said Tonya to herself.

"Nah dog, I don't get down like that," answered the rapper. "Yo, trust me. I love women. This hating crack head ass rapper from Y.O. put that bullshit rumor out there."

"Well, he's on my show next week and we'll get down to the bottom of this shit. Do you have another album coming out?"

"Oh yeah, the shit is hot! It'll be in stores next month. I want everybody to go out and cop that, especially the ladies out there."

The women in the audience yelled, clapped and called the rapper's name out as Gangster Larry shook the rapper's hand as the show went off.

For a brief moment, Tonya escaped the reality of her life. The show made Tonya laugh and feel better, but she still couldn't get Shameek and T-bone out of her head; she wanted them dead. She snapped back when her grandmother entered the living room.

"Child, what in the world are you watching?" asked her grandmother as she put on her coat.

"Nothing mommy, it's going off now."

"I don't know what you sitting around the house sulking about, but get up and clean that kitchen. I have to go out and I'll be back around ten, so don't be calling all around town looking for me like you always do."

Tonya laughed as her grandmother walked out of the apartment with a smile on her face.

Tonya got up off the couch and grabbed her phone book. She began looking through it to see which thug she could call to do a favor. She knew it would be easy to get the two workers killed, but it was Shameek and T-bone that she wanted dead.

Chapter Twenty-Four

Richard sat at the defense table as nervous as hell. His lawyer Mr. Atkins sat next to him discussing strategy before the judge appeared at his bench. His lawyer Mr. Atkins was dressed as sharp as ever. He had his royal blue briefcase on the defense table as it matched his expensive suit. The district attorney had on his usual cheap get-up. His black briefcase sat on the floor and he had prosecution papers scattered all over the table.

Richard anxiously wanted for the trial to continue. He scanned the courtroom. There were seven women and seven men, two of which were alternates, on the jury: four black women, three white women, five white men and two black men. Seated behind the prosecutor were the two arresting officers. Behind them, with sad looks on their faces, sat Rashien's wife Kim and his older sister Tammy. Kim sat looking at Richard like she was ready to kill him for killing her husband. Tammy just sat there as if she were trying to find out what this was all about, Tammy didn't fool herself. She knew her brother Rashien was no angel. She heard all about the people that he killed when he was alive, but he was still her brother and she couldn't believe that he was gone. Tammy was a nurse at a hospital in Manhattan, and she had always told her brother to do something positive with his life. But her brother would laugh as if she had just told the world's funniest joke. Positivity was not a part of his life. All he knew was murder and mayhem, he loved it because he was so good at causing it. She always told him what comes around goes around. But what surprised her most was that her brother had got killed by someone so young. So she came to the trial to find out why her brother was dead and why this young boy was in jail. Rashien's wife Kim came for different reasons. She knew her husband was in the street killing people as well, but she loved that fact and even encouraged it because his behavior gave her prestige over other women and even over most guys in Fort Greene Projects and surrounding areas. She also knew Rashien was seeing other women, but for the respect she got in the 'hood she didn't let that bother her. Her reason for coming to court was so she could report the whole trial to Shameek and T-bone. She wanted Richard dead just like her husband died and she would play her part to make sure it got carried out. Tammy did not care for Kim at all, because she knew Kim's whole purpose for being with her brother. She saw many women like Kim and knew she would be with another gangster before the year was over. Tammy was not dumb, but was openly respectful to nearly everyone, so she sat next to her sister-in-law as if they were the best of friends.

Sitting on the other side of the courtroom behind Richard and his lawyer, sat his mother Maria, Lisa and her best friend Gina.

The Honorable Joseph Clark were presiding, so far he and everyone else in the courtroom heard the testimony of the medical examiner concerning the autopsy report, and the testimony of the arresting officers as to who was the decease, what the witnesses had told them and who was the person arrested for the murder of Alex Steward also known as Rashien.

"Okay, let's get on with this case," said Judge Clark. "What is your witness's name?"

"My first witness," answered the DA, "is Anthony Parker."

Ant-live entered the courtroom walking tough like he was on Nostrand Avenue.

"Mr. Parker," said Judge Clark. "Come up the steps, stand along side the chair, face the clerk and raise your right hand."

After being called as a witness on behalf of the People, Ant-live was sworn in by the clerk of the court.

"Please have a seat," said the clerk.

"Look at this snitch ass nigga," Gina whispered to Lisa. "He definitely need two to the head."

Lisa looked at Gina and shook her head with a smirk on her face. Gina is so gangster, she thought to herself.

Ant-live sat down and looked at Richard with a smile on his face. Maria couldn't believe Anthony was turning on her son, but she was curious to know what happened that day. She only knew what the police had told her and that wasn't much; they said that Richard was accused of killing someone. She did figure that it had something to do with the beating he took in front of the supermarket that day and knew from Richard that it also had to do with his friend Kenny being killed. But that's all she knew. She just hoped he would beat the case because she knew in her heart that he was a good boy.

"Speak into the mic," said Judge Clark, "and give us your full name."

"Anthony Peter Parker," said Ant-live.

"Okay you may now inquire," said Judge Clark to the DA.

"Thank you judge," said the DA. "Mr. Parker, good morning. Mr. Parker, where do you live?"

"102 Nostrand and Gates."

"Here in Brooklyn?"

"Yeah, for sho' "

"Okay, I'm going to direct your attention to July 28th of this year. Where were you at 10:45 P.M. on this day?"

"I was with Richard in front of his building."

"Mr. Parker, do you see Richard in this courtroom?"

"For sho', that's him right there," said Ant-live pointing at Richard.

"Let the record reflect that the witness pointed out the defendant. Okay, then what happen Mr. Parker?"

"I told him to walk with me to Murder Ave. I mean, Myrtle Ave. So when we got there we saw Rashien-"

"Do you know Rashien's real name?"

"Nah, I only knew him as Rashien." "Okay, continue the story."

"We saw Rashien talking to a girl. Richard pulled out a gun and the girl ran. I can't remember what Rashien said, but Richard shot him and that's when I ran up Myrtle Avenue."

Richard looked at Ant-live enraged. He couldn't believe that Ant-live was lying on him like this.

"Do they call Richard anything else?" asked the DA.

"Yeah, they call him Bishop." "Bishop. Do you know why they call him that?"

"Yeah, my man gave him that name, because he goes to church like every Saturday and Sunday."

"Okay, did you see the defendant pull out a gun and shoot the decease?"

"Oh yeah, for sho'. I told you that already."

"What color was this gun?"

"The gun was black."

"Was there anything blocking your vision?"

"No sir," smiled Ant-live.

"Okay thank you. No further questions your Honor."

"The defense may now cross examine," said the judge to Mr. Atkins.

"Thank you your Honor," said Mr. Atkins.

He got out of his chair, looked at the jury and then walked over to Ant-live on the witness stand. "Mr. Parker, you say my client is the one that killed the decease. Is that correct?"

"Oh yeah, for sho!"

"About how long did you know my client?"

"About two months before he killed Rashien."

"Was Rashien your friend?"

"Hello no! I never dealt with him."

"It sounds as though you didn't like Rashien."

"Objection your Honor!" shouted the DA. "We're not here to talk about what sounds like what."

"Sustained," replied the judge looking at the jury. "Jury, disregard that comment. Defense continue."

"Okay, was Richard your friend?" asked Mr. Atkins.

"Yeah you can say that," answered Ant-live.

"With friends like this, who needs enemies?" Before the DA had a chance to object, Mr. Atkins continued.

"You said they call my client Bishop, because he goes to church every Saturday and Sunday. When was the last time you saw Bishop before he allegedly killed Rashien?"

"I saw him a day before the incident."

"Did he seem like the usual church going Bishop?"

"Yeah, for sho'. Homie is corny like that."

"So you're telling me that in twenty four hours or less, this church going Christian turned into a cold blooded thug?"

"I don't know man."

"Okay, when he allegedly pulled this gun out, how long will you say everything transpired?"

"It was real quick. He pulled out and shot 'em. It wasn't even a minute. I took off running."

"You said the decease said something. Did Richard have the gun out when the decease was talking?"

"No. After Rashien said something, Richard pulled out and shot him."

"Did you see the gun? If so, what color was it?"

"I answered that already. It was a black three fifty seven revolver."

"A black three fifty seven revolver you say. It was dark outside, but you can see that it was a black three fifty seven revolver?"

"It was a big revolver, alright?!" said Ant-live becoming very angry.

"And that makes it a three fifty seven revolver?"

Ant-live knew he said the wrong thing so he decided not to

answer the question.

"Mr. Parker, don't worry, you don't have to answer that question, but answer this. Did you run when you heard the shot?"

"Yeah man, I told you that already."

"So you didn't see my client shoot the decease?"

"Yeah I saw him shoot Rashien."

"You ran when you saw him shoot Rashien or when you heard the shot?"

"Come on man," Ant-live said angrily. "You got me confused. I don't know. I heard the shot and ran."

"Well, you must be a very very fast runner, because the decease was shot twice and you keep mentioning a single shot. No further questions your Honor."

"Does the prosecution have any questions for this witness?" asked Judge Clark.

"No your Honor," smiled the DA. He knew the defense did not make his witness look too bad.

"Okay, the witness may be excused," said Judge Clark.

Ant-live walked to the back of the courtroom with the same hard rock walk he entered with and sat down without even glancing at Richard.

"You may call your next witness," Judge Clark told the DA.

"Your Honor, I now call Michelle Jackson to the stand," the DA said as Michelle walked into the courtroom and approached the bench.

"I know that bitch," Lisa whispered to Gina. "She used to fuck with my brother."

Michelle looked at Richard and walked to the stand. She was instructed the same way Ant-live had been and was sworn in by the clerk of the court.

"Speak into the mic and give your full name." said Judge Clark.

"Michelle Karen Jackson."

"Okay," Judge Clark told the DA. "You may now inquire."

"Thank you your Honor. Ms. Jackson, good morning. Can you please tell the court where you live."

"999 Willoughby Avenue here in Brooklyn, New York."

"Okay, I'm going to direct your attention back to July 11th of this year. Where were you at 10:45 P.M. on that night?"

"I was talking to Rashien in front of the supermarket on Myrtle Avenue."

"Did you know Rashien's real name?"

"No. He was always known to me as Rashien."

"Did there come a time when the defendant approach you and Rashien on this particular night?"

"Yes, he and another guy approached us."

"Okay, please tell the court what took place when you two were approached."

"Well, the other guy the defendant was with had a gun out, and told me if I didn't wanna die I better leave so I left."

"But you saw the defendant with a gun, right?"

"No. That's why when the police told me to say he pulled a gun out," said Michelle pointing at Richard, "I tried to tell you he didn't have a gun. But you said stick to the story that the police had."

Ant-live was sitting in the back of the courtroom scared to death. He began to sweat and realized he should have left after testifying. It was too late now. He didn't want to get up and draw any attention to himself, so he just sat there.

"Ms. Jackson, do you know that you can be put in jail for perjury? Do you know what perjury is, Ms. Jackson?" asked the worried looking DA.

"Yes. It means giving a false statement under oath. But I'm telling the truth so I'm not worried about going to jail."

"I have no more questions for this hostile witness your Honor," said the angry DA, as he walked back to the prosecution table.

"The defense may cross examine," said Judge Clark.

"Thank you your Honor," smiled Mr. Atkins as he approached the witness. "Good morning Ms. Jackson. I'll try not to take up too much more of your time. I assume you have other things to do. You say you never saw my client pull out a gun?"

"No. He didn't have a gun."

"Okay, good. Now, I want you to look around this courtroom and see if you see the person that had the gun that night and shot the decease."

Michelle looked around the courtroom before her eyes rested on Ant-live. She slowly raised her arm and pointed at him.

"I didn't see him shoot," said Michelle, "but he's the one that had the gun that night and told me if I didn't wanna die, I had better leave."

"Thank you. No further questions," said Mr. Atkins.

Michelle was excused and the jurors were led to a room to deliberate.

Two hours later, the jury came back to the courtroom and issued a not guilty verdict. Richard was free to go. He turned around to the joyous, smiling faces of his mother, Lisa and Gina, but he noticed that Ant-live was no where in sight. The arresting officers left the courtroom shortly after Ant-live's testimony. The last ones to leave the courtroom were Rashien's sister, his wife and the district attorney, all with looks of anger and injustice on their faces.

Chapter Twenty-Five

"So what's up? What you wanna do?" asked Omar.

"I wanna get some money. I'm talking major money," answered Richard. "Put me in the game. I need to make it happen and I need to make it happen fast. I still got beef with Shameek, so I need a gun; one with a silencer. I also need to get my man out of jail."

"Damn kid, you changed like a motherfucker," said Omar. "Before you went to jail, you was a straight church boy. I seen jail change niggas, but it changed you quick! I don't know why you wanna get into this bullshit ass game, but I know what time it is. I came out of jail back in the days the same way, but I wasn't no church nigga before I got knocked either. But then again, I didn't come home to no major beef back then. I'm not really with putting you into this drug shit, but I know I gotta do it. I see your plan nigga. It won't be long before Shameek and T-bone find out your whereabouts, so you can't stay here too long duke. Not here. But like I said, I see your plan and I like a young nigga that plans ahead. Reminds me of myself when I was younger. What's your man's bail, kiddo?"

"It's a body but it's a weak case. They set his bail at fifty thousand dollars."

Omar laughed and said, "Fifty thousand dollars is a bit too much for a weak case. The last time I got knocked back in the days, bail for a weak case was like two gee's homie."

"Yeah," said Richard, "but he got a body."

"What?!" Omar said with a smirk. "Niggas was getting shit like probation, and two to fours for bodies back then."

It was Richard's turn to laugh as he looked at Omar and said, "I hope you're not going to give me an old-timer's speech about how good the eighties was. I met an old-timer that came from up north in the court pens when I was on trial, and all he talked about was '87. Digging pockets in mid-town, going to Latin Quarters and throwing garbage cans through the jewelry store windows."

"Nah, nah, nah," laughed Omar. "But check it, how long your man been on the Island?"

"A few months," answered Richard.

"Do you really believe this nigga is for you?" askedOmar looking at Richard intently. "I don't like putting my money on losers."

"Omega, I trust him like a brother, and I wouldn't ask you to do it for me if I had doubts about him."

Omar stared at Richard for what felt like an eternity.

He then smiled and said, "Give me his information. I'll have him out in two months."

"Thanks Omega. When I start making money, I'll pay you back everything you gave me."

"Of course you will," smiled Omar.

"Do either of you want something to drink? Lemonade, soda, juice, beer?" asked Gloria Patterson.

When Richard beat his case, he didn't want to go back to Fort Greene. He knew he had no chance if he went straight there. He took Kendu's mother up on her offer and had been staying in the LG projects for the past two weeks. Richard's mother had agreed to the situation because she didn't want her son back in Fort Greene so soon either. Richard knew that not many people in LG had love for Shameek because he killed Kendu, so it was the perfect place to chill for a minute. The first week Richard was there, Omar came to see him and from that first moment Omar and Gloria really hit it off.

"No baby, we're okay," said Omar.

Gloria sat on his lap as Richard continued talking.

"Plus, I'm tired of Lisa taking care of me. As much as I hated being in jail, I learned a lot in there, Omega. Especially some people you love like family turn their back on you, like Ant-live did me."

"I knew that boy wasn't shit," said Gloria. "I used to tell Kendu all the time not to trust him. But you know how Kendu was; he always gave people the benefit of the doubt. But I could look in that boy's eyes and tell he was no good. You could see the lust in his face; you don't lust after your friend's mother."

Omar laughed and said, "Shit, if my friend's mother looked as good as you, I wouldn't give a rat's ass about the friendship we have."

Gloria laughed and slapped Omar playfully on the head.

"I just need to get my own money," said Richard getting back to what he was saying. "There's a few things I need done and to make them happen takes money."

"I feel you and I feel your situation," said Omar. "I was going to surprise Big Lord and give him a few spots, but I'll give it to you and I'll give you something to play the game with. I got plans to leave this bullshit ass game, so I'll give you three of my spots. Big Lord will teach you the game before you start moving them thangs. I don't want Lisa to know or be involve with anything. Did she give you the twenty I sent as your coming home present?"

"Yeah, I got it. I had to give somebody eight thousand of it to take care of something for me."

"Okay, that's cool, I can dig it," said Omar as he began kissing Gloria's neck.

$

Richard had been out of jail for the past month and a half, and things were already looking up. It took Big Lord two weeks to teach Richard the basics of the game, but to survive Richard knew he would have to use his instincts. He decided against putting drugs in LG. The first thing he learned was to never do dirt where he ate. Richard showed people in the projects mad love, and spoiled the little kids rotten with ice cream and candy. People in LG called him Richie Rich and showed him mad love back. They had no idea that he was becoming a real heavyweight in the game.

After taking over three of Omar's spots, it seemed as if he was buying more cocaine and heroin everyday. He had good workers and he showed his appreciation by giving bonuses to the best ones. But he still needed a trustworthy lieutenant and the only person that kept coming to mind was Divine. He now had the money to bail Divine out himself, but Omar told him he'd take care of it without drawing any heat.

Richard wasn't sure if Shameek knew he was staying in LG, so whenever he had time he would be in the projects protecting Kendu's mother. He made plans to move from LG that following week. He wanted no harm to come to her on his account. He found a nice apartment in Flushing, Queens and would no longer be anywhere around LG after the weekend.

One day, Richard was standing in front of Gloria's building talking to a few old-timers. Seven blocks away Ant-live walked down Quincy Street between Nostrand and Marcy Avenue. A stocky white guy in his late thirties approached him. At first Ant-live thought the white guy was a cop because you did not see white guys in the area just walking around. When the white guy pulled out a stack of money, Ant-live didn't care if he was a cop or not.

"Excuse me, would you like to make some money? I'm trying to find this address. If you help me find it I'll pay you very kindly."

"What address you're looking for?" asked Ant-live thinking of a way to take all of the white man's money.

"I'm looking for 1206 Quincy Street."

"Nah, I think 1206 is on Gates Avenue," said Ant-live hoping to get the white guy around the corner. He knew he would see someone with a gun to help him take the money the white boy carried.

"So let's go to Gates Avenue. I've got my van parked across the street," said the white guy.

"Okay, let's go," said Ant-live scheming.

The van was black with tinted windows. The white guy jumped in the driver's seat and Ant-live got in the passenger's seat without looking in the back of the van. The van drove away and Ant-live was looking out of the window searching for someone he knew when suddenly he felt something cold and hard on the back of his neck.

"Get the fuck in the back and if you try to open that door boy,

I'll blow your fucking head off!" said a deep voice from the back of the van.

Ant-live was half-dragged to the back of the van and his mind raced as to who wanted him this bad. Maybe it was the guy he robbed the other day for his drugs. If that was the case, he knew he would be able to talk his way out of the situation. When he got to the back of the van, he saw a baldhead dark-skinned guy with a thick beard that he never saw before.

"Lay face down and put your hands behind your back," the black guy ordered.

When Ant-live felt the handcuffs on his wrist he knew these two guys were the police. When Richard beat that murder case, Ant-live slipped out of the courtroom. The police finally caught him he thought, but he had the case beat because the bitch, Michelle never saw him shoot anyone, he thought to himself.

"Y'all fucking pigs didn't read me my rights! I'm beating this bullshit case anyway!"

The white guy driving started laughing and then he spoke. "You have the right to die slow motherfucker! Moe-dog, this bitch nigga thinks we're cops."

When Ant-live heard the name Moe-dog, his heart began to beat faster and faster. He had heard a lot of stories about the infamous Moe-dog, but he never knew what he looked like, until now. For that matter, very few people knew what Moe-dog looked like. They just knew whenever his name was mentioned bodies were left behind. Ant-live also noticed how much the white guy driving sounded black. Moe-dog finally spoke to the white guy driving.

"Pull into the garage, Whitey."

Ant-live didn't know where he was. They drove around for a half hour before Whitey finally pulled up in what appeared to be a garage with a single light bulb hanging from the ceiling.

"What the fuck you gonna do to me? What the fuck did I do? At least tell me that," said Ant-live with tears running down his face.

"Ant, you're a snitch," said Moe-dog. "You have to be punished for telling on the Bishop."

Ant-live's fear turned to anger. He looked at Moe-dog with contempt and said, "Fuck Bishop, fuck you and fuck that white boy too! All y'all can suck my dick!"

"Suck your dick, huh?" asked Whitey as he looked at Moe-dog with a smile. "He wants us to suck his dick. We'll see how tough you are by the time we're done with you. You rat bastard."

Moe-dog went into the house that was connected to the dark garage and returned with two pairs of rubber gloves. He passed Whitey a pair. He was also carrying two ice packs, two ace bandages, and a metal hanger. He put one of the ice packs on Ant-live's neck and then wrapped the ace bandage around his neck to keep it in place.

"You want somebody to suck your dick, huh?" asked Moe-dog as he put the other ice pack under Ant-live's nuts and used the other ace bandage to hold it in place.

"What the fuck you doing?!" asked Ant-live. "You freak ass motherfucker!"

"Yeah, I'm a freak," said Moe-dog as he bent the hanger straight. He then grabbed Ant-live's dick and stuck the hanger into the slit at the head of his penis.

"Ahhh, you're killing me! Oh shit it hurts! Please stop, I'm sorry. Oh God!" yelled Ant-live with tears running down his face. Moe-dog and Whitey continued torturing Ant-live for two more hours. They pulled all of his teeth out with a pair of pliers and did the same to his finger nails. The ice packs on his neck and nuts were to keep him from passing out.

Two days later, Richard came out of building 456 in L.G. and then crossed the street to purchase a newspaper from the corner store. The front page headlines screamed out in big words, "MAN FOUND DEAD." Richard crossed back across the street and stood in front of the building, smiling as he read the story.

"The headless, decomposing body of a man was found in an open lot in the Brownsville section of Brooklyn. The body was naked and appeared to have been tortured. Reports from the police indicated that about 7:30 am, a passerby came upon the gruesome find and contacted authorities. On arrival, the police found the body that was partially covered with a piece of cardboard. The police investigating said the fingerprints of the body are believed to be that of Anthony Peter Parker, an 18 year old from the Bedford Stuyvesant section of Brooklyn. Anyone with information is urged to contact the police at..."

Chapter Twenty-Six

The party was packed but it wasn't Richard's type of atmosphere. He and Lisa sat in the back of the club. Lisa sipped on her glass of Cristal while Richard nursed a glass of orange juice hoping the party would end soon. A banging song called "Put your hands up" by a rap group called The O.G.'s had the club jumping. And after the DJ played "You got it bad" by Usher, he put on a song by the hot new artist O-Fella called "Bank Stop."

"Oh shit, that's my song," yelled the off-duty CO Lynette Davidson as she made her way to the dance floor. Divine smacked her on the ass and walked over to Richard and Lisa's table.

Lynette Davidson laughed and kept dancing. She was enjoying herself. She had met two big time drug dealers, an NFL player and the night had just begun for her. She was looking good as usual and the blue FRANKIE B jeans she wore showed off her butt to the point where every brother in the club was staring and trying to push up on her. She also wore black shoes and a low cut Anne Kline shirt that showed off her flat Janet Jackson type stomach. A few heavy-set girls in the club were hating her and made it a point not to hide it. But Lynette paid them no attention as she danced to another one of O-Fella's songs, catching eye contact with a tall brother wearing a long platinum chain and cross, flooded with diamonds.

Lynette always went after the money getters. She was very materialistic but at times she was generous too. She always looked out for her friends, and would spend her last dime to impress a man she wanted to be with. But he would have to have money as well because she felt she was born to be spoiled and treated like a queen. To maintain her mental health, there were things she just had to have. The world was her stage and her appearance that she showed to everyone had to be the very best. Beauty and luxury was the religion she invented, but she was very impatient and that's what Divine did not like about her. He told her many of times that things would start looking up for him financially and when it did, she would be his one and only woman but she refused the offer. She told herself that "later" never promised anything.

"O-Fella get the money, I swear it, pay to see a gator die before I wear it..." Lynette rapped with O-Fella's song as the tall brother with the platinum chain walked up and began dancing with her staring into her eyes with a smile.

This was Divine's coming home present from Big Lord and he was enjoying every minute of it. As soon as he was released from jail Richard took him shopping. Anything Divine wanted he paid for. He had stacks of money in the brown paper bag he carried. Money was not a thing to Richard. The three drug spots he had were making serious money.

Richard had two spots in New London, Connecticut locked down, Federal Projects and Crystal Projects and both of them were making a lot of money. He also had a spot in Jamaica, Queens. He bought a condo in Flushing and he was no longer staying in L.G. with Gloria. But he did stop through there on a regular basis to make sure she was okay. Most of the time Omar was there or she would be on the phone with him making plans for that night.

Richard was already pushing a black BMW 745i sitting on 20 inch rims. He was probably the only drug dealer that didn't sell drugs on Sundays and if he saw any of his workers on that day he would make them go to church with him and Lisa. All of his workers made sure not to run into him on Sundays. Everything was good, his connections were giving him drugs at a good price and the product was high quality. Richard was making a killing, but when Lisa found out that he was moving drugs, she had a fit.

When Richard dropped out of school, Lisa and his mother cried, shouted and pleaded with him, but to no avail. He knew if he went to school it would be suicide. He was well known now, and it would only be a matter of time before word got back to Shameek that he was in school. Shameek definitely would've gotten him there. Just two days prior, Richard saw T-bone; T-bone pulled a gun and started shooting, but luckily Richard got away. It was a very close call. He was leaving Junior's restaurant on Flatbush Avenue and didn't notice T-bone sneaking up on him. The only thing that alerted Richard to the sneak attack was a white woman who saw T-bone with his gun drawn and began screaming. When Richard turned around and saw him, he pulled for his own gun and let off two shots but missed. Richard ran up Flatbush to his car on Lafayette Avenue, when he heard four shots. He kept running and knew he would have to get out of this area because this was not the place to have a shoot-out. The police would soon be all over the place. T-bone must've realized the same thing because Richard didn't hear any more shots as he made it to his car.

T-bone was very dangerous and Richard knew he would have to come up with a plan to get him out of the picture. Richard heard that Shameek and his 1soldiers were coming down to LG a lot hoping to catch him. He knew he would have to make his move soon and get them before they got him.

"What up son?" asked Divine interrupting Richard's thoughts. "You ain't enjoying the party?"

"Divine, you know this ain't my thing."

"Well, if you want I'll have the DJ play some hurch songs in this motherfucker. What you wanna hear, some Kirk Franklin?"

Richard and Lisa laughed, and Richard said, "No I'm alright Divine. Enjoy yourself. I'm just relaxing and spending time with my baby."

"Lisa, your homegirl Gina is type proper," said Divine. "Fuck around she might be wifey."

"Boy, I saw you talking to at least ten girls since you've been here," said Lisa. "Especially that bitch that's over there dancing."

"Who? What bitch?"

"She's talking about CO Davidson," smiled Richard.

"Come on Lisa baby," said Divine. "That bitch don't love me. None of these bitches do. They just love my doggy style."

"Your doggy style?" asked Lisa curling her lips. "Nigga please."

"I'm telling you Lisa, that's all it is. They just love the way the dog buries his bone."

Richard and Lisa both started laughing.

"Your boy is crazy, boo," Lisa said to Richard. "I'll be right back. I'm going to the bar. I need to talk to Gina, anyway."

She leaned over to kiss Richard and excused herself from the table.

"Do me a favor," said Divine to Lisa. "Tell Gina, I said I need a girl that's mine, mine, mine. I need a girl to make her my wife. I need a girl-"

"Nigga shut up," smiled Lisa. "That song just went off. You're stupid."

She then walked to the bar with all eyes on her. Her long hair came down her back; rocking the cream color Moschino pant-suit and cream color Prada shoes like no other woman could.

The club was in lower Manhattan and it was packed. Women were everywhere and Divine was truly enjoying himself. He already made plans to have a menage a trios with two beautiful women after leaving the club.

"So, what's up kid?" asked Divine.

"Ain't nothing," answered Richard. "I was just thinking about a few things. How did you get to the party?"

"I'm pushing Lynette's Acura. So, I gotta drop her off and then slide back through and scoop up these two bitches for a sandwich."

"I pick up my Cadillac Escalade tomorrow, so you can push the BMW until you cop a whip if you want."

"No doubt, I'm feeling that."

"Divine, I want you to be my lieutenant. Are you with it?"

"Hell yeah, I'm all for it kiddo. I got a little clique too and they all carry these," said Divine pulling two 44 bulldogs up under the table so only Richard could see them. "We're called the Bulldog Crew and kats thirsty for paper."

"It's bigger than that Divine. This ain't no hand to hand street level stuff. I deal with spots 'cause it pulls in good money, but I'm also moving weight and I'm about to make major moves so I need you to collect the money and make sure everything runs smoothly. I can put your clique on too, but I don't want to know them. You handle that. "

"I'm feeling you kid. Let's make things happen baby boy." "Gina is looking at you," said Richard, changing the subject.

Divine looked towards the bar and sure enough, Gina and Lisa were looking at him and Richard. Gina was smiling and was she ever the vision.

"Damn kid, she's type proper. Fuck them other two bitches, I'm coming back for Gina."

The DJ threw on Truth Hurts' song "Contagious" featuring Rakim. Lisa sat at the bar listening to the words. As she listened to the song, she realized that she felt the same way about Richard. And when she heard Rakim's part forget about it. Mentally she was not even in the club.

"Lisa. Lisa. Lisa-"

"Oh what's up, Gina? What did you say?"

"Damn bitch, what the fuck you thinking about? I was calling you for like three minutes. You zoned out on me and did not hear a word I said."

"No, I heard you. I was just listening to the song. You was saying something about Divine being fine."

"Yeah, that nigga look good. Come on let's go over there."

Richard and Divine watched them make their way back to the table. They were by far the best looking women in the club. A few guys spoke to them as they past, but they just smiled and continued walking. A few jealous women acknowledged their presence with up turned lips and stares.

"What's up, baby?" asked Lisa as she sat on Richard's lap and gave him a kiss. She knew that would really piss the jealous chicks off because they were the ones looking at and trying to get with Richard all night.

Gina slid in the seat next to Divine and began speaking.

"What's up Divine? All the bitches in here got their eyes on you, but when you're ready to get with a real woman, let me know."

"Gina, these bitches ain't shit," said Divine. "I was just waiting for your invitation, that's all."

"It looks like you've been getting invitations all night," said Gina as she nodded her head in the direction of the two pretty young girls he had earlier planned to take home.

"Come on Gina," said Divine. "That shit ain't about too much of nothing."

"Oh yeah, what about the CO bitch on the dance floor Lisa was telling me about?"

"Damn bitch, why the fuck you tell him I told you about that?" asked Lisa. "You can't keep a secret for shit!"

As Richard and Gina started laughing, Divine grabbed Gina's hand to get her full attention. When she looked him in his eyes he said, "Let me be real with you, ma. Homegirl is cool people. She's with me but she ain't for me. Trust me, it's a very big difference. Right now she's checking for the biggest balla in here to go home with. She ain't sweating me and you know I ain't sweating that bitch."

Just then Richard's cell phone started ringing and Lisa leaned forward so he could get it out of his jacket pocket. She was hoping that it wasn't a business call because she wasn't trying to hear that he was leaving her for the rest of the night.

"Hello?" Richard said into the phone. "What?!-When?!... I'll be right there!"

Lisa knew something was not right.

"What's wrong?" She asked as she and Richard hurried out of the club. Gina and Divine trailed closely behind them.

"Somebody just shot up my mother's door. I know it was

Shameek and them," said Richard.

Chapter Twenty-Seven

The strip club was located in the Bronx off of University Avenue at a club called Brillante Cafe. The place was huge with three big sections. A twenty foot bar and a stage surrounded by a hundred tables where people came to dine and dance. And they also had their own kitchen and full restaurant serving twelve tables.

Shameek and T-bone sat in the VIP room getting lap dances from two beautiful, thick dancers. They were throwing hundred dollar bills around as if they were singles. They had it like that, especially Shameek. He now had four girls transporting kilos of cocaine to Philadelphia and South Carolina. He was moving keys faster than Allen Iverson pushed the ball on a fast break. He had plans to open up shop in Richmond, Virginia. He had met a few girls from there that said he could make a killing on the drug side in VA and Shameek went wherever the money was with no fear. He figured he'd take T-bone and a few of his soldiers with him to hold him down, and of course he would have a girl from Virginia show him around and point him in the right direction to the money-making ghettos.

Shameek was already making a lot of money. Besides his Cadillac Escalade and 600 Mercedes Benz, he also had a Mercedes CL 55 AMG, a Maxima GLE, an Acura CL, a Mustang GT convertible and a yellow Hummer H2. He loved his cars and trucks and did not understand why T-bone had never bought a vehicle to get around in. T-bone always took cabs or rode the train to get around. Shameek knew T-bone could drive because he once drove one of Shameek's cars. In fact, Shameek didn't know what T-bone did with the money he made at all. He didn't buy expensive clothes, all the jewelry he wore came from the guys he robbed, and he definitely was not known to spend it on girls, except a rare occasion like this night at the strip club.

The reason T-bone never wanted to own a car was because he figured it made you an easy target for your enemies. All they had to

173

do was know your car and they would find a way to catch you getting in or out of it. T-bone had killed many guys in their cars because he always planned their deaths by trapping them where they couldn't get out of their cars. Shameek never knew why T-bone referred to himself as a foot soldier and he had never bothered to ask. All T-bone wanted to do was continue putting in work and having fun. He stayed in Fort Greene with his girl, Monique. His family lived in Coney Island and he would once in a while visit them. He made sure his family was provided for financially and he spoiled his nieces and nephews rotten. Just about anything they wanted or needed, Uncle T would provide. That's what he did with his money but he never told Shameek or anyone else because he felt it was no one's business what he did with his paper.

The dancer giving Shameek the lap dance was light-skinned with long hair, slanted eyes and a body that left brothers with the feeling that they were being hypnotized. Her stage name was Sunshine. She stood before Shameek in a red thong and nothing else. The DJ put on Busta Rhyme's song "Make it clap" and she stood up and made her ass clap like someone was applauding.

"Damn baby, do that shit," smiled Shameek. She sat back down on his lap and he whispered into her ear, "When you retire this scene tonight, let's bounce over to the Marriot."

"I don't do the dating a customer thing," she said.

"I'm not asking you to fuck for free. Shit, nothing is free baby. I got two thousand for you and two for your friend, what's up?"

Sunshine smiled, got up and walked over to her friend who was giving T-bone a lap dance. She whispered in her friend's ear and the smile her friend gave answered Shameek's question. The girl T-bone was with was a tall Puerto Rican girl with long hair. She was the spitting image of Jennifer Lopez but with an ass to put Jenny's to shame. And to top it off, her stage name was J-Ho and the customers loved it. Sunshine whispered in Shameek's ear that she and her friend were with it and they would be ready at 4:30 am.

Shameek gave her two hundred dollars for the lap dances, got up from his chair and gave T-bone the signal that it was time to leave. They put on their jackets and exited the club. The cold outside air greeted them like a friend who'd been betrayed. They hurried to Shameek's Mercedes parked across the street.

"A yo, shorty was bad," said T-bone as Shameek pulled from the curb. "I was trying to hit that but she was playing games. If she knew me outside of that fucking club, that bitch would be sucking my dick for free just to say she know a nigga."

"We already got that lined up," said Shameek. "We coming back at 4:30 to pick them hoes up."

"Word?!" asked T-bone laughing. "Oh shit, you that nigga. Remember when we saw that bitch Jennifer Lopez at that awards show? I was trying to push up on her sexy ass but she was all over that white dude." T-bone laughed and said, "Fuck it, J-Ho look better than her anyway. Yo, get back on University, I wanna get some weed."

"Nah , that shit gotta wait. Them niggas on Tremont still owe me for them two kilos and they act like they can't get my money to me quicker."

T-bone got very serious and pulled out two nine millimeters from his waist band. They rode in silence, each man with his own thoughts. They pulled onto Anthony Avenue and Tremont, and they noticed the block was packed with people as always. After double parking, Shameek and T-bone exited the car. Shameek walked to the building and stood outside while T-bone made his way into the building alone. Ten minutes later, Shameek heard someone yelling in Spanish followed by five shots. He pulled his gun and looked up at the window and then glanced quickly back to the street. People hustling on the block started dispersing at the sound of the gun shots.

Shameek knew things could get ugly on this block so he hoped T-bone was okay. Just then, T-bone came out of the building at breakneck speed. He tossed Shameek a big blue duffel bag and jumped into the passenger's seat. Shameek hurried to the car and pulled away. Gunshots were fired and three bullets hit the side of Shameek's car.

"Stop the car!" yelled T-bone.

Shameek stopped and T-bone got out of the car between Anthony and Echo Place and shot his nines with bad intentions. People ran everywhere. Someone was firing back but T-bone kept firing and wasn't satisfied until he saw two people drop to the ground. He walked backwards quickly to the car, got in and Shameek pulled off. After making a few turns he made his way to Webster Avenue towards Fordham Road. He pulled over on 184th Street and emerged from the car. T-bone did the same.

"Yo, what happened up there?" asked Shameek. "You was just suppose to go up there to see why I ain't get my money yet."

"Yo, everything was cool until the motherfucker said some shit in Spanish and him and the bitch he was with started laughing. I smacked the shit out of him with the gun and when the bitch yelled, they both caught it."

"Yo, you don't even speak Spanish, how do you know he was dissing you, baby boy?"

"Man, I don't know what he said," said an agitated T-bone. "Fuck him, he's dead. If the bitch didn't yell, she wouldn't be dead either. The bag in the car is full of money," said T-bone as he got back into the passenger's seat.

Shameek shook his head sadly, got in the car and drove away. T-bone put in the new Tupac CD and was bobbing his head to "Thug Mansion". Shameek paid no attention to the music; he was into his own thoughts. He knew he should've gone upstairs instead. T-bone was too trigger happy and killed without thinking. That's why so many people were afraid of him.

$

Shameek drove down Fordham Road thinking of how he began in the game. He started as a look-out man to selling hand-to-hand on Myrtle Avenue for a guy everyone called Pretty Tone. During that time, Pretty Tone was the guy that had things locked down in Fort Greene on the drug side. He never wore expensive clothes or drove expensive cars because he said it brought too much attention to you. All the young, up-and-coming dealers idolized him because of his longevity in the game.

Out of all of his soldiers, he liked Shameek the best of all, because of Shameek's thirst to climb to the top. He only wished that Shameek would stop hanging with the two idiot trigger happy boys; Rashien and T-bone. After selling hand-to-hand for Pretty Tone for a while, Shameek was promoted to the position of lieutenant. It wasn't long before he started going with Pretty Tone to handle all aspects of the business and even was able to secure large drug supplying deals without Pretty Tone even being there.

Pretty Tone saw so much of himself in Shameek, that he took him under his wing and taught him all aspects of the game. He loved Shameek like his little brother, but made it clear that he didn't want Rashien and T-bone around. Ever loyal to his friends, Shameek was forced to sneak around to hang with Rashien and T-bone. It was then that the plot began.

One day while bagging up some drugs, Shameek left the door of the drug den unlocked. Rashien and T-bone snuck in with guns drawn and killed every worker in the apartment, except for Shameek. Pretty Tone should have followed his number one rule. Never trust anyone and never let them know too much or you will become unneeded. Before killing him, Rashien and T-bone tortured Pretty Tone for hours. Pretty Tone was dead and so were all of his inner circle, except for Shameek. He became the number one man--Rashien and T-bone were his enforcers. The money started rolling in for him at that point and he never looked back. Six years later, Shameek smiled as he drove his Mercedes down the street, thinking of how far he had come.

"Yo, I saw that little bitch nigga that killed Ra," said T-bone snapping Shameek out of his thoughts. "I don't know how Ra let that little bitch ass nigga do him. I almost had the nigga on Flatbush

Avenue but the cops were all over the scene. Then I went to his mom's crib a few days later and knocked on the door, but the bitch wouldn't open up. So, I put a few holes through the door hoping she was standing right behind it. I can't wait to get that little nigga."

Shameek smiled and nodded his head. T-bone never changed. He was the same since junior high school when Shameek first met him, Shameek thought to himself. They pulled up in front of the strip club, just as Sunshine and J-Ho walked out of the club. Shameek sat in his car smiling at the two young women holding four thousand dollars in his hand.

"That's the best sight, I've seen all night," said Sunshine reaching for the money.

Shameek released the money into the girl's hand and they entered the car.

"A yo, y'all better hurry up and get in before my boy in the car have a heart attack," said Shameek.

"That's what I'm talking about," said T-bone. "Yo, stop at the weed spot, I want some trees."

"I have some right here," said a giggling Sunshine.

"That's what I'm talking about," yelled T-bone as he snatched the bag of weed out of her hand. He pulled a cigar out of his jacket pocket and began rolling a blunt as Shameek drove away with his eyes on the road listening to a banging song called "Desperado's" by Yukmouth and Young Noble from the Outlawz.

It wasn't long before they pulled up in front of the Marriot hotel on 44th and Broadway.

They got two rooms, and after T-bone opened the door to his room he threw Shameek the key and said, "Let me know when you're ready to pull outta here."

"Okay," said Shameek with a smile before entering his own room with Sunshine holding him close.

After two hours of talking and having sex, Shaneek was ready to leave. He left Sunshine in the bed sleeping and walked out of the room closing the door behind him. Before he put the key in the door of T-bone's room, he wondered why J-Ho was in there yelling. He stuck the key in, pushed the door open and began laughing holding his stomach, as he saw T-bone hitting J-Ho doggy-style as she yelled from the top of her lungs, "Fuck Puffy, fuck that nigga Puffy, I want you poppy, fuck Puffy!"

Chapter Twenty-Eight

The house in New Haven Connecticut was big. It was white with neatly trimmed bushes and freshly cut grass in front. A brand new yellow Lamborghini sat in the driveway. Inside of the house was well decorated with African paintings on the wall. The sounds of Missy's song "Work it" were coming from the sound system in the back yard. A beautiful five foot six brown-skinned woman with short hair, a nice body, and thick eye brows sat on Moe-dog's lap as he laid back on a yellow beach-type chair looking up at the sun. She had on a yellow two-piece bathing suit, and she had a sweet little laugh that made you smile every time you heard it. Her name was Tameeka but everyone called her Meka for short.

Another woman sat in a chair next to Moe-dog. She was light complexioned, five foot nine with long hair. She had a nice body and she wore her two-piece white bathing suit to perfection. Her name was Donna but everyone called her Diamond because she looked just like Lisa Raye but Donna didn't know a thing about the players club. She looked at Whitey as he swam across the big pool. He always came to Connecticut to relax. He loved CT. There were nice parts of Connecticut, even though you had your bad areas, like the jungle, but it was nothing new to Whitey. He was used to going through bad areas and making a name for himself. And many times, thugs in different places would try to front on him because he was white but he enjoyed making examples to let the rest of them know he was not the average white boy to mess with. Like the day he was in New Haven, Connecticut at the Freddi Fixer day parade. He was downtown by the fire station talking to a pretty light-skinned girl named Tamara, when three so-called thugs approached him. He knew it was going to be trouble so he told Tamara to step off.

As she walked away, a dark-skinned six foot three guy looked down at Whitey and said, "Yo white boy, what the fuck you doing over here, and why you talking to our bitches?"

The two other guys put their best screw faces on and moved closer to the one talking.

Whitey wanted to laugh but instead he said with a straight face, "I don't want no problems with y'all, and for the record, I prefer black bitches over white bitches."

The leader of the group did not appreciate Whitey calling black girls bitches and Whitey knew it, that's why he said it, because he wanted to get under the guy's skin. From Whitey's accent they knew he was from another state, and something in his demeanor had told them he was not the one to mess with, but the guy refused to be punked by a white boy, especially in front of his friends. So he made his worse mistake ever by reaching inside of his pants pocket, pulling out an orange box cutter. Whitey pulled out his nine millimeter and when the guys saw the gun, they all ran. Whitey laughed because they were stupid enough to run together instead of running in separate directions. Whitey squeezed off five shots hitting all three guys in the back before making his getaway. He knew it was real thugs in Connecticut though, because he had met a few of them. Especially, in Bridge Port also known as 'Little Brooklyn'. But Whitey always told himself that he was too big and dangerous for the state.

Whitey looked at Diamond and smiled. She was beautiful. And when he reached the edge of the pool to get out, Diamond walked up to him, kissed him and dried off his back with the big white bath towel she held.

Whitey walked to the empty chair with Diamond following behind. He then sat down and when Diamond sat on his lap she kissed him again.

"This is a nice spot you got here," said Moe-dog to Whitey. "I know it cost you a fortune."

"Nah, not really, " smiled Whitey. "It's much cheaper than living in New York. But you know I gotta keep a crib out there too. This is just the little hide-away spot. So how you like my new car out front?"

"Shit is hot," answered Moe-dog. "I wish I could afford one right now, but I have a lot of things to do in the future. Maybe you should start saving money too."

"Nah kid, you only live once," said Whitey kissing Diamond on the neck. "So eat, drink and be merry..."

"For tomorrow you will die," said Moe-dog, finishing the saying.

"Do we have any work to do today?" asked Whitey.

"None that I know of," answered Moe-dog smiling and rubbing Meka's ass. "All fun and relaxation today."

Moe-dog used to enjoy killing people for money and he specialized in taking contracts. But lately he was getting tired of it and knew he would not be doing it for too much longer. He did not do them for just anyone, because he knew there was always the possibility that someone who hired him would also be the one to put him in a tight situation. For some reason, he trusted Richard. There was just something about the church boy that made him feel at ease. A lot of people did not know how Moe-dog looked and they had only heard of him through whispers in the streets. No one knew where he came from or why he killed so many people and Moe-dog liked it that way. He was quiet and never told his business to anyone. He knew the only reason his name was in the streets was because of someone he once did work for opened their mouths to someone. Probably bragging on how they had someone murdered. Not many people knew of his past.

Moe-dog came from a nice middle class family, but he was always considered the black sheep, always fighting in the street. He would extort children his age and beat grown men with baseball bats in broad daylight in front of everyone just to get a little reputation. His family was Orthodox Muslims but Moe-dog never liked the idea of praying five times a day. He was too busy causing mayhem in the streets.

Unlike Richard, he would never allow anyone to tease him like they did his family for wearing the Muslim garb his father wore or the fact that his mother and sister covered their entire bodies and faces. When he was old enough, he traded his Muslim garments for the Polo,

Guess, and many other name brand clothes. His family could not reach him no matter how much they prayed for him or talked to him about the ways of Islam.

It wasn't until he was like fifteen years old that his life began to change. He was walking down the streets in the Flatbush section, where he lived, when he saw a well-dressed black man, under the hood of his car. As Moe-dog neared, the man lifted his head from under the hood and said, "Hey boy, you wanna make some money? Get in the car and try to start it." It sounded more like a demand than a request, enraging Moe-dog. He began thinking of getting into the car and running the man down, but he figured he would help the man and then rob him with the knife in his pocket. Moe-dog got into the car, turned the ignition and the car turned over smoothly. The man closed the hood and told Moe-dog to stay in the car. The man got into the car on the passenger's side and instructed him to turn off the car.

Moe-dog did as he was told, when the man suddenly pulled out a gun with a silencer on it and pointed it at Moe-dog's ribs. His eyes opened wider and wider in fear, as the man said in a quiet, serious tone, "I already know who you are. Your name is John Simmons, but people in the streets calls you Moe-dog, 'cause you run the streets like a dog with no sense. You got a dumb ass reputation for beating and robbing people. I know where you live. Your family is Muslims and you constantly put their lives in danger when you act the way you do in the streets. Your little reputation means nothing right now punk. If I put a bullet in your head right now, you'll be forgotten by the end of the year. You beat up a well-respected man with plenty of money and he offered me a nice amount of money to kill you, but I don't kill children. Enough of y'all is already doing that. Your dumb ass reminds me of myself when I was your age." The man lit a cigar and introduced himself. "My name is Tommy Jones. Have you ever heard of me?"

Moe-dog shook his head "no" quickly. For some reason he wasn't scared of the man anymore; he was now fascinated with the black gangster.

"The reason you never heard of me," continued Tommy Jones, "is because I don't let people know my business. Only those who pay me, ever know me. The best way to be is low-key, you stay alive and stay out of prison that way."

Tommy Jones put his gun away and gave Moe-dog a piece of paper with a name and number on it. From that moment on, Moe-dog was changed forever. He was now a quiet and sneaky boy and didn't terrorize his neighborhood anymore. Tommy became like a father to him, teaching him everything he knew, up until the day he died from cancer. His death crushed Moe-dog but he always remembered everything Tommy taught him and it was then that Moe-dog started taking hits for big time drug dealers and business men.

The most important thing Tommy ever taught him was to follow the three rules of any illegal game-know how to play the game; follow the rules of the game; and know when to quit the game. Moe-dog had plans to pull out of the game because he knew he couldn't do hits forever. Once he reached his savings goal of three hundred thousand dollars, he was retiring. It wouldn't be long now, because he was almost there; the end was in sight.

When he met Whitey, his hits and robberies became easier. Because Whitey was white, people would let him into places that Moe-dog would never be allowed to enter. Hits and robberies were their hustle and both paid well. Whitey was just as dangerous if not more so than Moe-dog and he loved Whitey because he was always down for whatever.

Moe-dog smiled and thought about the day he met Whitey. A big time drug dealer had gotten robbed and called Moe-dog to take out the white guy that robbed him. Before Moe-dog could take care of the situation, the white guy popped up again, this time kidnapping the drug dealer. After torturing him, Whitey learned that a hit was put out on his head and got the number of the hitman who was to kill him. He had the drug dealer tied to a chair with stab wounds all over his body. But the drug dealer was still alive. Whitey paced back and forth with a hunting knife in his hand. He then dialed the number he obtained from the drug dealer.

"Hello, can I speak to Moe-dog?"

"Moe-dog, doesn't live here anymore. Who is this?"

"Listen Moe-dog, this is Whitey, a guy you were paid to kill. I have a present here for you."

"Why are you calling me? I have no idea what you speak of."

"You know what the fuck I'm talking about!" Whitey yelled into the phone. "Let's stop playing games. From time to time, I do the same shit you do. But I'm going to be honest with you. You make me a little nervous, because I know you did your homework on me before you took the hit and I don't know anything about you. I only heard your name in passing a few times. I want the hit taken off."

There was silence on the phone for a full minute and then Moe-dog replied, "The hit is off."

"Why should I believe that shit?" asked Whitey.

"Because I'm a man of my word," answered Moe-dog.

"Didn't you give this piece of shit your word too?" asked Whitey looking at the bloody drug dealer.

"My word means nothing to him. It's because of guys like him why my name is in the streets. Why couldn't he just die with honor? He just had to give up my name and number. Lucky you was not the police. I would like to meet you in person. I have big things we can get into. You have my cell number. Give me a call tomorrow and we'll hook up. Oh yeah, is the present you have for me dead or alive?"

Whitey looked at the drug dealer and said, "Alive with a few stab wounds."

"I don't like presents, kill it and get at me tomorrow."

Whitey hung up the phone, walked over to the drug dealer and slit his throat without so much as a word. Ever since then, Whitey and Moe-dog have been best friends and partners in crime.

Whitey was raised in the Crown Heights section of Brooklyn. He was the only white boy in the Albany Housing Projects that was raised around blacks and he made it his business to be respected like the rest of the black and Spanish thugs. He came from a good family that was not well off with money just like the rest of those that lived in the projects. All of his friends were black and Puerto Rican and even his girlfriends. He loved white women equally, but at this time there were no white girls anywhere near Albany Projects and he was not going out of his way to be with a white girl. He was not prejudice, so all women were the same to him.

Even though his father and mother provided the basic things he needed, the streets was calling him and he was curious to hear what it had to say. By the time he was seventeen years old, he had killed many thugs and robbed even more. He used to wear gold teeth in his mouth until Moe-dog convinced him that gold teeth would be unproductive to the hits and robberies that they had planned. Moe-dog just wanted to reach his goal and stop doing hits and robberies, but Whitey saw it as a life-time career and he was ready to do whatever it took to keep the money coming in.

$

"I have to jet back to New York," said Whitey snapping Moe-dog out of his thoughts. "But I might just wait 'til tomorrow night."

The telephone on the patio began ringing. Diamond got up, answered it and then handed it to Whitey. Whitey passed the phone to Moe-dog and said, "It's Bishop. I guess our plans for the day may change after all."

Chapter Twenty-Nine

Nobody paid any attention to the housing worker with dreads on his head, a thick mustache and full beard. He casually walked in his blue uniform, carrying a clipboard. It was a cold morning, but the sun was shining down. Few people were outside this early in the morning. Just a mixture of those going to work, hanging out, selling drugs and purchasing their morning highs.

The elevators were broken again, so the housing worker had to take the stairs, but that's what he had planned to do anyway. As he made his way up the stairs, two young kids came running down the stairs almost knocking him backwards. Building 79 was known for having off the hook kids running around at all hours of the day. The tall housing worker finally made it to the fifth floor and knocked hard on the apartment door.

"Who is it?!" asked an angry female voice.

"Housing. I need to check the radiators."

The woman looked through the peephole and then opened the door. She was light-skinned, five foot four, short curly hair and thick in all the right places. Even wearing burgundy house shoes and a burgundy house coat, she was looking good.

"Damn, why the fuck y'all come so early for?"

"Sorry miss. I won't take long. I'll be out of your way in five minutes."

"Come on in."

The housing worker entered the apartment and walked over to the radiator in the living room. He felt it with his hand and then wrote something down on his clipboard.

"You can check the radiators in the other rooms," said the woman. "I have to use the bathroom. My man is in the last room on the left so you better check the radiator in there very quickly 'cause if he wakes up and sees you, you're done."

She then laughed thinking of the scene if her man was to wake up

187

and see the housing worker.

As she entered the bathroom leaving the housing man alone, she hoped the housing worker wouldn't get shot just for doing his job. She thought about going in the room with the housing man to make sure everything turned out alright, but decided against it because she had to use the bathroom badly, so he was on his own.

After she closed and locked the bathroom door, the housing worker stealthily walked to the last room on the left and opened the door.

The room was small with a queen-sized bed taking up most of the space, a big brown dresser with two big mirrors attached to it, and a color TV rested on a stand. The TV was turned down low and when the housing man looked at the screen, he saw the singer Ashanti talking to a white lady with blonde hair about her career as a singer. The housing man quickly looked away from the TV and his eyes focused on the male figure sleeping peacefully in the bed with his hands behind his head. T-bone was sound asleep when he felt something hard pressing down on his forehead. He wished this stupid bitch would stop playing games, he thought to himself as he opened his eyes slowly. What he saw instead of Monique was a dark-skinned, dreadlocked man holding a nine millimeter with a silencer attached to it. He looked so familiar but T-bone could not place where he knew him from. If only he could reach under his bed he would be okay, he thought to himself. He knew that would be a stupid move. He wondered what he could possibly have done to have a housing worker with a gun to his head. T-bone knew it was a professional hit. Looking hard at the man, T-bone was finally able to place him, but seconds too late. Before he could speak, the housing worker shot him four times in the head. He then knelt down next to T-bone's body and said a quick prayer of forgiveness. After he was done, he opened the door with the gun in his hand. Walking down the hallway, he noticed that Monique was still in the bathroom. He stopped at the bathroom door and thought about killing Monique, but decided against it as he left the apartment quickly and quietly.

He ran down the stairs still carrying his clipboard and putting his gun in his waist. When he reached the lobby, the same two kids ran past him again almost knocking the clipboard out of his hand. There was no one else in the lobby as he made his quick escape. No one outside paid any attention to him leaving the building. He was just another housing man doing his job early in the morning. After walking quickly to Willoughby Avenue, he got in his black Cadillac Escalade and didn't feel safe until he had pulled over on Willoughby and Skillman Street. He then took off the fake beard, mustache, dreads, latex gloves and the housing uniform. He put everything inside of a black duffel bag and threw the bag in the passenger's seat. He tucked the gun into his Tommy Hilfiger jeans. He then drove away and kept driving until he got to Brownsville. He pulled up in front of a big house on Prospect and Saratoga.

When Richard rung the doorbell carrying the black duffel bag in his left hand, Divine opened the door with a smile on his face and large bills in his hands. The sounds of the rap group M.O.P. song, "Ante Up" was playing on the stereo in the living room.

"Bishop, my boy. What brings the kid over here this early in the morning?"

"I need to talk to you."

"Come on in baby boy."

They walked past the living room and entered Divine's bedroom. Richard looked back over his shoulder at the couch where not long ago Divine had killed his sister's boyfriend. He shook his head, entered the bedroom and sat in the black leather chair located in the corner of the room as Divine sat on his bed.

"Damn baby," smiled Divine stuffing the money under the mattress that he had in his hands. "This money is coming in real quick. Shit keep coming like this, I'ma be the biggest balla in Brownsville."

"You might be the biggest balla in Brooklyn," corrected Richard with a smile. "Especially the way this money is coming in. Divine, I never thought we'll make so much money. Especially so quick. Majority of people work their whole lives and still don't make what we make in one month."

"Yeah, you're right about that," smiled Divine, "and it only gets better."

Even though Richard was talking like everything was okay, Divine could tell that there was something on his friend's mind so he looked at Richard and said, "Bishop, what's up? You want me to take care of that nigga Shameek and T-bone this week or what homie?"

Richard took the gun out of his waist and threw it on the bed. Divine picked it up, smelled the barrel and began smiling.

"It smells like you just got done cooking."

"I did. Your boy T-bone is history. When Omega told me he found out that T-bone was the one that shot up my mom's door, I had to get at him."

"Damn churchboy, you really do put in work huh?" asked Divine with a smile.

"I had to get him Divine."

"I hear that but check it out kid," Divine frowned. "Next time let me handle that part of our business. That's part of what I get paid for and I don't like when someone else does my job."

"Alright," smiled Richard. "You got that."

"How is moms doing anyway?"

"She's doing okay. She's staying at my condo in Queens, and I'm just happy that the bullets hit the door
and not her. If something had happened to her I would go crazy."

"So what's up with Shameek? You know he's gonna be out for blood when he finds out that T-bone is Frank Sinatra. You want me to handle him?"

"Nah, just handle the money coming in. Don't worry about Shameek."

The phone began ringing and Divine picked it up on the third ring.

"Hello? Who dis?" asked Divine.

He then looked at Richard and said, "This my man on the phone. He's up north in Clinton. Give me a minute."

After pressing three, Divine spoke into the phone.

"Yeah, what's up?...Word?...You want me to handle that?...Alright... Yeah nigga, I just sent you and your brother a thousand dollars... Yeah, you should have it by Friday... Hell no nigga, I ain't taking no pictures... What the fuck I look like a model?... I ain't that Tyson kat nigga... I'll be up there next weekend...Oh, honey is bouncing?... Tell her to hit me before she leaves. I'll smash her wit' some trees... Alright, what's the number? Aiight check, I'm talking to my man right now. I'll call her on the three-way and she...Yeah, if she picks up the phone you can kick it and I'll pick it up in a half an hour, aiight? What's the number again?...Hold on."

Divine dialed the number, listened for a few seconds and then put the phone under his pillow.

"Yeah, like I was saying," Divine said to Richard, "it's a good thing moms got away from the Fort."

"Yeah, but on another note, them other four spots we opened is bringing in a lot of money also."

"Yo Bishop, I'm thinking about buying a crib myself. Yo, Mr. Atkins gotta hook up the paperwork for me first."

"Divine, go ahead and get that crib. You ready to cop the Bentleys or what?"

"No doubt baby," answered Divine through his laughter. "No doubt. Yo kid, I'm feeling Gina. She was over here last night. Man, that pussy is good! She know how to make a motherfucker feel special son. I think I'm in love."

Richard started laughing and said, "You in love already, huh?"

"Yeah man, it's deeper than sex. I love her personality and everything. You know I don't give a fuck about no bitches, but I think she's the one son."

"What about Lynette?"

"Fuck Lynette! I was at her crib the other day. After I smashed

191

her out I went to sleep and shit. I heard mad noises so I get up to see what's going on and this stupid bitch got some lame ass drug dealing hand to hand nigga up in there beefing. I ain't say shit to none of 'em. I just broke out. I tried to put the idiot bitch on but she's too greedy for paper. And all she wanna do is fuck for it. I should've put her stink ass up on the hoe stroll in Hunts Point or somewhere. Now she be calling me like every fucking hour and shit. I mean, I got mad love for her, but it's not the kind of love I can have for Gina."

"I hear you but check it, take the nine," said Richard changing the subject and pointing to the gun on the bed, "and hold it down for me."

"Aiight, I got you. The Bulldog Crew is putting in mad work kid. You see they got us them four diamond mines. And they about to kill some rich niggas for they spots so we should have five more by next week. The only problem is they kill too many niggas in the streets over nothing. Like them Columbian kats uptown that was moving weight in Bushwick. They didn't have to kill them niggas, we didn't even have shit on that block. The area was too hot for us. We don't need that kind of heat so I gotta talk to them."

"Yeah, talk to them before it gets out of control. What are you doing today?"

"Well, after I take care of our business," Divine answered with a smile. "I'm taking Gina wherever she wants to go."

"Tricking already, huh?" Richard asked with a smile.

"Call it what you want nigga," laughed Divine. "Whatever my baby Gina wants, she gets."

When they entered the living room, on the stereo M.O.P. was singing, "Cold as ice."

Chapter Thirty

Everyone attended the wedding. Lisa's mother, Mrs. Alice Thompson sat next to Richard's mother in the front row. She never thought she would see the day when her baby girl would be getting married. She could remember getting married at the same age as her daughter and when she saw Lisa glide down the aisle in the same wedding dress she wore twenty-one years prior, tears welled in her eyes. She truly wished at the moment, more so than any other, that her husband was still alive to see this day.

Lisa was her father's little angel and there was nothing he wouldn't do to make her happy. Barry Thompson was a handsome man with a sense of humor unparalleled by most. He was a tall, burly, truck driver with curly brown hair. Whenever he was not on the road working, he was home, spending time with his family. Everyone said Omar looked just like him, but Lisa was his world.

As Mrs. Alice continued to watch her daughter make her way down the aisle filled with joy that her baby was getting married, she also thought about the day she met her husband. She and Barry were in high school and he was the star of the basketball team. Everybody in the school knew that he was going to the NBA and every girl hoped to be the future Mrs. Thompson. But Barry wanted to be with the girl that every boy in the school was trying to date. Alice Hall was the most beautiful girl at school and her personality would make you smile on the inside.

For months, she ignored his overtures until one day everything in Barry's life changed. He severely injured his knee in a game and his career ended before it had begun. Down but not out, Barry approached Alice again, and this time she accepted his invitation for a date. The single date turned into a strong relationship. The two of them were in love and inseparable. Alice got pregnant two months before graduation and they decided to wait after they graduated to get married. They named their little boy Omar and thirteen years later, they had a baby girl named Lisa, who was the apple of her father's eye.

Alice wiped a tear from her eye as she looked at her baby marrying this handsome young man. She was happy for her baby girl and had liked her new son-in-law from the moment they'd met. She was even happier that Lisa did not marry Shameek. Alice couldn't stand Shameek. She had often seen him with young boys in the projects selling drugs. Alice couldn't figure out what Lisa had saw in him in the first place. So she was happy that her daughter had made the right decision to leave him alone. As tears rolled down her face she thought about how fast Lisa had grown up. It seemed as if it was only yesterday that she was changing Lisa's diapers. They were always as close as a mother and daughter could be, she knew she would miss her daughter terribly and Lisa would miss her as well. Lisa moved in with Richard to a new Long Island condo he bought, but she promised to visit her mother often.

Mrs. Alice and Maria took pictures of everything and were introduced to everyone except for the five thugs sitting in the back wearing tuxedos and dark shades. The five were best known as the 'Bulldog Crew. Richard insisted they show up, not only for protection in case Shameek and his boys decided to make an appearance, but also because he wanted to invite the guys who played such a big part in his becoming rich.

Gloria sat opposite Mrs. Thompson and Mrs. Brown. Sitting behind Gloria sat Divine. His thoughts were on the wedding he and Gina would have one day. Everything was going well for Divine, especially the money that was coming his way as Richard's lieutenant. He kept his money stashed in a safe hidden in the floor of the new house he bought and Richard was the only one who knew where Divine's earnings were stored. Not even Gina knew where the money was.

Omar was the best man and was very happy to see his baby sister marry someone like Richard. But he wanted Richard to pull out of the game and go legit before the game closed in on him as he saw it happen to so many others. His thoughts wandered to the trip to Jamaica he and Gloria planned as he began to smile. He had taken other girls to the island but had never took someone he loved, until now. Gina stood next to Lisa, she was the bridesmaid and was enjoying every minute of it.

The wedding was beautiful and the reverend announced the newlyweds--Mr. & Mrs. Richard & Lisa Brown. The young couple left immediately after the ceremony for their honeymoon in Cancun.

$

Divine's phone began to ring and when he answered it, he heard a familiar voice. "Divine, what's up boy?"

"Who dis calling."

"Who it sound like sinner?" Richard asked with a smile.

"Oh shit, Bishop what's popping baby? I thought you wasn't coming back 'til next week."

"We were, but Lisa had a bad dream about moms so we just came back early. So what's been going on?"

"Man, the money is still flowing lovely but the Bulldog Crew is trippin'. I thought money would slow these fools down a bit, but these niggas is worse than ever. They just bodied some Blood kats down on Flatbush Avenue. And the police found some nigga dead down in Sumner Projects, dead from eighty two stab wounds. Everybody in the streets are talking about Bishop and the Bulldog Crew and they looking at me like I'm the head BDC. Maybe it wasn't a good idea for you to meet them. I would hate to see you get jammed up fucking wit' these niggas."

"No, don't worry about me. My alibi is good. I can prove where I was when the bodies fell if need be. The money I'm getting and the way they're moving we would've met eventually. I'm just glad they're on our side."

"My alibi is tight too. I was at Mr. Atkins' office taking care of some business when both bodies dropped. But check it, being that these fools are killing everyone, you want them to get that nigga

Shameek?" asked Divine.

"No," Richard answered quickly. "Leave him alone. Because of what happened to T-bone, he probably don't even want anymore beef. I know when we were locked up, I said I would never forgive him for what he did and that I was going to make him pay, but I have to forgive him because that's what my father would want me to do."

"You can't forgive niggas like that," said Divine sounding like Kendu. "Nigga, the first chance he gets, he'll kill you. Dudes on this level is dangerous. As soon as you slip up, he'll be right there to kill you."

"Yeah well, let come what comes. I'm getting tired of this game anyway. It's weighing too much on me. When I was in Cancun, I did a lot of thinking. I thought getting money and being someone that everyone knew would make me happy. That's something that I always wished for and when the opportunity presented itself I took it. But you know what? It didn't make me happy. The only thing that makes me happy is being with Lisa and she wants the old Richard back. She hates what I do. You understand? Divine, the game doesn't last forever and with all the gossip and telling going on, it's just a matter of time before we get killed or get put in jail for life. Don't get me wrong, I enjoy the money, but that's not what I'm about. Every time I think about the way I make my living, I get disgusted with myself. Because I know it's wrong, and if my pops was alive I couldn't look him in the eyes and continue to do what I do. When he died, in a sense that gave me courage to get in the game because if he was alive, I would've been scared to death just thinking about the drug game. So I just totally disrespected my mother because she wasn't the authority figure my pops was. Divine, I'm thinking about getting my life together and becoming a preacher. You know, following in my pops foot steps and chill out now. I'm pulling out of the game like Omega."

"Listen man," said Divine becoming angry. "Don't start talking like a sucker. You got in the game and it paid off but if you think you can walk away from it while Shameek is still alive, you bugging kid. The nigga got mad heart and it won't be long before he flip on Omega and kill you, Lisa and whoever else gets in his way. He's already talking shit about Omega, because he knows the nigga Omega left the game in a sense and his clique in the streets is becoming weak. So, it's just a matter of time. What you gonna do, move to another state? He's a major nigga just like we are, which means he gets around. So there's always a chance that you will see him, and trust me, looking over your shoulder is not the best way to live. If I was him I wouldn't stop 'til I got you. Come on, think like the enemy for a change. I don't overestimate Shameek, but you can't underestimate a nigga either. I say we kill the nigga and then you can do what the fuck you wanna do. Let come what comes? Man, I don't wanna hear that suicidal bullshit!"

"Okay, I hear you," said Richard thinking about everything Divine said. "I hadn't thought about it like that. But for now, don't do anything. I'll get back to you on that later. Okay?"

"Yeah, okay," said Divine now calming down. "Regardless of your decision homie, I'm wit' you. Just holla. I'm just making sure that we keep each other on point because the game is too deep and serious to start slipping up now. I got a lot of plans for the future, Bishop. After a year of getting this paper, we'll both be able to pull up outta this game smelling like roses. By then, I'll be ready to get into that legit shit you keep talking about. The only thing that stops you from pulling out of the game right now is that bird ass nigga Shameek."

"I know man," said Richard sadly. "And I'm thinking about everything you're saying. But like I said before, I have to pull out of this very soon, because in a sense it's killing me worse than what Shameek could ever do. Just give me a month and if it'll make you feel better, we can get rid of him together."

"That's what I'm talking about nigga," smiled Divine. "That's the Bishop I know. But check this, I've been thinking about marrying Gina but I don't know if she's one hundred percent loyal to me. Feel me?"

"Yeah, I feel you, but I think I got a way for you to find out. I'll get back to you on it."

"No doubt baby," said Divine wondering what Richard had in mind. "Bishop, get back at me. One."

Richard hung up the phone, looked around his big bedroom and thought about the situation he was in. He knew when he shot and killed Rashien the beef would never end until he or Shameek were dead. It was only a matter of who would die. Then, when he killed T-bone the beef only intensified. After thinking about what he'd done for the hundredth time, he knew he made the right decision. The thing he now most regretted was getting into the drug game. When he first started, he rationalized selling drugs to his people by looking at all the pharmacies and liquor stores in his neighborhood as being no different than what he was doing. But deep down, he knew that he was still wrong. His father had always told him to be himself and not become like those other people. He wanted to tell his father so many things but now that he was no longer here, he wouldn't have the opportunity to tell him anything. He wanted to explain that if he told the police in the beginning, things would have only been worse. Because the police cannot and will not protect a poor black family twenty four hours a day from a rich thug with a thousand soldiers. The only way to beat a thug with power is to become a thug with power. All of these things he wanted to tell his father. But most of all, he wanted to say that he loved him.

Richard pushed his situation to the back of his mind and reached for the phone. As he dialed a number, he smiled and was now thinking about Divine and Gina.

Chapter Thirty-One

Divine was feeling good and was enjoying life to the fullest, for the first time in his life. He was making more money than he'd ever made before. He had to hire his sister to count and keep track of the huge amount of money he brought home. Whenever he wasn't taking care of business or spending time with Gina, he would go upstate to the prisons to visit his fallen comrades. He would always take them packages and even marijuana, to brighten their days inside of the dark gloomy prisons. He would also send girls up north to visit his friends; sometimes he sent so many girls up north, he often forgot who he sent to see who. But his generosity, also benefited the many women who'd found themselves behind bars. He would send a bus load of guys from his neighborhood upstate lugging packages to the Bedford Hills women's prison to visit girls he didn't even know. But he would do it because he knew that they did not have the outside support that men had the privilege of having. For the children in his neighborhood, he would sponsor free bus trips to Great Adventures or any other event he'd thought they would enjoy. Those in prison and people in the streets now spoke of Divine as if he were a celebrity. But he did not do any of these things to get attention. It was simply just another side of who he was as a person.

Tonight was just about Divine though. It was his night to go out to a club and enjoy himself. He took his time to get dressed and made sure he was perfect. He was rocking a pair of black alligator shoes, a pair of tailor-made pants, a black alligator belt with the initial 'D' flooded with diamonds in the belt buckle, a black expensive dress shirt and a long white mink coat. He was smelling good. He had on Angel cologne. He also had his diamond infested Rolex on his left wrist, an iced out pinky ring and a platinum chain with a flooded out diamond cross he had tucked inside of his shirt. He stuck his nine millimeter inside the back of his pants and checked himself once more in the mirror before leaving his house to make sure he was looking as good as he felt. He opened the door of his brand new black Bentley sitting on 20-inch Giovanni chrome rims and settled into the driver's seat. The car was nice. It had a navigational system a 13inch TV in the headliner, an in-dash-pull-out TV, and tan soft leather seats. When the car was started the sounds of O-Fella's song "Bank Stop" came blasting through the twenty thousand dollar system. He pulled onto the street and as he took off, he thought about going to pick up the Bulldog Crew. He decided against that idea, because he didn't need any unnecessary bodies dropping. He was definitely not going to take Gina to the club either. He figured why take sand to the beach. He knew there would be a lot of girls flocking around him. He was not going to have sex with any of the girls he met though. He could only think of Gina nowadays and for some reason that made him uncomfortable. He had never been in love so it was a new experience that made him feel too vulnerable. He was going to the club tonight with the hopes that there would be gorgeous women there to snap him out of this thing called love.

It was very hard for Divine to put his total trust in any woman. He remembered the day his friend Keith had gotten killed over a girl. Divine was sixteen years old and could not get along with Keith's girl at all. In fact, he hated Laura. He knew she was still seeing her baby's father on the down-low and everytime he mentioned it to Keith he would ignore what Divine was telling him. Laura's baby's father was a thug from Coney Island that everyone called Animal. He and Keith never liked each other and they even had a few shoot-outs without any of them ever getting hit.

Divine remembered that Keith had called him on that fatal morning. He picked up the phone and in a groggy voice said, "Yo, who is this?"

"It's me baby boy," said Keith. "You just getting up?"

"Yeah man," answered Divine wiping the sleep from his eyes. "I was fucking this bitch late last night, and then I had to go uptown to re-up. So, what's up?"

"Ain't nothing. I'm about to head over to Laura's crib."

"Yo Keith man," Divine said angrily. "Why you keep fucking with that bitch? You know she still fucking that nigga Animal."

"No she ain't," laughed Keith. "Trust me kid, I know what I'm doing. Anyway, I'm out, I'll see you later,"

Something just didn't seem right. Keith stayed on Divine's mind that whole morning. Then four hours later he got the phone call. Keith's sister Levette said through her tears and anguish that when Keith went to Laura's apartment, Animal was there and Keith had died from two gunshots to the chest.

Four days later, Animal and Laura was both found dead in Coney Island with a bullet in each of their heads. Even though no one could prove it, they knew it was Divine who had done it.

Since that tragic day, it was very hard for Divine to put his complete trust in women. And falling in love with Gina, had only made things a bit more complicated.

Divine looked down at the Rolex on his wrist and smiled. He was finally coming up in the game. He never in his life had it this good.

When he was ten years old, he and his family lived in a rat infested, perpetually cold, two bedroom apartment. His mother had her own room and he shared the other room with his older sister. His father was a good man, but when he lost his job at Avis car services, he started staying out on the streets drinking and getting high. Shortly after, his father died of a crack-induced heart attack and that left Divine colder than the no heat apartment they lived in.

Even as a child Divine always took things seriously. He was a thinker that didn't like to be told what to do. He began hanging out in the streets with boys that had his same mentality. It wasn't long before he started robbing people to buy the things he wanted. Nobody could tell him anything. He liked to do everything his way even if it caused chaos and confusion. He was very independent, he loved his freedom to do whatever he wanted and he always thought ahead.

When his mother began working a second job and was finally able to move her family into a decent house, it was already too late. Divine was addicted to the streets. He had dropped out of school and got his own apartment.

Divine eventually lost his apartment because he was constantly in and out of jail. He found that it was just easier to stay with the various girls he was having sex with. He had seen so many of his friends become victims of homicides. He vowed then to take all threats seriously. His fighting days were over. He began carrying a gun and before he knew it, Divine had a body count that was so great that the police commissioner thought there was a new gang in the area. He started selling drugs and for many years he was still what they called a low-level petty drug dealer. But now that Richard had put him on, he didn't even deal with small weight anymore. He was a big deal in the drug world. On a daily basis he was pushing ten kilos and better.

Divine rolled down his window and lit a cigar as he pulled in front of the club. The block was crowded with people and everyone was waiting to get into Cheetas on 21st Street between 5th and 6th Avenue in Manhattan-Everyone turned to see who was driving the expensive car. Girls peered into his car to see if he was a celebrity and some of the guys looked at him as if they was figuring out whether or not they could rob him. It was dangerous for Divine to come by himself but he was a true thug that always traveled solo. He felt that the thugs in the streets needed to be protected from him and not the other way around. He parked the car, took the gun from the back of his pants and slipped it into his mink coat pocket.

He patted his other pocket to make sure he had his cell phone and stepped out of the car.

When Divine stepped out of the car, the guys that knew who he was, began jocking him. Most of them showed fear, and the ones that did not know him, had quickly gotten the word that he was definitely not the one to mess with. The girls did not care about his reputation.

They recognized that he was a big balla now and most of them would try to compete with one another to be in his presence tonight and hopefully forever. They knew being his girl would put them on top of the world and bring them nothing but respect from their peers and others in the streets.

Divine walked past the line of people waiting to get inside of the club, when he spotted one of the bouncers he knew. He walked over to the bouncer and whispered into his ear. The huge bouncer laughed, patted Divine on the back and escorted him into the club without searching him. As Divine entered the club, all eyes were on him. He noticed a few rappers were also in the club. They looked upset because his presence stole the spotlight from everyone of them. He casually walked over to an empty table and spotted five beautiful women talking to Hip-Hop's biggest superstar. Divine waved the girls over to his table. The girls walked away from the rapper, leaving him wondering, who was this guy who had damn near the whole club watching him.

The pissed off rapper and his entourage walked past the table where Divine and the girls sat, and he overheard Divine telling one of the girls, "Nah baby, don't get it twisted. I'm not a VIP nigga. That's for them faggot ass rappers and sports celebs."

The girls laughed as if he had just said the funniest thing in the world. The rapper looked at Divine as if he was ready to live out one of his songs.

Divine ordered six bottles of Cristal at six hundred bills a bottle. The rapper watched him and did the same, matching him dollar for dollar. Divine laughed and kept buying and conversing as if the rapper didn't even exist.

The speakers was blasting Fifty Cent's song "Wankster" and every so-called thug in the club added five percent more to their screw faces.

Divine noticed the rapper's bodyguard face fighting him, so he yelled out to the bodyguard, "A stupid, what the fuck you keep looking at?"

"What duke?" asked the bodyguard with his face screwed up. "You talking to me nigga?"

"Yeah, I'm talking to you, stupid," answered Divine. "You big dumb fuck. Here I am trying to enjoy my motherfucking self and you looking in my face like you wanna suck my dick or something, nigga."

The bodyguard became enraged and had a look of murder in his eyes. He grabbed a glass of wine from a girl, walked towards Divine and threw the drink in his face. Divine grabbed for his gun but the club's bouncers quickly reacted, as the five girls quickly got up and backed away from Divine's table.

"Yo Divine," said the bouncer who had escorted him in. "Yo, please don't shoot that nigga in here. The other bouncers know you're peoples, so we ain't gonna throw you out. Just please do not shoot that nigga in here. He just don't know who you are."

The rapper started laughing and began talking to the girls who were just sitting with Divine. "Baby, I told y'all I'm that nigga," said the rapper. "Who's a thug baby? That nigga tried to diss my man Big Bear? My boy don't give a fuck about that motherfucker!"

Divine wiped his face with his hand and looked the bouncer holding him back in the eyes and said, "Yo, that nigga is dead. He just signed his death certificate."

"Damn Divine," said the bouncer. "I know he's a dead man, but please just don't do it here. Plus this place is full of witnesses."

"You're right kid," said Divine, as he sat back into his chair. "Don't worry, I won't do nothin in here. You got my word on that."

The bouncer walked away from Divine with a worried look on his face because he knew how Divine can get.

Divine pulled his cell phone from his pocket and made a phone call, as the rapper and his entourage continued to party and laugh. After a few minutes of yelling into the phone, Divine hung up and ordered another bottle of Cristal. But instead of opening this bottle, he had it sent over to the bodyguard Big Bear.

Big Bear approached Divine's table and said, "Yo, you sent me this bottle kid?"

"Yeah homie," said Divine. "It's sort of an apology. I was way out of line. I never should've invited you to my dick. That shit ain't cool, dig?"

"Yeah son," said Big Bear as he sipped from the bottle. "I just came home from up north and we didn't play that up there."

"You right homie," said Divine. "No beef?"

"Nah, it ain't no beef," said Big Bear as he extended his hand. Divine gave him a five, smiled and said, "I like your style homie."

Big Bear laughed and then turned around and walked away.

Divine finished enjoying his night out, full with drinking and dancing. He was leaving the club when he saw the rapper, Big Bear and a few other guys leaving too. When he made it outside, he walked over to Big Bear and said, "Yo stay up homie" and they shook hands again.

No one noticed the two members of the Bulldog Crew until it was too late. They pulled out their forty-four bulldogs and shot Big Bear in the face damn near blowing his whole head off. Divine made a quick escape. As he pulled away in his Bentley, he saw the rapper crouched over crying and vomiting.

Chapter Thirty-Two

Gloria was truly enjoying herself in Jamaica. This was the first time she had ever left New York. She was born and raised in Brooklyn and her travel had been limited to the five boroughs. When she moved to the Lafayette Gardens Housing Projects, she met a tall, handsome, smooth-talking brother that also lived in the building. It wasn't long before they became an item. Shortly after, she became pregnant and eventually gave birth to a beautiful little boy she named Kenny. Kenny's father began sniffing dope and supported his habit by robbing people. At any given time, Gloria could look out of her bedroom window and see her son's father, Georgie, buying a bag of dope or trying to sell something on Dekalb Avenue.

She often wondered what had caused him to change so much. When they first met, he was very respectful, polite and always had money in his pockets. But one day, he made a sudden change and Gloria did not know where this new person had come from. People in the projects had tried to warn her that Georgie was no good, but she could not see him that way until one day a hundred dollars was missing from her rent money. She went outside to look for him and when she got to the back of her building, she could hardly believe her eyes. Georgie was sitting on a bench wearing dirty clothes, going into a nod. Gloria had never felt so embarrassed in her life. She had seen enough dopefiends in her life to know that Georgie was high on heroin. She walked towards him and yelled angrily at him. "What the hell are you doing to yourself and where is my money?!"

Georgie looked at her through glazed eyes and said, "What the fuck you talkin bout? Go upstairs, I'll be there in a minute to give you this dope dick. You know you want it."

Gloria could hardly believe her ears. This was the first time Georgie had ever talked to her that way. She looked at the man she loved and suddenly all of her anger dissipated. Her face softened and she quietly said, "Georgie, baby, I can't do this. Since I've known you,

I have never asked you where your money comes from. I never disrespected you and I have truly loved you."

She sat next to him on the bench, stroked his head and continued.

"But I love my baby Kenny more. I refuse to let you hurt him because of this foolishness you are involved in out in these streets."

Georgie looked at her and smiled.

"Nothing won't happen to Kenny. That's my little nigga right there and if any of these punks around here even think about hurting my boy, I'll put a cap in their ass. Now come on, let's go upstairs."

They walked into the building and made their way back into the apartment. They made up by making love and Gloria hated herself for it because she knew Georgie would continue with his behavior. Their being together didn't last long. During one of Georgie's robberies, things got out of control and he ended up killing his victim. He was quickly caught by the police and was sentenced to thirty years to life. Their relationship was over and Gloria was not going to waste any more time on him. She always told him to leave the streets alone and get his life together but he didn't listen, so she was not pausing her life for him.

After he left, all she did was go to work as a home attendant, come home and spend her time with her baby Kenny, after picking him up from the babysitter. Even as a baby, she talked to him as if he was a man and made sure they were able to communicate with each other about anything. She didn't bring men she dated around her son and before she knew it, he was a teenager always telling her about all of the pretty girls he was seeing. She always told him to respect women and if he slipped up and got any girl pregnant, he better do right by her. When her son Kenny died, she didn't even think about a man until she met the handsome mystery man that Richard called Omega. He made her feel so alive and loved. Before him, only her son Kenny made her feel so special and now he was gone.

$

Gloria was having the time of her life in Jamaica. She and Omar were staying at a beautiful resort in Negril and everyday was spent doing something new and exciting. They even explored the different ways of making love as the days went forward. She relaxed in a beach chair by the pool doing a crossword puzzle. She was startled when she heard Omar's voice.

"Hey mon, what are you doing?" asked Omar with a smile. He stood in front of her with drops of water cascading down his chiseled abdomen. "I thought you were coming into the water with me. Don't tell me you're tired of me already," he said.

Gloria smiled and looked adoringly into his eyes.

"Not hardly. But I was wondering how long will all of this last."

Gloria was beautiful. She had on a two-piece sky blue bathing suit, her long hair in a ponytail and she wore a light bluish pair of shades. And she was smelling good wearing the Gucci women's fragrance she loved wearing.

"What do you mean, how long will this last?" asked Omar as he lifted her legs and placed them on his lap to sit down on the beach chair.

"I mean," Gloria paused before she continued on. "I'm falling in love with you and I don't want this to end. But I know there's a possibility that it can end as quickly as it began."

"Baby, just love me," smiled Omar before he leaned in and kissed her gently on the nose. "If it ends, I shall leave you in possession of the feeling."

"Oh, how romantic, but that's not what I mean. I don't want it to end. I couldn't take another broken heart. I was with Kendu's father for three years. I gave my heart to that man and he never loved me. He left me with my baby and now my baby is also gone. Sometimes, I feel so empty. But you've brought the happiness back into my life and I don't ever want to lose that. I don't want to lose you. Omar, remember the first time we met?"

Omar smiled as he thought about the first time they met.

Richard had just beaten his case and called to give Omar the good news, in case he hadn't heard it already from Lisa. He told Omar that he was staying in Lafayette Gardens and would like to talk to him in person, so he went to the projects to see Richard. Omar knocked on the door of the apartment where Richard were staying and could hardly believe his eyes when Gloria answered the door. She was so gorgeous that he opened his mouth to speak, but no words came. He was speechless and had forgotten who he'd came to see. It was a good thing Richard came to the door and told him to come in. He entered the apartment and talked to Gloria for so long that he and Richard never got the chance to speak that day. He and Gloria had so much in common that before he left her apartment that day, he was already calling her his woman.

"You're as beautiful as the first day I saw you," answered Omar with a smile. "Pretty lady, I'm not going anywhere. I'm in this relationship for keeps. I love you. Now come on."

Omar grabbed her hand, stood up and led her to the nude section of the beach. It was getting dark as they made their way to the water. There were a few people still on the beach but for the first time in her life Gloria did not care. She pushed Omar away from her, took off her bathing suit and ran into the water laughing.

Omar looked around at the envious men and women. Smiling, he shrugged his broad shoulders, took off his trunks and ran into the water after her. He disappeared under the water and she felt him exploring her private parts before coming up for air. They were waist deep in the water and Omar looked into her eyes with his strong arms wrapped around her waist and began kissing her. The few people still on the beach watched them make love. Gloria came again and again with her legs wrapped around Omar's waist.

A fat middle-aged butt-naked white guy yelled out, "Hey you two, get a hotel room, for crying out loud."

Omar and Gloria laughed while walking out of the water holding hands as the few people on the beach applauded them. After putting their bathing suits back on, they headed to their hotel room. They reached their room and Omar looked at Gloria and asked, "What do you wanna do tonight, baby?"

"I was thinking after we eat we can go dancing. I heard there's some kind of party in the dining area tonight."

She then gave him her brightest smile.

"But first let's get this shower going. Baby, you are truly Superman."

"Yeah, you made me put a lot of work in, out there," said Omar taking off his swimming trunks and heading towards the bathroom with a smile on his face.

Gloria laughed and followed him to the shower peeling out of her bathing suit.

After freshening up and changing their clothes, they finally made it down to the hotel's restaurant. Omar ate the seafood salad with a glass of Alize Cognac on the rocks. And Gloria had the prime rib and a virgin pina colada. They were the perfect couple. They enjoyed the delicious meal and then headed to the party off the main dining area. All day, people in the hotel were talking about the party like it was going to be Jamaica's greatest event. They arrived hand in hand at the door of the party. Before the door even opened you could hear the sounds of Sean Paul singing, "Give me the light."

They pushed the big quilted door open and when they entered, the party was already in full swing. The room was big and it looked as if it were spring break. There were so many college kids dancing with their shirts off and drinking.

Gloria inched closer to Omar when she felt someone touch her arm. The party was off the hook. A few NBA basketball players stood near the DJ booth with a gang of female groupies willing to do anything requested.

Gloria had never seen so many different nationalities in one room in her life. Whites, Blacks, Latinos and Chinese people partied, laughed, conversed, hugged and kissed as if racism never existed.

Gloria smiled at the sight. The DJ put on Missy Elliot's song, "Work it" and Omar pulled Gloria by the hand onto the dance floor.

It was obvious that Omar hadn't danced since the mid-eighties by the way he was dancing. When he did the wop, Gloria busted out laughing.

"What are you doing?" she asked with a smile. "This is not the eighties, baby."

"What?" asked Omar with a smirk on his face as he continued dancing. "I'm the best dancer in here."

Gloria laughed and said, "No baby, you're not. Stick to the Brooklyn gangster dance."

"The Brooklyn gangster who?" asked Omar.

"You know," answered Gloria. "When gangsters in Brooklyn go to parties, they're too gangster to dance so they do the unofficial two step."

"The unofficial two step?"

"Yeah, I'll show you. They do it like this."

Gloria put one foot forward and brought it back with a real mean look on her face and then did the same thing with the other foot. Omar bust out laughing holding his stomach. When he was finally able to stop laughing, he said, "Baby, you're a trip. I love that about you. You're not afraid to show your true self. And who taught you the latest dance steps?"

"The best man that I ever had in my life," she answered with an expression of pain on her face. "Kendu."

Omar wrapped her up in his big, strong arms and gently rocked her slowly from side to side with her face buried in his chest. She felt so safe in his arms. She looked into his eyes and kissed him softly on the lips.

"I love you," said Omar. "And I enjoy every minute I'm with you baby."

"I love you too," Gloria whispered into Omar's ear.

When the DJ put on Nelly's song, "Hot in here" and started

rapping along with the song "It's getting hot in here, so take off all your clothes", the people in the party went bananas taking off every stitch of clothing they had on.

"Come on baby," said Omar taking Gloria's hand. "We're outta here. It's about to get crazy!"

"I'm right behind you," said Gloria as they headed for the exit.

They got back to their room still laughing at the spectacle of the party. "Did you see the white girl take off her bra and panties?" asked a wide-eyed Gloria.

"I had to see her," answered Omar laughing. "She shook her titties all in my face. I thought you was going to snuff her."

"I was," said Gloria with a frown. "She was about to get it Laila Ali style."

"Laila Ali style, huh?" asked Omar. "That's something y'all both have in common."

"What?"

"Both of you are quick to fight and both of you are too beautiful to be fighting."

"I take it you have a thing for Laila Ali."

"Yeah, but nothing like what I have for you. Plus it's only a matter of time before Laila catches a few knots on her head," smiled Omar as he laid back on the big king size bed and began staring at the ceiling.

"What are you thinking about?" asked Gloria climbing on top of him as she looked into his eyes.

"I was thinking about the future," answered Omar. "As soon as I get this record label off the ground I'm out of the game. I know you don't like what I do, and I'm getting tired of it myself baby. I see good things in my future, and I see you in my future. The drug game is over for me. I'm going to pull out of it so fast no one will even remember me being a part of it baby."

"What if certain people don't want you to leave the game yet?"

Omar smiled and said, "No mon can tell I and I what we fe do, seen? When mon try to tell I and I what we fe do, him violate, and I play for keeps."

Gloria laughed shaking her head from side to side looking at Omar. He then got serious, looked into Gloria's eyes and said, "But on a serious note, will you marry me?"

Gloria stared at him for a moment and then the tears fell as she answered, "Yes, I will marry you."

She leaned over, kissed Omar hungrily and began to undress the man she loved.

Chapter Thirty-Three

"That stupid little bitch. Didn't she know who the fuck I am," Shameek thought to himself as he sat alone on the bench in the middle of the Fort Greene projects. Two days ago he went up to Monique's apartment and questioned her about the looks of the housing worker that killed T-bone. When Shameek first heard about T-bone, he wanted to murder the first person that looked at him wrong. But he had to stay focused. It was the only way to get the person responsible for killing his friend if it was the last thing he did. He knew a lot of people were glad that T-bone had been killed. They were celebrating quietly. You could see the happiness in their faces. Someone had finally done what they were too afraid to do. When the word got out that it was someone in a housing uniform, everyone had wondered who the very intelligent hit man could be. Names of thugs from all over Brooklyn were thrown around in the streets and throughout the prisons. Especially the Bulldog Crew and some even said Moe-dog. And every time the name Bishop was mentioned, it was him paying someone to do it because no one believed that he had the heart or brains to do something like that.

When T-bone was killed, Shameek was in Philadelphia. One of his workers called him on his cell phone. He reached in his pocket to take out the ringing cell phone. "Hello?"

"Yo, Shameek, this is little Dee," said the obviously shaken young man on the other end. "They got 'em, they got 'em."

"Slow the fuck down nigga," said Shameek calmly. "Who got who?"

"They got T-bone man," the guy cried into the phone. "He... Somebody killed him in Monique's crib. There's police everywhere down here in the projects. We had to shut down shop for a minute. A yo..."

Shameek hung up the phone, got into his car and hurried back to New York. There was no doubt about it, someone was going to pay for this.

"What do you mean T-bone is dead? T-bone can not die," he told himself over and over on his way back to New York. He would gather up his little soldiers and kill whoever was responsible for killing T-bone and that was all there was to it. He wanted to know about the person that killed his right hand man and Monique was going to tell him everything she knew.

Shameek sat down on the couch in Monique's living room. She had on a long white tee-shirt and French cut lace panties. He noticed that she kept flirting with him but he had no interest in having sex with her. Not right now anyway. The only thing he had on his mind was murder. Of course, T-bone had a lot of enemies, but the only one that kept coming to Shameek's mind was Richard. He heard all about Richard's climb in the game. He now knew he underestimated the young quiet churchboy. Already he lost two of his most dangerous comrades to a young boy that just came out of the house. But Shameek still felt that it would be a matter of time before he and his soldiers would catch up to Richard. And when he did, he would make sure to dump every bullet he had into him.

"So how the fuck do the nigga look, Mo?"

"I told you before," said Monique licking her lips. "He was dark-skinned with dreads, The same shit I told the police."

"And where the fuck you was at when my nigga got killed?"

"I was in the bathroom. The housing man was checking the radiators so I didn't think nothing of it. When I came out of the bathroom nothing looked out of order. I mean Shameek, I didn't even hear a shot. And then I walked to the bedroom and," Monique said tearfully. "When I entered the bedroom, I saw him lying in a pool of blood on my bed. I couldn't believe it. That's when I called 9-1-1."

"You ain't hear no motherfucking shots? Unfucking believable! To me it sounds like you was down with the whole shit. That's why I don't trust none of y'all bitches around here."

"What nigga?!" yelled Monique angrily. "I don't get down like that! I don't have to put up with this bullshit! Get out my house motherfucker!"

"Who the fuck you talking to like that?" asked Shameek as he stood up from the couch with his face screwed up.

"You don't scare me!" yelled Monique. "I don't give a flying-"

Suddenly he swung at Monique before she could finish speaking. His large fist hit her squarely on the chin, knocking her over the small table sitting in front of the couch. Monique landed flat on her back and struggled to get up from Shameek's blow.

As she tried to kick, yell and get up, Shameek stomped and kicked her in the face like he was playing soccer. Blood dripped from Monique's nose and mouth. In her last struggle to get up, Shameek pulled her white blood stained tee-shirt around her neck and began to strangle her. In her attempt to breathe and fight, Monique kicked and tried to scratch as her big titties swung from side to side violently. She then pissed on herself as Shameek applied more pressure. And then Monique went limp. He removed the tee-shirt from Monique's lifeless body.

He used the tee-shirt to open her front door, threw it down the incinerator and casually walked, down the stairs to leave the building.

$

Two days later, Shameek sat on the bench, deep in thought and full of rage about the recent events. He had just finished distributing drugs to his workers on Park Avenue, and he was contemplating re-upping his other workers on Myrtle Avenue. He just couldn't get Omar out of his mind. 'I know that nigga Omega is behind that Bishop kid. It ain't nothing, that punk nigga Omega is gonna get his too. He wanna fuck wit' me and then try to pull outta the game? I'll kill that nigga and his whole family. My team's doing it and his team's getting weak as fuck. And I heard about those 44 boys. They get busy but like I always say, kill the head and the body is dead,' Shameek thought.

It was 8am on a Sunday morning, so no one was around. Most were still resting from what Saturday night offered. His thoughts were interrupted, as he saw Lisa walking into her mother's building. Shameek got off the bench and ran top speed to the building. She entered the building and as she reached the staircase, someone grabbed her arm from behind. Startled, Lisa swung her pocketbook as hard as she could to get the stranger off her. Shameek blocked the pocketbook and spun her around so they were face-to-face .

"What's up Lisa baby?" smiled Shameek. "This is the kind of greeting I get nowadays?"

"Oh my God, Shameek," said Lisa with her hand over her heart. "You scared the shit out of me. What the fuck you doing sneaking up on me like that for?"

Shameek began to laugh, ignoring her question.

"Lisa baby, what's popping? Can I get some love or what?"

"Boy my love is for my husband."

"Your husband?" asked Shameek with a confused look.

"Yeah, I'm married now," said Lisa flashing her diamond ring with a smile on her face. "And I love my baby."

"Who you married to?"

He already knew the answer, but he was seriously hoping that he was wrong this time. He became so angry that pictures of Rashien, T-bone and Monique flashed in his head. Three of his people were dead because of Lisa, he thought to himself. He was the one that killed Monique, but he had rationalized, that was because of Lisa too.

"Who you married to?" Shameek asked again.

"Shameek, you know who I'm married to. Stop acting stupid."

"You married my enemy?" asked Shameek enraged.

"Boy, y'all need to stop this nonsense," answered Lisa. "I don't know why y'all just-"

Shameek knocked her backwards onto the steps with a hard punch to the side of her head.

"You stupid motherfucker!" yelled Lisa as she fell on the steps, tears streaming down her face. "I'm telling my brother!"

When Lisa tried to get up, Shameek hit her with a left hook to the side of her face and his right hand followed to her ribs making her collapse back onto the stairs. She had never felt so much pain before. He then grabbed her by the neck.

"You think I give a fuck about your punk ass brother?" he asked through clenched teeth. "I run this side of the projects bitch! You wanna fuck with the enemy, huh?"

Shameek reached with his free hand under Lisa's skirt and pulled until her panties ripped clean away from her body. He threw the shreds of her panties to the ground and pulled out his penis. Lisa tried to yell and defend herself, but the pressure from his hand on her neck was too much. Shameek entered her with full force of anger and pumped and pumped and pumped.

Chapter Thirty-Four

Moe-dog and Whitey pulled into a parking lot in a brown four-door Dodge, To every street hustler, the sight of this team spelled police. They saw Gina getting out of the white CLK Benz that Divine gave her for her birthday. She was about to enter Carolina's Kitchen on Atlantic Avenue, but was abruptly stopped near the door. She had been craving the delicious food but had quickly lost her appetite, when Whitey flashed his forged badge in her face and grabbed her arm.

"Excuse me miss, are you Gina Randall?" asked Whitey.

"Yeah, that's me. Why?" Gina answered with an attitude.

She looked so good that Moe-dog wanted to step to her, but this was business so he pulled back and let Whitey continue with the interrogation.

"You're under arrest for conspiracy to distribute and sell narcotics," said Whitey.

"I ain't do shit!" said Gina with her hands on her hip. "So y'all do what the fuck y'all gotta do!"

"Miss, please put your hands behind your back."

Gina put her hands behind her back and Whitey slapped handcuffs on her delicate wrist. They knew they would have to hurry up and get her out of the area before the real police drove by. There weren't too many people in the restaurant yet, so they did not have to worry about a crowd forming. Moe-dog and Whitey then escorted her to the brown Dodge and put her in the back seat. They entered the car and drove off.

"You didn't read me my rights!" snapped Gina.

"Your rights?" asked Whitey. "You have the right to answer my fucking questions. Do you have kids?"

Gina didn't say anything, so Whitey continued.

"Well I have kids, and you're selling drugs to children to keep you in minks and Benzes, huh? By the time you come home they'll have the new Benz that fly in the air. Them big dykes up in Bedford Hills are waiting for your pretty ass to come through. You may not have a pussy by the time they're done with you."

"Why don't you just shut the fuck up and get me to the precinct already?" said Gina.

"Bitch, I'll get you to the fucking precinct alright," said Whitey.

"Hey be easy on the lady," said Moe-dog speaking for the first time. "Pull over on that side block."

Whitey pulled over to the curb as Moe-dog twisted his body over the front seat so he could speak with Gina. He loved her attitude towards the police and the fire that she had in her eyes. She had a look as if she was ready to die for the ones she loved. Moe-dog hadn't seen that look in a woman's eyes in a very long time. Every girl he had been with was afraid of thugs and was afraid of the police even more, but Gina seemed different. He was determined to see how far she would go before breaking down and telling them everything.

"Look," said Moe-dog. "Excuse my partner here. I don't want to take you in, and you're way too pretty to be doing a hundred years for someone else. We know you don't have a job. You're in college and you can't afford the new Mercedes Benz you got out of. You have my word on it, we'll let you go. All we're asking you is, are you aware that Divine is selling drugs?"

"I ain't telling y'all shit! Fuck y'all! I ain't no snitch, y'all can kiss my ass! And why the fuck you keep looking at me like you wanna lick my asshole or something?! You Uncle Tom bastard!"

"Drive," Moe-dog told a laughing Whitey as he turned around to face the front. Inwardly, he smiled to himself, admiring the strength of Gina. Why he couldn't find a girl like that? But he knew once they got to the garage, she would break down and tell everything. As they pulled into the garage, Gina knew something was wrong. This was not a police station.

"Where the fuck you taking me?" asked Gina beginning to get scared. "I heard about y'all crooked cops. This is really fucked up!"

They took her out of the car and the first thing she saw was the chair in the middle of the garage. They made her sit in the chair and when she sat down she looked at the floor and saw stains of blood and what appeared to be teeth.

"Listen bitch. Let's try this again," said Whitey. "Where does your man keep his money?"

"I don't know what you're talking about," said Gina. "I don't have a man."

"Don't play games with me!" Whitey said angrily. "We know all about you and Divine."

Gina knew these crooked cops would not be satisfied with any information she would give them. They would still kill her or put her in jail. Gina hated snitches more than anything, so no matter what happened to her, she made up her mind not to tell them anything. She saw many snitches in her projects get killed for telling on someone and even after they were dead and gone, people in the streets laughed about their death and their names were never spoken of with honor or kindness. It was like being killed again and again and again. Gina never wanted to die that kind of death and she knew she had no control over how long she lived, but she definitely had control over how she lived. So she made up her mind to live with honor even if it was to end in two minutes.

Moe-dog sat a human skull on her lap, threatened her, yelled at her, and tried everything possible without physically assaulting her to get her to spill; but Gina remained strong. The average nineteen year old girl would have cried, told everything and would possibly have been mentally scarred for life. But not Gina, seeing her mother die from a heroin overdose at sixteen, Gina felt that she could take almost anything. With her mother gone, it was just her and her older sister who she did not see eye to eye with. When her mother passed away, her sister Natalie took care of her, but they rarely spoke because they had nothing in common. Natalie was a white woman in a black woman's body. She only dated white men that never attempted to help her out of the projects and she looked down on every black person that did not think like she did. She was so far gone, that she believed everything that she heard on the news and was quick to side with the police whenever she heard about an altercation involving blacks and police officers. Gina knew her sister was very brainwashed, so instead of wasting her time arguing or debating with her she stayed as far away from her as possible to avoid a fight. It was the happiest day of Gina's life when she moved out of the small Fort Greene apartment she shared with her sister to move in with Divine. Gina loved living with Divine, and most of all she loved him. She looked at the two crooked cops standing in front of her and at that moment realized that she would die for him if she had to.

"I'm going to give you one more chance," said Moe-dog. "And if you don't cooperate, I'm going to kill you nice and slow. Now, are you aware that Divine is a drug dealer?"

"You know what?" asked Gina with an attitude. "Do what the fuck you have to do, because I'm not telling you shit!"

Moe-dog went to the car and came back with a black plastic bag. He put it over Gina's head so she couldn't see. She then was led back to the car and Moe-dog laid her head on his lap as his partner Whitey got into the driver's seat and drove out of the garage.

Gina knew she was going to die. She wondered how they would kill her. Would they shoot her or stab her to death? Would they set her on fire? Would they rape her before killing her? Would they pour acid all over her body after she was dead to get rid of the evidence? Would they let her body float in the lake? All of these questions were going through her head as the car drove on.

She wondered why the two crooked cops had become so quiet. She could feel one of them rubbing her head through the plastic bag in soft caressing motions. It wasn't long before the car stopped and Gina was being led out of the car. She felt the handcuffs being removed from her wrist and she waited for the gunshots to follow. She made no attempts to pull the black bag from her head. She did not want to see when they pulled the trigger. Tears rolled down her face as she heard a car drive away. She then heard the laughter of children. She removed the plastic bag from her head and realized she was standing back in front of Carolina's Kitchen. Her appetite was completely gone and she desperately wanted to be home. She hoped that Divine would be there as she wiped the tears from her eyes. Gina got into her car and drove away, obviously shaken, but determined to stay strong. She had no idea the skull that sat on her lap earlier was actually Ant-live's. She wanted to get home, relax and put the day's event behind her, once and for all.

Gina entered her home and hung her mink coat in the walk-in closet. She sat on the beautiful plush green couch and took off her Prada boots. She put on slippers and walked into her spacious kitchen. As she made her way around the kitchen, she saw a small note hanging from the refrigerator.

"Baby I was waiting for you to come home but I had to go out and take care of something. I'll see you when I get home. I love you boo. Hit me on the cell when you get in."

Daddy Big Dick Divine

Gina folded the note and smiled. She opened the small green box on the counter, took out a blunt and then lit it. She knew she would have the munchies afterwards so she decided to cook after taking a long nice hot bath. As she smoked her blunt she thought about calling Divine to warn him about the two crooked cops, but hesitated. She couldn't put her finger on why they seemed so peculiar. She stood standing with the phone in her hand deciding on what to do. The phone began to ring and she answered it immediately.

"Hello?...What's wrong?...Why you sound like that?...What happened?...Shameek did what to you?!" Gina yelled into the phone. "I'll be right there!"

Gina hung up the phone, put her boots back on, grabbed her coat and keys and ran out of the house with the blunt still in her mouth.

Chapter Thirty-Five

The comedy club in Atlanta was off the hook, it reminded you of Comic View on BET. There were so many beautiful women in the audience, and the ten best looking ones sat on stage at small tables. The ballas, players and regular men were also in attendance enjoying themselves. The comedians performing kept looking at Pam wondering how the club missed her, because she was definitely better looking than any of the women sitting on stage. They were all bad, but Pam easily outshined them. She sat in the front row, looking lovely as ever next to her man Big Gee, who was rocking a pair of white and blue shell toe Adidas.

Big Gee didn't really care for sneakers too much but earlier that day he told Pam that he was wearing them in memory of Jam Master Jay from the legendary rap group RUN DMC. He told Pam how years ago he remembered being in Jamaica, Queens when a few guys had him surrounded about to rob him when Jam Master Jay saw what was going on, got out of his car and approached the group of thugs. Knowing all of them, he told them to chill and black men had to stop killing and robbing one another for the little things that they possessed. Big Gee walked away untouched that day and he was grateful that Jam Master Jay had stepped up for him.

They sat in the front row of seats. The comedy club held over two hundred and fifty seats, and they were all occupied. The rap group Out-kast and a few other celebrities were also in attendance. All of the comedians were funny, but there was one who stood out. Tammy Green had just received a standing ovation because she was the funniest so far. The host of the show came out and the crowd applauded him. His name was Ramel Thompson and he held up his hands for the audience to stop applauding so he can speak and introduce the last comedian for the night.

"I'm glad to see you motherfuckers enjoying yourselves. Now we bring to you our last and very talented comedian. You may have seen him on Def Comedy Jam or in the best movie out there right now starring Sandra Bullock. Without further ado, please put your motherfucking hands together for the one and only Mr. Joe 'Funny Man' Fletcher!"

The audience clapped, yelled and laughed before he even came out on stage. Joe Fletcher was a very funny man and he always made fun of those in the audience. He was dark-skinned, tall, slim and swore he was God's gift to women. He wore all white. Even his hard bottom shoes were white.

"Damn! My people look good in this motherfucker tonight. But some of you are some ugly motherfuckers and I ain't lying." The audience looked around at each other, laughed and clapped. "Look at this nigga," continued Joe Fletcher pointing at a guy wearing pimp clothes. "He look like Bishop Don Magic Juan on crack. He sold his cup for a blast before he came in here. Bishop strong faggot gone. And look at this skinny nigga here," he said pointing at another guy in the audience. "Looking like a back in the day ten-cent icey."

The audience was in tears laughing at the guys Joe Fletcher was picking on, "Oh shit, I see we have Out—Kast in the house," he continued as the crowd applauded for the ATL legends. "I love y'all niggas. What's up Big Boi? Tell the truth nigga. You get embarrassed as hell being with old crazy ass dressing Dre. The nigga got on a yellow hat, a blue shirt, orange pants and red bowling shoes. Where you shop at nigga, Weirdo's R Us?"

The audience was rolling in their seats. Even Dre laughed and waved his hand at the comedian. Suddenly, Joe Fletcher saw Pam sitting in the front row and said , "Damn baby, you look good as fuck. Might be the best looking woman up in here. Bitch, what strip club you work at?"

"Your broke J.J. Evans looking ass couldn't even afford this pussy nigga!" Pam yelled out before the audience could drown her out with their laughter.

"Oh, you trying to come back?" asked Joe Fletcher. He then

looked to the back of the curtains and said, "Somebody please come out here and give this bitch a mic, being that she loves to have things close up to her mouth. This is going to be fun."

A fat white man came from the back of the stage and handed Pam a mic. Big Gee looked at Pam like she was crazy because she didn't refuse the microphone. She took it with a smile as the audience laughed and clapped.

Big Gee knew Pam would get embarrassed tonight because Joe Fletcher was a very funny professional comedian. He looked around hoping that he could grab Pam's hand and make it to the quickest exit, but that would really put him out there to get joked on, so he slid down in his chair hoping that Joe Fletcher would not recognize that he was with Pam, and get on him as well.

"Girl, if your pussy is as big as your mouth, you are ruined baby," said Joe Fletcher.

The crowd roared with laughter and when it died down, Pam said, "If your dick is bigger than your mouth give me your number nigga. Wait a minute, I can tell how big you are from your shoes. Ladies, the nigga still wearing infant walkers."

The audience was bent over in laughter looking at his white hard-bottomed shoes. Even the show's promoter was laughing and wiping tears from his eyes.

Joe Fletcher smiled and said, "My dick is four inches, but that's from the floor bitch."

The audience laughed and then Pam said, "You chubby head motherfucker, if you do got a big dick you ain't got enough ass to sink that motherfucker with."

The women in the audience were in tears laughing at Joe. He looked around nervously and started saying old jokes aimed at Pam.

"This bitch is so dumb I told her to take the four train, and she took the two train twice."

The crowd laughed and then Pam said, "Your teeth are so yellow Joe, every time you smile traffic slows down."

The crowd erupted in laughter. Joe Fletcher looked at the crowd and said, "The bitch is so dumb, she cook Minute rice for hours."

The audience laughed at the old joke.

Pam smiled and asked, "Your black ashy ass got jokes? Joe, has anybody ever told you that you look like a struck match, motherfucker?"

The audience was rolling in their seats laughing so much that the fat white man had to come back out and save Joe Fletcher by taking the mic back from Pam.

Joe Fletcher said a few more funny jokes but he did not aim any of them at Pam. He knew the audience would want to hear what this talented woman had to say back to him and he knew it would not look good if he continued to get on Pam without her being able to respond. He was upset that the man took the mic from her, but something told him Pam would have killed him if he continued to go back and forth. His ego was badly bruised. Wasn't he Joe Fletcher, the funniest comedian around? He told himself that he would never do what he had done tonight in a club again.

Joe Fletcher looked out to the crowd and said, "Thank you for coming out. I had a good time tonight and I hope you all had a good time too. Y'all have a good night."

He then turned to walk off stage and glanced at Pam over his shoulder. The DJ put on TLC's song, "Girl Talk" as the crowd exited the club. On the way out, people stopped Pam to give her crazy props. She smiled it off and continued to walk hand in hand with Big Gee who was still laughing.

Pam was no stranger to cracking jokes on people and making them laugh. She came from a very funny family. Her mother and father were very humorous and naturally it was passed down to their five children. Pam had two older brothers and two younger sisters. Growing up, whenever they were bored the Jones' house would turn into Def Comedy Jam. After graduating high school, Pam got a job at Bell Atlantic Telephone Company. She made extra money doing hookups for a few people, selling phone numbers they did not have to pay the bill for. She was also boosting, dealing with credit cards and every other small time scheme that brought in the money. She was now twenty years old and had her own place in the Flatbush section of Brooklyn. But being that her friends and family were still in Fort Greene, most of her time was spent in the projects. Pam, Tonya, Lisa and Gina went to public school, junior high school and graduated from Boys and Girls High School together, but only Lisa and Gina decided to go to college. That was not for Pam. She did not see the point in paying all of that money to attend school and after graduating only possibly being able to find a good job. She knew a lot of unemployed college graduates.

Now they were talking about how bad the economy was and despite what the politicians were saying, people were desperately trying to find work more than ever before. The government had the nerve to raise taxes and fare hikes as if people had it like that. Pam was so disgusted with the governor and mayor that she wondered how anyone could vote for them year after year for doing nothing. All they did was offer empty promises and spend more money on prisons instead of education and employment. And whenever it was election time again, they would play on the people's emotions by mentioning their support for the families of those who died in the World Trade Center tragedy. She was tired of hearing it.

Pam was still young so she figured she had plenty of time to decide what she wanted to do with her life. But just because Pam did not go to college didn't mean that she was not a smart person. Talking to her, you would think she knew about everything. And even when she didn't know about something you would still think she did. With her winsome little smile, she would say the first thing that came to her mind, but made it sound so terribly accurate. Pam liked to play mind games and she always came out ahead. She hadn't been in New York in almost a year and she was definitely missing the Big Apple. Especially the fast traffic, the faster men, and of course her three best friends.

Big Gee did not spend too much time with her. He stayed on the move getting his hustle on. Even though some of the men down in Atlanta were handsome and wanted to talk to the beautiful, fly sexy New York girl, Pam gave conversation to none of them. Most of them were too slow with thick southern accents and a mouth full of played out gold teeth. New York finished with that fad long ago, Pam thought to herself. The people down here spoke to you in the streets whether they knew you or not and Pam just was not used to that. If she didn't know you she preferred not to say anything to you. Some would say it was rude, but Pam figured it was just the New York way. Atlanta was beautiful but it wasn't for her. The best time she had down there was when Big Gee taught her how to ride his Honda CBR929RR motorcycle. The bike was red, black and white and Pam bought a red and white outfit that clung to her every delicious curve as she rode all over the ATL. But she still could not wait to get back to New York City. She had been down in the south for way too long, she thought as she packed her luggage to go back home. She was waiting for Big Gee to come back from his last run. One thing was for sure, he had made a killing down here on the drug side, she thought. Pam looked at the gold Gucci bracelet watch with the gold dial Big Gee bought her and wondered why he was late. They had to be at the airport in two hours and Pam was not trying to miss her flight for anyone. She took off her clothes and headed for the shower.

In the shower, she started thinking about what her sister had told her over the phone the night before. She told Pam how Richard was no longer the nerdy churchboy and that Lisa had married him. That blew Pam's mind and she couldn't believe her ears when she heard that Richard went to jail for killing the notorious killer Rashien. Not the big time gangster Rashien, she thought to herself with a smile. She knew his day was coming, but Richard was the last one she thought would do it. Pam left New York right after Kendu was killed. All of this was news to her, especially that Richard had beaten his case and was now one of the biggest drug dealers in Brooklyn. She was also shocked to hear that T-bone had been killed. All of this was too much, Pam just had to get back to Brooklyn. Thinking about Lisa, Gina and Tonya made her want to hurry up and get back even more.

Pam got out of the shower, dried off with the big red bath towel that was hanging on the back of the bathroom door and then walked into the bedroom. She sat on the bed and grabbed her Neutrogena body oil and applied it all over her body. Then she put on a white thong and bra before putting on her deodorant. She knew it would be cold in New York and she was not changing on the plane so she put on a wool-blend blouse, a wool skirt with a seamed back, a pair of black knee-high Prada boots and she grabbed her distressed leather jacket off of the bed and sat in the chair at the foot of the bed. She then put her Prada shielding balm on her lips and sprayed on some Chanel's Chance perfume.

As soon as she was about to reach for the phone, Big Gee walked into the room. Pam put the phone down and said, "Come on, we have to get out of here."

"What's up baby girl?" asked Big Gee with a smile. "Damn, we got time. I ain't even pack my clothes yet."

"I did it for you. Your luggage is on the other side of the bed."

Big Gee looked on the other side of the bed and sure enough, his clothes were sitting there in the Louis Vuitton luggage.

Big Gee laughed and said, "Damn, you feening to get back to New York. Yo, I had mad fun at the comedy club last night. I knew you were funny but I didn't know you were that damn funny. You should really think about being a comedian."

Pam screwed up her pretty face and said, "I don't have time to be no fucking comedian. Now let's hurry up and get the fuck outta here."

She was tired of people telling her to be a comedian all of the time. She cursed Joe Fletcher out under her breath for making her snap on him. The only time she felt comfortable making people laugh was when she was around her friends and family.

"Come on Gee," continued Pam. "Let's get outta here!"

"What you in a rush for Pam? A nigga in New York waiting on you or what?"

"Yeah, a nigga waiting on me," said Pam sarcastically. "He been sitting in front of my house on my door step since I been down here. Damn, you starting to sound like these country ass niggas."

Big Gee laughed, grabbed his and her luggage, and headed for the car parked out in front.

They finally got to the airport, boarded the plane and as they sat in their seats preparing for take-off, Pam put on her CD walk man, closed her eyes and dozed off to the sounds of Lenny Kravitz greatest hits, thinking about New York.

Chapter Thirty-Six

The rich drug dealer was trapped inside of his car. It was no sense in trying to drive away. The Bulldog Crew had the car surrounded with their guns drawn. All five of the Bulldog gunmen were there. The brown-skinned six foot three baldhead guy they called Big Dave. The light-skinned five foot nine slim guy they called Light because of his complexion. The brown-skinned five foot eight chubby guy they called Fats. The brown-skinned six foot tall curly hair guy they called Tommy Guns because all he did with his money was buy more and more guns. The last one being the five foot nine stocky guy with corn-row braids named Lamont but everyone called him L for short.

Fats and Light always liked to joke around, but they were the two most dangerous out of the Bulldog Crew. They were the ones that killed the rapper's bodyguard Big Bear at the club, and they were also the ones that killed the guy in Sumner Projects. The guy name was Jimmy, and he was known in Sumner Projects for getting drug money. Plus he had caught a few bodies before. Most people did not call him Jimmy. They called him Jay for short and he really thought he was the toughest guy in the projects.

One day while chilling in the front of his building, he saw Light's girl Kia come out of the building.

He stood in front of her and said, "What's the deal Kia? Damn, you looking all good and shit. When you gonna let me tap that?"

"Boy, I'm not fucking with you," said Kia with an attitude. "I have a man and if he finds out that you pushed up on me, you might get tapped."

"You serious?!" asked Jay with his face twisted. "I ain't scared of no nigga. Mrs. Hawkin's son ain't never been scared of a motherfucker. You hear me, you stupid bitch?"

Kia didn't even answer him. She just screwed up her face and walked around him. She couldn't wait to tell Light what he said. She couldn't stand Jay anyway. He disrespected almost every girl in the projects that didn't give him any play. Like the day his man Don from Red-Hook pushed up on a girl in the projects and just because the girl didn't want to talk to Don, Jay punched her in the face knocking her out cold. And all the guys in the P.J.'s that stood around, began laughing as if that couldn't had been one of their sisters. Kia was so disgusted with them and she would make sure to tell Light what Jay said to her. It was a week later when she told Light about Jay. Light had showed no signs of anger. He laughed it off and said he'll see Jay.

Walking through Sumner Projects two days later, he and Fats saw Jay walking into his building on Park Avenue. They increased their speed and when they entered the building Jay was waiting on the elevator.

When he saw Light and Fats he didn't pull for his gun, because he didn't think they were coming for him. But when Light pulled his gun and pointed it at Jay's head he knew it was too late to pull for his own gun. He cursed himself for letting them get the drop on him.

He held up both hands and said, "What's up kid? What's the gun for? I ain't got no beef with y'all. If it's a robbery take everything, just don't kill me."

Jay thought they were coming to rob him. He forgot about the whole incident with Kia. He figured he could take a loss with a robbery and blamed himself because he slept, but he knew it would never happen again and he would seek revenge for them robbing him like this.

"Shut the fuck up, you punk ass nigga," said Fats searching him and finding the gun. "Get on the elevator coward."

The elevator door opened and Jay was hoping someone was on the elevator but was disappointed to find an empty elevator for the first time at this time of morning.

Fats shoved him inside the elevator, then he and Light stepped in behind him.

"You was trying to push up on my bitch, huh?" asked Light as they rode up to the top floor.

"Nah, I wasn't trying to talk to your girl Light," said Jay in a pleading voice.

He forgot that Kia was Light's girl. It was just one of those days when he was feeling himself, but he meant no harm by what he told Kia. But he was now too late.

Light put his gun away and pulled out two 007 knives from his black leather jacket pocket. Fats still had Jay's gun in his hand.

"You knew that was my bitch," Light said calmly. "I told y'all niggas around here don't fuck wit' me or mines, didn't I?"

"Yeah Light, but I forgot that was your-"

Light stabbed him in the eye stopping him from completing what he was trying to say.

"Ahhh!" yelled Jay falling to the elevator floor holding his eye with blood all over his hands. "I can't see, I can't see!"

Fats laughed and took the other knife from Light after putting Jay's gun in his waist. He then stabbed Jay two times in the neck. While the elevator rode to the top floor, they stabbed Jay all over his body hitting him in the head, neck, face and body. He was dead before they reached the top floor. When the elevator door opened up, Fats held it open with his back while Light continued to stab the dead body all over. They had blood all over them and knew they would have to get back to Fats's black BMW parked on Myrtle Avenue without being seen. After Light was done, he pressed all of the floors in the elevator with his forearm and they both took off running down the stairway to get out of the building.

They walked through the projects quickly, laughing and joking about how Jay screamed like a girl after getting stabbed in the eye. They got in the car and went to Fats's house to wash up and change clothes before meeting up with the rest of the Bulldog Crew.

Everyone was talking about the murder. It was the most gruesome killing in New York City in a long time and it made the front page of every major newspaper. The newspapers stated the police had very few clues about the murderers, and they were looking for the people responsible for the killing. But the police were frustrated because no one was willing to step forward with information. They even thought putting out a reward would help, but no one came with any information. All the police knew was that people in the streets were saying that the Bulldog Crew had done it, but out of fear for their own lives none cooperated. The police figured the same murderers were responsible for the Flatbush Blood killing.

Actually, it was Big Dave, Tommy Guns and L that killed seven Bloods in Flatbush. They were at Tommy Guns uncle's house on Beverly Road and East 21st Street when a sixteen year old Blood member said something to them as they were leaving the Flatbush area. They were just about to get in L's Benz. They had to meet Divine downtown near the mall and they did not have time to be wasting with the Blood's gang. They had more important things to take care of.

"Who the fuck is y'all niggas?" asked the young Blood. "And what the fuck y'all doing over here in my 'hood."

There were seven Blood members behind him leaning on cars.

"Yo shorty," said Tommy Guns. "We ain't the ones little nigga. Now take your punk ass in the house."

"What nigga?" asked the young Blood. He had his young face screwed up and when he walked closer to the Bulldog Crew the rest of the Bloods leaned up off of the cars to see what was going on.

"Y'all faggot ass niggas," said the young Blood making sure his Blood brothers heard him, "better recognize where the fuck y'all at."

Before Tommy Guns could say anything to the young Blood, Big Dave pulled out his .44 bulldog and began firing.

The young Blood died instantly with a bullet to the chest, and the rest of the Bloods went for cover pulling for their own guns. But they were easily out-matched. Tommy Guns, Big Dave and L riddled the Bloods with bullets. Only one of them got away with a bullet to the shoulder.

They knew their beef with the Bloods would never end, but they were thugs that didn't care about that. They had a lot of beef already, and the Bloods were just another group of guys on the list that wanted revenge. The Bulldog Crew were bloodthirsty murderers with money and they didn't care who they got into beef with.

That was two weeks ago and the Bloods in Flatbush and the police were out for them and the Bulldog Crew were ready for either encounter.

$

"What did I do?" asked the scared drug dealer sitting in the cranberry colored Jaguar.

"Listen bitch," smiled Fats. "Climb your punk ass in the back seat and if you try to pull out or drive off, we'll swiss cheese this car so bad, you'll be able to see your toes by just looking at the hood."

The drug dealer climbed quickly to the back of the car. He could tell by looking in Fats' eyes that he was ruthless. Light and Fats then got in the back seat with the trapped drug dealer sitting in the middle of the two.

Big Dave got into the driver's seat and Tommy Guns got in the passenger's side of the car. They drove away with L following them in his black and gold Mercedes Benz - Light and Fats searched the drug dealer in the back seat. They took a thousand dollars and a pinky ring with diamonds in it from him. It was 11:30pm on a cold Friday night and not too many people were out on the streets. It seemed as if everyone was in their houses, enjoying the warmth their homes provided. But for the Bulldog Crew, it was a beautiful and perfect night for them to pull off their murder because not many people were out in this cold weather.

When Big Dave got the call from Divine that the rich drug dealer, Pete, was at a girl's house in East New York, they all jumped inside of L's Benz and made it to the girl's house in ten minutes time. Once there they didn't come out of the shadows until Pete got behind the wheel of his brand new Jaguar. He started the car and the sounds of Jay-Z came out of the system nice and clear as if Jigga was in the back seat performing live. Just as he was about to pull out of his parking space, a guy with a big gun pointed at him stood at the driver's side window with his gun cocked back. And then four more thugs came out of the shadows brandishing guns and Pete knew if he pressed the gas pedal, he wouldn't make it a few feet before being gunned down. He took his hands off of the steering wheel as L opened the door. Pete had been robbed before, so he didn't worry about these guys robbing him. He just hoped they wouldn't kill him because he had so much to live for.

Big Dave drove the car out to Jamaica, Queens and when he got near Forty Projects, he parked the car and got out. Fats and Light also got out of the car.

After they were out, Tommy Guns spun around in his seat with his .44 pointed at the drug dealer's head and said, "What up kid? You know you outta here right?"

The drug dealer looked at Tommy Guns with pleading eyes and said, "What did I do? If it's money you want, I'll give it to you. Just don't kill me please."

"I'm not getting trapped off trying to get your money. But what I want is them three money-making dope spots you got. Them shits is pulling in a lot of paper."

"Fuck them spots," said the drug dealer. "You can have them all. What happened to the days when I was told that I couldn't sell no more and I packed up and left?"

"Them days are long gone," answered Tommy Guns.

Big Dave, Light and Fats looked into the car wondering what was taking Tommy Guns so long to kill the drug dealer. Tommy Guns looked at them holding up one finger and they turned back around watching everything in the area.

"There's only one way you can save yourself," said Tommy Guns to the drug dealer, Pete. "Tell me where money-making John rest his head."

Tears fell from the drug dealer's eyes and then he said, "That's my man but fuck it. Better him than me. He and his girl stay in a house on Jefferson and Lewis in Bed-Sty. The address is 1140. The third house from the corner."

"Thanks and oh yeah," said Tommy Guns, "You can't sell no more." He then pulled the trigger two times hitting the drug dealer in the head and chest. He put the gun in his waist and quickly grabbed his ears. They were ringing so bad it felt as if his head was going to bust open.

Fats and Light stood outside of the car laughing and cracking jokes on him. Big Dave was taking the gasoline out of the trunk of L's Benz.

When Tommy Guns got out of the car, he angrily said, "What the fuck y'all laughing at? Shit ain't funny."

They were still laughing and through his laughter Light managed to say, "You dumb motherfucker. All them guns your ass stay buying, you should've known the sound of that big ass gun would fuck your ears up. You about a dumb motherfucker. I hope you go deaf."

"Fuck you," said Tommy Guns screwing up his face as Fats and Light kept laughing.

Big Dave came towards them with the gasoline in a big metal container and said, "Won't y'all chill the fuck out for a minute, and let's take care of this business and be out. I gotta shoot by my crib and get my ride. Divine want me to pick up his little man Murder Mike."

Light and Fats stopped laughing, took the gasoline from Big Dave, opened the car door and threw the gasoline all over the car and the dead drug dealer, Pete. They then set Pete and the car on fire and then piled into L's Benz and, headed back to Brooklyn. But the ride going back was not quiet. Fats and Light was still snapping on Tommy Guns.

L said, "Both of y'all need to shut the fuck up in my car. Y'all niggas stupid."

Fats and Light looked at each other and started laughing again.

When the laughter and jokes subsided, Tommy Guns said, "Y'all bitch ass niggas better be ready tomorrow, because we gonna get the big balla, Money-Making John."

The whole car erupted into laughter as they discussed what they had planned for Money-Making John.

Chapter Thirty-Seven

It was a cold windy day outside, but the warmth in the house was inviting. Lisa had no plans to go anywhere. She was just not in the mood to go anywhere or do anything. She did contemplate calling her mother; they hadn't spoken since the incident with Shameek. She wanted to let her mother know what happened but she knew all it would have done was worry her mother needlessly. She knew it would also cause an argument because Lisa did not want to involve the police.

Mrs. Alice Thompson was a citizen that never got involved with the going-ons in the streets, so she couldn't understand why so many of the younger generation were always so quick to take matters into their own hands. She told Lisa time and time again that it was the reason why so many young black men were out there killing other black men.

Lisa couldn't argue that, because she knew her mother had a point but she also knew that calling the police was not the answer to black people's problems. If anything, she felt they added to it with their racial profiling, police brutality and unlawful shootings. And of course it was the police that killed black children for acting like children playing with toy guns that the white manufacturers promoted to the black communities. To make matters worse, the police commissioner and the mayor always took the side of the police, causing more tension to the situation. Lisa always told herself that until the world changed its racist, one-sided thinking, black people would have to handle their own problems by whatever solutions were available.

Channel 9 news played on the television. They were talking about the war in Pakistan, but Lisa didn't hear a word they said as she laid on her bed consumed with her hatred for Shameek. She didn't want to tell Richard what Shameek did to her because she knew out of his anger that he would go to Fort Greene without thinking and Shameek would probably kill him. Lisa underestimated her husband.

She had no idea that Richard was the one that killed T-bone; all she heard on the news was that it was a man dressed in a housing uniform with dreads. Lisa decided to tell her brother what happened and she knew he would definitely handle Shameek. The only problem was contacting Omar. The last she heard, he was in Jamaica with Gloria, and his cell phone kept saying he was out of the area and could not be reached.

When Lisa called Gina and told her what happened, Gina rushed over right away. Upon arrival, Gina started cursing and yelling so loud, Lisa had to tell her to shut the hell up. They hugged and sat on the couch for twenty minutes, both of them not saying a word. They just hugged and let the tears flow. They spoke without words, each knowing what the other was thinking. The swelling on Lisa's face slowly reduced and you could barely notice it now, unless you knew what you were looking for. But the real pain was internal and she wanted Shameek to pay. After he raped her and ran away, Lisa cried all the way to her car and drove home, without stopping to see her mother. She took a long hot shower, when she got home, trying to scrub his scent off of her body. She felt dirty and low knowing she would eventually have to tell Richard what happened to her.

Richard laid in the living room on the burgundy couch with a towel over his face. He was stressed out and was trying to gather his thoughts. He longed to get out of the game and go back to being the old Richard. It seemed as if every hour he was praying to God for forgiveness and he felt guilty after praying because he was unable to stop his sinful actions. There was only one obstacle stopping him from leaving the game-Shameek. But Richard knew if he continued to pray, God would guide him in the right direction. Richard wondered what was going on with Lisa. She seemed so withdrawn lately. Every time he touched her, she would jump. Her behavior was erratic. They hadn't had sex in two weeks and he was beginning to get fed up. He knew now was the time to talk to his wife and straighten things out no matter what. Richard got off of the couch, threw the towel at the television and walked into the bedroom.

"What's up dirty?" Richard asked with a smile.

Dirty was the name he called Lisa when they were alone. He gave her that name because he said she always had dirty thoughts. Every time he called her that, she would laugh, but today she just looked at him as if she was contemplating telling him something.

"We need to talk," said Richard. "I'm not your boyfriend anymore. I'm your husband and if something is wrong, then we need to talk about it."

Richard sat on the bed, held Lisa's hand and looked into her eyes. She became teary eyed and then worked up the nerve to speak.

"You're right. We do need to talk Boo, please don't be upset with me."

"You're asking me not to be upset but I don't even know what's going on. Every time I kiss you, it's like I'm scaring you."

"Okay, I'll tell you," began Lisa. "I went to see mommy two weeks ago and when I went in the building Shameek, he, he."

"What did he say?" asked Richard angrily.

His heart began to beat faster and faster, knowing what followed would be bad news.

"What did he say?" Richard repeated.

"He...he...he raped me in the staircase."

"He did what?!" yelled Richard.

He had blood in his eyes and murder on his mind. Lisa had never saw him like this. If Shameek had been standing in front of him right then, he would have killed him with his bare hands. He knew he should have had Shameek killed when Divine requested to do it. It was more personal now than ever before and he wanted to get Shameek on his own. First he would have to get the nine millimeter with the silencer from Divine. He figured maybe he'd take a member of the Bulldog Crew with hi m down to Fort Greene Projects to hold him down if needed. But Shameek would die.

"Please don't do anything," pleaded Lisa. "I don't want you to go back to jail again. I called Omar but I think he's still in Jamaica with Gloria."

"Forget Omar!" said Richard angrily. "I'm your husband and I'll take care of it. The Bible said a man that cannot control his own household is less than anything. Trust me, I'll take care of Shameek once and for all!"

As Richard reached for the phone to call Divine, the door bell and the phone began to ring almost simultaneously. He left the phone alone and went to answer the door.

Lisa answered the phone.

"What's up girl? Are you okay?" asked Gina.

"Yeah Gee, I'm hanging on. I'm just laying here watching the news."

"Word? I know you probably don't care, but I'm on my way to Brooklyn Hospital."

"What's going on Gee?"

"Somebody beat Tonya into a coma."

"Who the fuck beat Tonya into a coma?" asked a very shocked Lisa.

Even though she and Tonya didn't speak anymore, Lisa still loved her like a sister. She thought about getting in touch with her and squashing the little beef they had, but her pride would-not allow her to pick up the telephone. Now guilt consumed her. What if Tonya never comes out of the coma, she thought.

"I don't know what's going on," said Gina. "But word I got from someone in the projects is that Tonya heard about what had happened to you and when she saw Shameek, she tried to hit him in the head with a bottle. You know Shameek keep them little dirty niggas with him. They'll do anything he say, like he's God or something. I heard they did that to Tonya. And check this out, the same nigga that told me about that, also told me one day Shameek called Tonya upstairs and when she got up there, him and his niggas straight took the pussy."

Lisa really felt guilty now. She blamed Tonya for something she should have known her best friend would never have done. She should've listened to what Tonya was trying to tell her. That was just like Tonya to try and hit Shameek in the head with a bottle because of her. Tonya always tried to fight Lisa's battles. Even in public school, when girls tried to pick on Lisa because she looked better, Tonya would be the first one to help her fight. Lisa now felt bad for flipping on Tonya. She had no idea that Shameek had also raped Tonya.

"Come pick me up. I'm going with you to the hospital," said Lisa. "I need to get out of this house for a minute anyway."

"Why? What's going on over there?"

"I told Richard what Shameek did, and Gee, I saw murder in that boy's eyes. I've never seen him like that before. I tried to call Omar but I can't reach him."

"I'm ten minutes from your house, so I'll see you soon. Oh, I've got a surprise for you."

"What is it? You know I don't like surprises."

"Bitch, you gotta wait to see this."

Lisa heard a dial tone and then hung up. She then went to her closet and grabbed the first thing she saw. She did not feel up to getting dressed up.

$

Richard opened the front door, and Divine stood there with a big smile on his face.

"What's up fool?" asked Divine. "What's the angry look about? The wife still ain't break you off?"

"That's not funny," said Richard. "Come on in, I was just about to call you."

They entered the living room and sat on the couch. Divine looked at Richard and knew something was seriously bothering his friend.

"Okay, we never kept anything from each other," said Divine. "Now tell me what's going on."

"I'll handle it. I just need to pick up that nine with the silencer you got at your house."

"Yo Bishop, I know you ain't hiding shit from your brother. Now I'm gonna ask you again. What's going on?"

Richard looked at the closed bedroom door and then put his hands over his face. He finally looked up at Divine with tears in his eyes.

"That punk Shameek raped Lisa."

"He did what?!" Divine yelled angrily. "That nigga is dead! Word to my mother, son. That's why I been wanted to murder that faggot ass nigga."

"I got this," said Richard hoping to calm Divine down.

He didn't want Lisa to hear what was going on.

"I got this," Richard repeated. "I'll take care of him once and for all."

"You sure you got it?" Divine asked with his face contorted,

"Yeah, Divine. One week and he's dead. If I need help, I'll call you. Just let me plan this thing out before we move."

The doorbell rang and Richard got up to answer it. It was Gina and Pam. As soon as they walked into the house, Gina made introductions.

"Richard this is Pam and Pam, that's Richard. Hey, I didn't know my baby was here," said Gina as she walked to the couch and sat on Divine's lap.

"It's nice to meet you," smiled Richard. "I've heard so much about you."

"Likewise," smiled Pam. "You probably don't remember, but I was with Lisa when you first met her."

"Oh, you were one of them on the bench laughing at me, huh?" asked Richard with a smile.

Pam laughed and said, "No, I wasn't laughing at you. Let me stop lying, yes I was. But it wasn't to diss you 'cause I don't get down like that."

Richard laughed and shook her hand.

Divine sat on the couch kissing Gina on her neck. His eyes widened at the sight of Pam. Damn, all of Gina's friends were bad he thought to himself.

Lisa then entered the living room. She could hardly believe her eyes when she saw Pam.

"Oh my God!" she screamed as she rushed over to hug Pam. "Where the hell have you been?!"

Pam smiled, took a step back and said, "What's up, you in politics now? Because you sure look Patacky."

"Bitch, shut up," laughed Lisa.

Lisa and Gina gave their men a kiss before heading towards the front door. They said nothing about where they were going because they didn't want to upset Richard and Divine anymore than what they already were. The three women left the house with Lisa talking a mile a minute to Pam.

Richard and Divine remained seated on the couch in their own thoughts.

"A yo, I'm about to pull outta here myself," said Divine. "You're sure you don't want me to go and handle that nigga Shameek?"

"No, I got it," answered Richard. "I'll take care of it. I got so much on my mind right now but I'll get him. Oh yeah, Gina passed the test. "

"Yeah, I knew she would," Divine said with a smirk on his face. "I'll slide back through tomorrow afternoon."

"Okay, I'll be here," said Richard giving Divine five and a hug.

"I love you bro," said Divine as he walked out of the house and back to his Bentley blasting Ja Rule and Ashanti's song, "Always on time" with a frown on his face.

Chapter Thirty-Eight

"What's up Gina? What are you doing?"

"Nothing at all Pam. I just came back from the clinic. Where are you?"

"I'm down here in the Fort and it's still boring as hell down here. Why were you in the clinic?"

"Bitch, you'll never believe it. I'm pregnant, and don't tell anybody. I didn't even tell my man yet. He's going to be so happy. What's up with your man Big Gee from Crown Heights?"

"Gina, I dumped that egghead nigga. I walked in his house and caught a young bitch sucking his dick like she was bobbing for apples. The dumb fuck left his front door unlocked. Somebody could've killed his dumb ass. And you know the stupid fuck had actually thought I would stay with him because he got money? Now come on, do I look like Tonya? Speaking of which, she's out of the coma. She's doing well. I just came from seeing her, and when I told her that Lisa came with us to see her, she was so happy I thought the bitch was gonna go back into a coma," laughed Pam. "I told her we'll all come back to see her this week. I see Lisa's husband stepped up in the game. "

"Yeah, but he's trying to step out," said Gina. "And it's hard to do that when you got beef with stupid ass Shameek."

"Old Pizza face is still acting up huh? Remember when we first saw Richard? He was always handsome, but that boy was churched out. I come back and the nigga is a rich gangster. Nah, let me change that, he's a rich young thugged out T.D. Jake," said Pam as she and Gina began laughing.

"No forreal," said Gina. "You have to get to know him. He is too sweet, oh yeah, guess who Lisa's brother Omar fucks with?"

"Who?" asked Pam thirsty for gossip.

"Kendu from L.G. moms."

"Word? Damn, Kendu was my baby. Remember when he died I got his name tattooed on my leg? But I got it covered up when I heard every bitch in Brooklyn had his name tatted on their ass somewhere. I couldn't even go to the funeral. I didn't want to see my boo like that. I would've married that nigga if he didn't have so many girls."

"Yeah I feel you," said Gina. "Anyway, call me tonight and I'll come through there and pick you up. I'll talk to you later. Bye." Gina hung up the phone and began thinking about Divine.

He had picked Gina up from the clinic earlier. She told him she'd been having cramps but didn't think it was anything serious. He took her home and got three of his guns: two .44s and the nine millimeter with the silencer. He then got a pen, paper and scribbled a note then left it on the dresser. He gave Gina a long passionate kiss, told her he loved her, and said he was going to see Richard. He left the house with a frown on his face. He got in his black 2001 GMC Yukon Denali and left as Gina sat on the couch eating grapes out of a big red bowl and watching TV. Something did not feel right to Gina, but she didn't know what it was. She couldn't put her finger on it. When Divine brought her home from the clinic, she took off all her clothes. All she had on was a pair of white panties and one of Divine's long sleeve Polo shirts. After talking to Pam, Gina still felt a bit uneasy as she reached for the phone and began dialing Lisa's number.

The phone rang and Richard answered. "Hello, who may I ask is calling?"

"Hello? Oh, what's up Richard?"

"Hey, what's up Gina? How are you doing?"

"I'm okay. Did Divine get there yet?"

"No, I haven't seen Divine. I called his cell phone about a minute ago, but he didn't answer. Did he say he was coming over here?" "Yeah, he said he was going to see you. He left about an hour ago. He should've been there by now."

"If he's not here in ten minutes, I'll make a few calls to track him down. Okay?"

"Alright. Where's Lisa?"

"She's in the other room watching television."

"Let me speak to her."

"Sure, hang on a second."

Gina was searching her mind as to what was troubling her as she waited for Lisa to come to the phone. Every time she felt this way, something always went wrong. She wished that Divine had just stayed at home with her.

"What's up Gee?"

"Hello?" said Gina.

"Yeah, I'm here," said Lisa.

"What're you doing?"

"Nothing. Just watching TV."

"Have you talked to Omar yet?"

"No, I can't even get in touch with him. I think he's still in Jamaica with Gloria. I saw Richard a few minutes ago loading a gun. I know he's going to Fort Greene."

"I hope Richard don't get himself hurt or get put back in jail."

"You're right about that," Lisa said softly. "Gee, did you go to the clinic?"

"Yeah, I went to the clinic today. It's official, I am pregnant. I haven't told Divine yet. I'm going to tell him over dinner tonight."

"Why didn't you tell him right after you saw the doctor?"

"I was going to tell him, but he had something on his mind that he didn't want to talk about, but I'll talk to him when he gets back. He should've been at your house by now. Lisa, I'm stressed out. I don't feel right and I don't know what it is, but shit just doesn't seem right."

"What doesn't seem right? What's going on?"

"I don't know. Ever since Divine left, I've been thinking about him like crazy. I hope nothing is wrong."

"Everything is fine," said Lisa. "Maybe you're just thinking about telling him about the baby."

"You're probably right. I don't know..." Gina drifted off.

$

Divine and Murder Mike, one of the youngest members of the Bulldog Crew, drove in silence towards the Fort Greene Projects. Murder Mike was sixteen years old and was very short in height. He always had a smile on his face, but his eyes told a different story. He was from Brooklyn's Pink Houses in East New York and was raised by his grandparents. His grandfather had died two years earlier and ever since then, he had been running the streets. Anyone he didn't like was eliminated and in such a small amount of time, he had a large body count. It was easy for him to get close to whoever he wanted murdered because he looked so young and innocent. But he was not seeing no real money until Divine recently put him down with the Bulldog Crew. He never ran with the rest of them. But meeting up with them after the drug dealer Pete was killed, he immediately took a liking to them. Especially Light and Fats. Already, Divine had looked out for him buying him a brand new Cadillac Escalade and putting him on the Bulldog Crew's payroll.

They reached the Fort Greene Projects and saw Shameek and three of his soldiers standing on the avenue. He pointed Shameek out to Murder Mike and pulled the truck up on Carlton Avenue. They adjusted their guns and exited the truck.

"I'm cutting through the projects," said Divine. "You go to the corner and do your thing. I'll meet you there and back you up."

"Alight kid, that's cool," said Murder Mike with a boyish grin on his face.

Divine cut through the projects as Murder Mike made his way up Carlton towards Myrtle Avenue.

Murder Mike approached Shameek and his boys and none of them paid him any attention. He looked more like ten than sixteen years old. But they paid attention when they saw the big .44 handgun pointed at Shameek.

One of Shameek's soldiers pushed Shameek out of the way and was rewarded with a .44 slug to the head. Half of his head looked as if it was gone as he fell dead to the sidewalk.

Shameek and his other two soldiers quickly pulled out their guns and began firing. Murder Mike ran in the street behind a parked car and returned fire. He hit one of Shameek's soldiers in the face. The bullet removed his whole mouth as he fell to the concrete. Murder Mike pulled his other gun and kept firing. Shameek's last soldier ran up Myrtle Avenue but was cut off by a single gunshot from Divine's gun. The bullet entered his head. Divine walked over to him and fired two more shots into what was left of it.

Murder Mike ran out of bullets and cursed himself. He knew he should've brought his two nine millimeters with him. But he thought this was going to be a simple Bulldog Crew hit. He tried to run, but Shameek shot him in the back. Murder Mike stumbled forward for a few paces before the next shot entered the back of his head.

People on the avenue were running every which way. Girls pushing baby strollers dragged their babies to safety. Officer Tom O 'Ryan and his partner Martin Harrison also known as Rambo were the first officers to arrive on the scene.

As the two police officers jumped out of an unmarked car, Divine ran after Shameek as he tried to escape. Divine fired his gun hitting Shameek in the back.

As Shameek stumbled, he spun around, firing off a shot of his own that hit Divine square in the shoulder. It was as if Divine was obsessed with killing Shameek, because he paid no attention to his arm or to the police. He fired off one more shot hitting Shameek in the head. Shameek fell to the ground. Divine stood over his dead body and shot him two more times in the back of the head, and then kicked him in the ass.

He threw the .44 on the ground and pulled out the nine millimeter with the silencer attached as police cars came from everywhere surrounding him. Divine turned around and pointed his gun at Officer 'Rambo' Harrison. Officer Harrison was as well known in this area as the gangsters were. Behind him and everywhere surrounding were police officers with their guns pointed at Divine.

"Drop the gun!" yelled Officer Harrison. "And put your hands on your head, Divine!" Officer Harrison knew most of the Brooklyn thugs by their street names because he either had shoot-outs with them, arrested them or identified their bodies.

Divine had a sick smile on his face because he knew this was the end. He pulled the trigger but no one heard the shot. Officer Harrison fell to the ground as blood gushed from his eye. Realizing he had been hit Officer Harrison's partner immediately opened fire on Divine. The first bullet hit his leg. The second hit Divine in the chest as he fell to the ground with a smile on his face. As he laid there dying, he thought about Richard, Lisa and his baby Gina. The other officers on the scene opened fire emptying their guns as bullets entered Divine from all angles.

Chapter Thirty-Nine

Gina was having a hard time without Divine. She hadn't cried so much since her mother passed away. Gina loved Divine more than life itself and just thinking about him made her hysterical.

She also wondered how would she be able to pay the bills. Divine left her no money, the house was in his mother's name and the car notes would have to be paid. She also had a baby on the way. That would not be a problem. Even if she had to apply for welfare she was having the baby. Plus she figured she'd sell the Bentley being that it was in her name. Richard told her that he had to talk to her and it was very important. She wondered what could be so important. Maybe she could ask him for some money. No, that wouldn't be right to get money from her best friend's husband, she thought.

Gina grabbed her car keys off of the kitchen counter and headed out of the door. She was suppose to pick up Tonya first; but decided to do that after leaving Lisa's house. Gina was in a very sad mood so she wore a pair of black high heels, a black and white Christian Dior dress and her black mink coat. She got inside of her white Benz and drove off to the sounds of Aaliyah's song, "I miss you". As she headed to Richard and Lisa's house she could not stop thinking about Divine's funeral. They had a closed casket, and the church was crowded with people from all over. Gina didn't know Divine knew that many people. It reminded her of the day they drove the Notorious B.I.G.'s body through Brooklyn. It was crazy.

The media portrayed Divine as a cop killing, career criminal that held no regards for human life. The Mayor called him a coward, and the Police Commissioner said he was an animal that killed a good cop that everyone loved. But the thugs in the streets and people that were constantly oppressed did not see things that way. To them Divine was a loyal, good stand up individual that handled his business and had rid the streets of one of Brooklyn's most corrupt pigs. He was a hero to the thugs and those who claimed to live by the codes of the game.

Richard spoke at the funeral and Gina was truly impressed by the way he quoted Biblical scriptures by memory. After the funeral, thugs approached Richard and offered their condolences and services. Richard gave thanks but declined any offers. He said he was no longer part of that kind of life. As far as he was concerned, the game died with Divine.

Divine's mother and sister were also at the funeral. Richard made it his business to let them know that he would always be there for them if they needed him. Gina had never been very close with them, but once they found out she was pregnant, they welcomed and supported her with open arms. They both treated her nice and told her she was part of the family now. Gina had appreciated their support and love, but her strength came from her three best friends, Lisa, Tonya and Pam. Lisa was the shoulder she knew she could cry on, Tonya was the mother she needed but hadn't had in so long and Pam managed to make her laugh and smile even under the current circumstances. They were not just her friends, they were her family.

Gina pulled up in front of Richard and Lisa's house. She noticed the brand new yellow 2001 Lamborghini Diablo VT6.0 sitting on 19-inch rims parked in front of the house as she exited her car. Gina checked her mink coat to make sure she possessed the note that Divine left on the dresser before he got killed. It was addressed to Richard, but all it said was 15:13 John with Divine's signature at the bottom.

Gina rang the doorbell. Lisa appeared moments later at the door.

"Come in. What's up?" smiled Lisa.

They entered the living room and Gina heart sank. "What the fuck are the police doing here?" Gina asked Lisa angrily. "These are the same corrupt cops I told you about. They kidnapped me and tried to make me flip on Divine."

"Cops? They ain't no cops," said Lisa. "That's Moe-dog and his friend Whitey."

Moe-dog looked at Gina with a smile, showing all of his pearly whites. Gina was attracted to him, but her heart belonged to Divine in life and death.

"Hello," said Whitey.

"Don't speak to me motherfucker. I don't know you," said Gina. "And you don't know me, you cracker devil, little dick fucker."

Moe-dog burst out laughing with his hands over his mouth.

Gina's mind was racing. What kind of game was Richard playing on her, she thought. Did Divine know about these two fake cops? Did Richard have Divine's money? All of these questions were running through her mind and she was becoming increasingly more upset.

Lisa knew Gina had a bad temper and wanted no part of what was going on. She slipped off to her bedroom and turned on the TV, wondering what was going on and why Richard had kept this a secret.

"Richard, what is this all about?" asked Gina pointing her finger at Moe-dog and Whitey. "Are they cops?"

"No, they're not cops, but they were just leaving. Wait here, and I'll come back and explain everything."

Moe-dog and Whitey stood up and Richard escorted them to the door.

"Hopefully, I'll see you again beautiful," smiled Moe-dog. "We didn't mean to put you through what we put you through. I sincerely apologize."

Gina didn't answer him. She took off her coat and sat on the couch. Richard closed the door behind Moe-dog and Whitey as they pulled off in the yellow Lamborghini, he sat next to Gina on the couch. He looked her in the eyes.

"Like I was saying before, they are not cops. Divine wanted to marry you, but he wasn't sure how loyal you were to him, so I put that situation together with Divine's permission. He told me only a thug chick with class could truly love him."

Gina now understood why Moe-dog and Whitey didn't try to harm her physically.

"Oh my God," she said with a look of exhaustion on her face. "My baby should've known that I would have died for him."

"He knew," smiled Richard. "I told him everything that took place before he died. He was so proud of you, even though he wanted to kill them for taking it so far. I only wish that he could have lived to see the baby you're carrying."

"Who told you I was pregnant? That big mouth wife of yours, huh?"

Richard didn't answer, he only smiled.

"Besides us losing someone who was very special, is everything else alright with you?"

"Well to be honest," Gina started. "I don't know how I'm going to be able to pay the bills. I got these cars, the baby is coming and trust me, I can't pay it with my looks."

"You're serious?" Richard asked with a smile. "You think I paid your man with my looks? Divine left you a fortune. I'll show you where it is. Plus his mother told me you can keep the house. She just wants to see her grandbaby on the regular. He left money with his mother and his sister too, so they're alright."

Gina was in shock; she couldn't believe what she was hearing. She lowered her head and began to cry in her hands. Once she regained some composure, she reached into her pocket and pulled out the note that Divine had left for Richard.

"I don't know what this means, but before Divine died he left this note in the house addressed to you."

Richard took the note and saw it was addressed to him in Divine's handwriting. He unfolded the note and read what it said. Tears formed in his eyes and fell onto the page.

"What does it mean?" asked Gina.

"It's a scripture from the Bible. It says, 'Greater love hath no man than this, that a man lay down his life for his friends.'"

Epilogue

Two and a half years past and a lot had changed. Richard was no longer part of the game. He sold all of his cars and the only thing he drove now was a back in the days Cherokee Jeep. He did not want anymore attention. Too many people knew who he was, so he packed up everything he owned and moved to North Carolina. He completed his GED and followed his dream. Richard was now an ordained minister. He built a nice church in N.C. and preached about issues like his father did. But he did not make anyone in the church angry because he knew first hand about the pressures of life and how easy it was to fall into sin, so he judged no one. He preached the Word and the conditions of the world. Before he left New York, he read a story in the newspaper about a boy being killed by an off-duty police officer after a failed robbery attempt. Looking at the boy's picture, he realized that it was no one other than Krazy Kay.

Lisa was a happy mother to she and Richard's one year old baby girl, Dejanay Shakira Brown. Lisa had one more year in college and was majoring in corporate law, she figured somebody had to learn how to clean the money Richard still possessed. Also, since she was the preacher's wife, she made it her business to be in church every Sunday.

Omar had pulled out of the game completely. He was now the CEO of the new banging Record Label "Untouchable Records". He and Gloria had plans to be married by the end of the year. They also started "Kendu's Youth Center" to help children get out of the street life.

Lisa's mother Mrs. Alice Thompson finally moved out of the notorious Fort Greene Projects. She and Richard's mother Maria Ann Brown became best friends and they both attended church whenever the time permitted them to do so.

Tonya did a one-eighty. She was no longer the money hungry young girl she once was. She was saved in a small church and became a born-again Christian. And everyone was surprised when she married one of the deacons in the church and swore this was the happiest she'd ever been in her life.

Gina was the mother of a healthy, handsome two-year-old boy named Robert James Scott, Jr. His nickname was Divine and he was the spitting image of his father. Gina only had one more year left of college and when she attended school her little boy stayed with Divine's mother and sister.

Moe-dog had finally gotten his wishes. He was now seriously dating Gina. He finally reached his financial goal and was no longer doing robberies and hits. He was also head of Omar's security team at the Record Label "Untouchable Records".

His man Whitey was still doing hits and robberies and it was said that he had two contracts out on his life but of course he didn't care about that.

Pam was the same old Pam. Always making people laugh and she was still boosting. Not that she had to, but she figured why pay for something when you can get it free. Everyone she knew had still tried to persuade her to become a comedian, but she always took it as an insult. She was now Big Lord's girl and everyone in the streets gave her the utmost respect. Big Lord was now the new rich thug in the streets. It was said that he was moving twenty kilos every two days in four different states. Also, the spots that Richard and Omar had, now belonged to Big Lord. Rappers that wanted street credibility always shouted his name out on their records.

Light, Fats and L of the Bulldog Crew are serving 25 to life up in Attica Correctional Facility for the murder of a well-known drug dealer from Harlem. And Big Dave and Tommy Guns were murdered executioner style by Brooklyn's notorious Bloods.

Forgiveness

I greet you my friends and my enemies,
those who love me and those who want to sentence me ...
to death.
But please save your breath because you must now know, that only
God can call me when it is my time to go.
There were times when you pointed your guns at me, pulled the
trigger and thought you had me.
Even I thought you had me, but my Father in Heaven decided to let
them bullets pass me.
So I am still here and I see it is my words you fear because I am not
blind,
I wear glasses but I see clearly without them because I don't need a
prescription for my mind.
Yes I have changed and rearranged my thought patterns but you
still judge me from my past, so I look at you and ask... Who are
you? I guess you are the one that never did anything wrong.
Everyone committed a sin before, and what makes mines greater
than yours?
I shot a gun and you had an abortion,
you killed for the US Army and support legal extortion.
And we all know you lied before which makes you a liar, and you
disregard our Father in Heaven by judging my past and keeping me
in the fire?
You hypocrite, out of my sight Satan right now. You read the Bible
and recite the words of Paul, but was not Paul the murderous Saul
at one time?
You speak of Moses but he also killed someone in his life time.
According to the Bible, David killed without a rifle. However, you
forgive them but you do not forgive me?
I cannot even get a decent J.O.B. because of my past history.

Do you even know who I am?
You say Jesus is coming back and when he does you will be
prepared, but what if I told you Jesus is here?
That he never left, because every righteous thought spoken is the
breath of Jesus.
I also do the work of our Father so I may be he whom you seek,
but you listen to the devil and don't listen to me when I speak.
So on judgment day you may see Jesus and you'll say,
"I went to church every Sunday, and I praised your name every day.
And if you would have came you would have seen with your own
eyes, that I was true and spoke no lies."
And Jesus may look at you and say:
"You waited for me to appear, but I was there. I saw that man that
was a murderer but I changed him by being within him.
And he spoke my words and you heard nothing he said, because
you wanted him dead.
You could not find it in your heart to forgive him, but haven't I
forgiven you?
Haven't I forgiven murderers, thieves, prostitutes and all those who
acknowledge me? And you say you follow me? You do not follow
me you follow the ways of the world and that is not living,
how many times must I tell you to forgive others for their sins and
yours shall be forgiven."

THE END!

(Sequel to Bishop)

Chapter One

The tension in Attica's yard was full with emotion and a tension that never ceased. It was always some kind of drama popping off in each yard, especially A-Block.

Every Block had its' own individual yard, and it was a regular routine to see someone getting cut, stabbed and even killed at times. Almost every inmate in the yard stayed close to their own individual cliques. The Muslims sat three tables deep in one area of the yard, the Bloods stood along the walls near the basketball courts, the Latin Kings and other Puerto-Ricans held one another down near the handball court while a few of them played a few games, the Jamaicans sat two tables deep chatting and banging on the table as some smoked their marijuana on the low, the White boys sat and stood around one table laughing and joking, and everyone else that belonged to no clique moved all around the yard freely doing whatever they did. Whether it was playing basketball, walking and talking, watching TV, talking on the phones, lifting weights, or doing pull-ups and dips to stay physically fit. There was no telling when something would jump off, so a person would have to definitely be ready for show time whenever it popped off!

The only inmates who enjoyed the music that played over the loud speaker in the yard were the White boys, being that the radio stayed on the Country station or some other station that the other nationalities did not really care for. And this was odd indeed, considering the White inmate population only made up ten percent of the General prison population. But to be fair, sometimes you might catch a Rap or something R&B you knew all the words to on the yard's radio. But more often than not, it would be some kind of Country or

Hillbilly song playing, and the funny thing is that you would hear it so much, you would find yourself one day singing all the words to the song and maybe even liking it.

On this hot particular day, Light was standing near the TV disrespecting a stocky brown-skinned brother wearing a brown crown on his head. The guy was a Muslim, but Light didn't care about any of that. He was Big Light from the Bulldog Crew and that's all that mattered.

A group of A-Block's most dangerous inmates stood around the TV laughing at the inmate taking the verbal assault from Light.

"You punk ass motherfucker," said Light. "You lucky I wasn't the nigga CB 'cause if your girl was looking all in my face on the visit floor, I would've bagged that bitch! But then again, that bitch is ugly. She look like a smoked out Daffy Duck, you bird ass nigga!"

All of the guys standing around laughed. Some laughed so hard, they were in tears. "Light is off the hook!" a few of them said.

The brown-skinned guy he was dissing said, "I'm saying though, she troop for a nigga. And I go down on the visit floor more than most of these niggas in this spot. Some of these niggas don't even know what the visiting room look like!"

The guys standing around knew he'd spoken the truth because some of them were the ones who never got visits.

"Motherfucker, my bitch troop too!" said Light with his face screwed up. "Plus I get trees nigga!"

"I'm saying," said the guy. "That's you. Drugs ain't my thing. "

Light's friend CB knew Light long enough to know when he was getting tight. He also knew Light was ready to put a steel shank in the boy. CB looked at Light and said, "Yo, come on man. Let's take a few laps around the yard before we work out. I need to talk to you anyway."

Light looked at the brown-skin guy he was dissing, and the guy knew he should've took Light's verbal assault quietly like most of the inmates did. When he looked in Light's eyes he saw danger, so he as glad that CB was successful in getting Light to walk away as he pulled his arm. Now he hoped Light would forget about the whole incident and not take it out on him at a later date.

"Yo man," said CB as they walked around the small yard, "you gotta chill out if you wanna go home. You should be on the low anyway. I mean, you just got that reversal on that 444.10, right? So, you might get time served. What did your lawyer say?"

"He said me and my crimes will get that appeal bail most likely," answered Light now calming down. "And he said he believe they'll throw it out or something. I don't know. But once I get outta here, I ain't coming back to this shit! That faggot ass Governor got motherfuckers going to their 4th, 5th and 6th parole board in this bitch! Before I come back to this shit, I'm going out like my nigga Divine."

"No doubt," said CB, "I hear you. Shit, I feel the same motherfucking way."

Light was part of a small gang of notorious thugs called the "Bulldog Crew" and Divine was basically the founder of it. The name came about because whenever they did a hit, the .44 Bulldog handgun was always the gun of choice. Of course they would have some kind of automatic weapon on them as well for back up, but when it came to a simple hit, the .44 Bulldog was favored.

Divine was always a well-known killer, but he wasn't seeing no real money until he met a church boy turned thug named Richard who everyone called Bishop. Richard got put on to the drug game by his wife Lisa's older brother Omar. Now Omar was a drug kingpin, a multi-millionaire from Fort Greene Projects that helped Richard with anything he needed. He retired from the drug game and became a CEO of one of the hottest record labels out. But whatever Richard wanted to do, Omar backed him all the way, until Richard himself decided to leave the game alone as well. But before that happened, Richard saw it as the right decision to make Divine his lieutenant in his multi-milliondollar drug operation. Not only did they become rich, but they also terrorized the New York City streets when Divine started a small gang called the "Bulldog Crew" that consisted of six very dangerous gunmen including himself. Three of them had gotten killed: Tommy Guns, Big Dave, and little Murder Mike. Divine had also gotten killed, but not before killing Richard's worse and most dangerous enemy Shameek, and also one of the police most corrupted detectives to ever walk the Brooklyn streets, Detective Martin "Rambo" Harrison. Divine was remembered as a hero to many thugs in the streets of almost every major city. After Divine's death, Richard quit the drug game and became a preacher down south in North Carolina. The three remaining Bulldog members: Light, Fats, and L, had just gotten a reversal on their conviction for killing a well-known Harlem drug dealer.

Light got his nickname because of his complexion, Fats got his from being chubby, and L was short for his name Lamont.

"Wha' mi say Light?" asked a dread sitting at the Jamaicans table with his friends.

Light and CB stopped walking, and Light approached the small metal table and all seated gave him a pound.

"Much respect," said Light to the dread with a smile. "Who got that good shit?"

The dread looked around making sure the COs weren't anywhere in the area as he gave Light another pound with three New York joints of weed in his hand.

"Good looking brethren," said Light as he pocketed the marijuana. "If you need anything, let me know."

"Cool," replied the dread as Light and CB continued walking around the small yard.

"Did you get the weed from your crimie?" asked CB.

"Nah," answered Light. "I'm good! Fats and L can keep that. And when Kia come up tomorrow, I'll send them some more over there. But what they need to do, is get up outta D-Block and come over here."

"Oh hell no nigga!" smiled CB. "I can put up with L. But you and Fats together? Forget about it!"

"Come on man," said Light changing the subject. "Let's go work out. Get a little chest in."

They walked over to the weights along the wall, and the inmates lifting weights greeted Light and CB and gave them enough room to work out.

"A yo, remember Karen from Kingston and St. Johns?" asked CB as Light put 245 pounds on the incline bench.

"Nah, I don't remember that bitch," answered Light. "The only one I remember from that block was Shanique."

"Damn, how you don't remember her? She had a crazy fat ass on her! But then again, she's older than you. She's my age."

"I still probably know her by face," said Light looking around for more weight. And then sitting down he said, "Come on, spot me!"

Light laid back on the incline bench and pressed the 245 pounds ten times before getting up.

"Damn kid!" smiled CB. "You getting strong. You was always a little skinny nigga, now you beefing it up! Remember when you was like twelve and I was fifteen, and we had that fight in the game room? Yo, you a funny nigga. That day I had to put it on you," CB laughed as Light gave him a little smirk as he also remembered the fight they had when they were children.

"Arr man," continued CB laughing. "That was crazy! And you know I still got it," he said, throwing a flurry of punches at the air before sitting down on the incline bench. He then looked up at Light and noticed that something was troubling his friend.

"A yo man," said CB with concern. "Don't let that bird ass nigga you was beefing with near the TV get to you homie. I can see it all in your face. Come on, let's just get this work out over with, and then we can blow a bone or something."

"Yeah, you right," smiled Light as he spotted CB helping him take the weight out of the rack.

CB pressed the 245 pounds six times and then felt a sharp pain in his side. He felt it again as he yelled and dropped the weight on the ground just barely missing his left foot. He then saw Light walking away quickly. He looked down at his side and recognized that he was bleeding badly. As he grimaced in pain, he got up and started to go after Light, but a brown-skin stocky baldhead guy that was working out named Mont-Mont saw everything that transpired. He pulled out a sharp looking icepick and told CB, "Don't blow it up bitch, take yours and heal up! If you try to walk behind 'em, I'ma kill you!"

CB thought about it for a second, and then walked towards the CO's bubble to let them know he'd been stabbed and was in need of some serious medical attention. He just couldn't believe that Light had stabbed him. He knew Light his whole life, and wondered why he flipped on him and stabbed him up. But for now he just hoped he wouldn't lose too much blood as the COs rushed him to the hospital.

Chapter Two

Fats and L walked around the yard in D- Block, and was making plans of what they were going to do when they got out of prison.

"The first thing I'ma do," smiled Fats, "is stick all of 'dem niggas up that's getting that drug money and rap money, except the nigga Omar."

"Man, we'll be back in jail faster than a motherfucker messing wit' them faggot ass rap niggas, "said L. "They talk all that gangsta shit and straight pussy. And they got the game hot as a motherfucker right now wit' all that snitching on records. 'He shot me and so and so shot him'. Yo, I hate them faggots! That's why the Feds is watching everything right now. Even most of the rap niggas signed to Omar is pussy! The only ones I like, is the O.G.'s and that's it."

Fats laughed and said, "Man, fuck all them niggas. Shit, if Omar wasn't peoples, I'll get that nigga too!"

"Nah," said L. "That's family right there."

Then changing the subject he asked, "You heard why Light hit the nigga CB?"

"Yeah I heard," laughed Fats. "He sent me a kite about it. You know the nigga Light never got over the fact that CB duffed him out when they was kids and shit. He said the nigga CB had the nerve to mention the fight and throw a few flurries at the air, so he blew 'em!"

L bust out laughing as he stopped walking and held his stomach. He knew Light was a bug out, but damn! When he was back in control of his laughter, the two of them started walking again.

"That nigga Light is stupid!" said L.

"He's on the visit right now," replied Fats. "Kia came up, and when he come back he said he'll send us some weed over."

"Aiight," smiled L. "That's what I'm talking about. Yo, you know he put the nigga Mont-Mont down wit' us, right?"

"Yeah, he told me he's BDC now. But I don't mind, he's a good nigga and I heard he don't hesitate to let his gun go in the town."

"I'm feeling that. But I don't know homie to feel him though," confessed L. "But I know what you're saying about letting that thang go. Fuck all that talking shit! Look what happen to Big Dave and Tommy Guns."

"Yeah," said Fats thinking about it. "You're right about that, man. You're right about that."

Big Dave, Tommy Guns and L, killed six Bloods in the Flatbush section of Brooklyn, as they came from visiting Tommy Gun's uncle. A little Blood kid who was looking for some kind of recognition, provoked the verbal exchange of heated words before Big Dave getting tired of shorty's mouth, pulled out and opened fire on the small group of Bloods. Of course the Bloods fired back, but they was outwitted and outgunned by the three dangerous Bulldog Crew members. But as the months passed, Big Dave and Tommy Guns found themselves visiting Tommy Gun's uncle once again. The rest of the Bloods in the area, had heard they were inside of the apartment, and decided to make their move by standing in front of his uncle's apartment waiting for the two gunmen to come out.

Big Dave looked at Tommy Guns and said, "Yo, it's a lot of them niggas outhere. Call Fats, Light and L, tell them niggas to get down here."

"I just tried to call Fats cell phone, but I'm not getting no answer. And you know they're all together."

Big Dave looked out of the window and said, "Aiight, this is what we gonna do. Them niggas got guns, but they aint pull out yet. So, just open the door and when I step out blazing, you follow behind me."

"Aiight bet!" said Tommy Guns pulling a nine millimeter and a .44 Bulldog handgun from his waist. He and Big Dave carried the same guns that day, so together they had four guns.

"Give me one of them guns," said Tommy Gun's uncle in a voice like he had too much to drink, as he looked out of the window. "I'm going out there with y'all. Come around my house with this bullshit! I'll show 'dem muh'fuckers, you don't fuck around with my family. Oh, hell nah!"

"Chill out Unc! I got this," said Tommy Guns looking out of the window. He then smiled when he saw a very familiar face. It belonged to a guy named Bo-Scagz that was close to his family. Theirs mothers were like sisters, which made them like first cousins being they grew up together since childhood. Bo-Scagz was a well-known and respected leader of the Bloods, and when Tommy Guns saw him arguing with a few Bloods, he knew his cousin was speaking in his defense.

Tommy Guns left the window, looked at Big Dave and said, "Yo, I'm feeling your plan. But I don't think we have to go out like that. My cousin Bo-Scagz is out there checking them niggas now. They scared of 'em. He's they leader or some shit."

"Where's Bo?" asked his drunken uncle. "Bo-Scagz out there?"

"We can just walk up out of here," said Tommy Guns to Big Dave, not paying his uncle any mind. "Trust me, my cousin got them niggas in check."

Big Dave didn't feel comfortable with Tommy Guns idea, because he was never a talker, and had no intentions of being one now. But he also did not want to possibly get his boy killed with his plan either, so he tucked his guns back into his waist.

"Come on," he said, "let's get this shit over with."

As soon as they walked out the door, almost all of the Bloods reached for their guns but none pulled out.

"Nobody better not shoot!" yelled out Bo-Scagz as he walked over and gave Tommy Guns a pound, and glancing at Big Dave with a funny look on his face.

Big Dave knew something wasn't right, and it was confirmed, when he saw one of the Bloods slowly inching his gun out, and Bo-Scagz trying to lead Tommy Guns away from everyone else. Big Dave had then knew what time it was. It was not hard to see that Bo-Scagz had made a deal to give him up, and save Tommy Guns. But he wasn't going out like a chump! Before the Blood could get his gun out, Big Dave went for his own. He pulled out and moved so swiftly, he caught the Bloods by surprise as he fired his weapon hitting the Blood that was pulling for his gun in the head. He then saw a way out and went for it, but caught a bullet in the back of his head from Bo-Scagz gun. But before Bo-Scagz could even turn around, Tommy Guns shot his fake cousin so many times it looked as if he was doing the 'Harlem Shake' dance. Tommy Guns had then tried to shoot it out with the rest of the Bloods and make a run for it, but got gunned down before he could let off a shot. He was dead before he hit the ground, and the Bloods ran in different directions because they all knew the police would be surrounding the area, probably before they could even get off of the block!

As the four dead bodies lay sprawled out on the concrete, Fats, L and Light was torturing a well-known Harlem drug dealer in a Brooklyn basement. They already got the whereabouts of where his money was kept, but Fats and Light was having fun breaking all the bones in his body with two small sledge hammers! A big time drug dealer from out of Brownsville named Hook, had put the hit out on the Harlem dealer. Being that Light knew Hook for years, the Bulldog Crew took the hit. All Hook told them to do was kill the drug dealer so he could come home from jail, being that the drug dealer was the only witness against him. But Light and Fats had other plans for the snitch besides what Hook had paid them to do.

"Just shoot the nigga and get it over with!" said L tired of hearing the guy yell in pain, and tired of seeing him pass out only to be awakened again by the bone cracking blows of the hammers as Fats and Light laughed with every sickening blows they delivered. It was blood everywhere and the guy was unrecognizable to the point where his own mother would not be able to identify him.

"Yo, just chill and try to call Big Dave and Tommy Guns back," instructed Fats.

"I just tried," said L. "I'm not getting no answer."

After being satisfied with the work they delivered to the dead drug dealer, they went to collect the money he would never need, as well as the money Hook was paying for their services. But when the Homicide police had discovered the murder victim, they knew it had to be the three remaining Bulldog Crew members that did the gruesome killing, so they paid a crack head off of the streets to lie and say that he saw Fats, L and Light enter the empty apartment building dragging the drug dealer. However, after a few years, the crack head cleaning up his act and now becoming religious, felt that it was the right thing to do by recanting his statement and letting the truth be known that he did not see anything, and was paid by the police to say what he said that caused three men to be wrongfully imprisoned. And because of that, Light, Fats and L was soon to be sent back down to Rikers Island on a reversal of their case.

$

"Yeah, I agree with you," Fats as he and L walked around the yard in Attica for at least the twentieth time today.

"From what Tommy Gun's uncle said," replied Fats, "they might've still been alive if they didn't go out there to talk to that faggot ass nigga Bo-Scagz. He lucky my boys killed him, before I could get my hands on 'em. Man, I would've tortured that boy so bad, they wouldn't be able to figure out was the nigga a human at one time or not."

"Yeah," said L knowing his friend had meant every word he'd spoken. Then changing the subject he said, "Yo, guess who wrote me yesterday."

"Who? Bishop?" laughed Fats.

"Yeah, how you know?" asked L, amazed at his guess.

"What is he talking about?" asked Fats with a smile, not answering his question.

"He always say I'm the more reasonable one out of all of us, because I'm the only one who writes him back," answered L. "He just sent me a bunch of 'Get in touch with Jesus' pamphlets. You want one?"

"Hell no!" laughed Fats. "That's why me and Light don't answer that nigga letters. Nobody wanna hear that shit!"

L laughed and said, "He's a good nigga though. He just wanna save everybody. But I ain't try'na be saved, I just wanna get the fuck outta here!"

"No doubt!" said Fats. "Yo, I thought you was going down on a V.I. today. What happened?"

"Everything is cool," answered L. "I told this bitch Sonia from outta Queens, to come next weekend. You want me to tell her to get one of her friends, to pull you down?"

"Nah I'm good," answered Fats as they continued walking around the small yard. "I ain't thinking about them bitches. A nigga just need some streets! And the nigga Hook said whatever cash we need to get outta here, he got us."

"Shit, that ain't no big offer," said L. "We got enough money individually to do that. All that money we made fucking wit' the big homie Divine and Bishop. But if the nigga Hook wanna give up some cash, fuck it I'll take it. A yo, what's up with your girl Denise? She ain't been up here in a minute."

"Man, I told you I'm not thinking about them bitches. Especially, that lying ass bitch! She's mad right now, 'cause I gave ten niggas in here her name and address. I'm saying, them niggas lie all fucking day and all her letters are lies, so I figured I'll just let them lie to each other."

L started laughing as Fats continued talking.

"The bitch is lucky, I ain't give them niggas the naked flicks she sent me."

L immediately stopped laughing and asked, "Word? You got naked flicks of her? Yo, bring them shits out tonight!"

Instead of answering, Fats just smiled as they continued walking around the small yard.

"The yard is closed!" yelled the CO over the loud speaker in the yard. "Line up near your company and prepare for the go back!"

All the inmates in the yard stopped whatever they were doing, and began to stand in certain areas of the yard. A few of them laughed and joked, some exchanged books of naked girls in yellow manila envelopes as if they were trading top secret information, some stood against the wall with their faces screwed up in a gangster glare, and the very few booty bandits that had sex with other men looked around for a possible weak or willing victim they could make a move on at a later date. The scene was actually comical, as well as very dangerous.

L and Fats were on the same company, and after going inside and locking in, the CO walked down the tier taking a list of those who wanted to go to chow as well as rec. He came back and stopped at L's cell and then going to Fat's cell telling them both that they had to pack up because they were going back down to court early Monday morning!

"Yo Fats!" yelled L through the bars. "You got the news, right?"

Fats laughed and yelled through the bars, "No doubt! New York City next stop! It's on boy!"

The whole tier erupted in noise celebrating the reversal of those fortunate enough to give the white oppressive system back their time.

ORDER FORM
Pen Cushion Publishers
PO Box 85
New York, NY 10116
(718)844 0686
www.pencushion

Bishop.............................$14.95
Shipping and Handling..............$3.20
Total................................$19.20

MONEY ORDERS ONLY

Purchaser Information

Name_____

Address_____

City_____   State_____   Zip_____

Quantity Ordered?

Orders shipped directly to Correctional Facilities, Pen Cushion
Publishers will deduct 25% of the sale price.

Bishop.............................$11.21
Sales Tax............................$.78
Shipping and Handling..............$3.20
Total................................$15.19